Negotiate Your Way to Riches

How to Convince Others to Give You What You Want

By

PETER WINK

CAREER PRESS
Franklin Lakes, NJ

Copyright © 2003 by Peter Wink

NEGOTIATE YOUR WAY TO RICHES
EDITED BY KRISTEN PARKES
TYPESET BY EILEEN DOW MUNSON
Cover design by DesignConcept
Printed in the U.S.A. by Book-mart Press

To order this title, please call toll-free 1-800-CAREER-1 (NJ and Canada: 201-848-0310) to order using VISA or MasterCard, or for further information on books from Career Press.

The Career Press, Inc., 3 Tice Road, PO Box 687,
Franklin Lakes, NJ 07417
www.careerpress.com

Library of Congress Cataloging-in-Publication Data

Wink, Peter, 1966-
    Negotiate your way to riches : how to convince others to give you what you want / by Peter Wink.
        p. cm.
    Includes index.
    ISBN 1-56414-690-1 (cloth)
    1. Negotiation in business. 2. Purchasing. 3. Shopping. I. Title.

HD58.6.W557 2003
650.1--dc22

                                                                2003054654

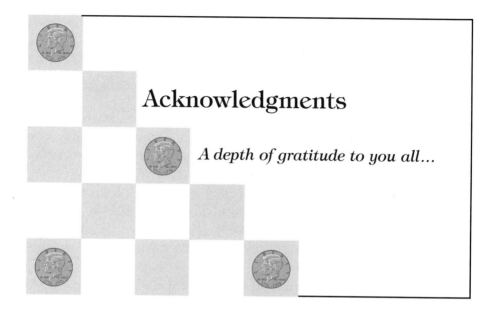

Acknowledgments

A depth of gratitude to you all...

$\mathcal{S}$pecial thanks to:

David Aaker, Jay Abraham, Debbie Allen, Robert Allen, Jim Bickford, Richard Branson, Bill Byrne, Nick "the Master Communicator" Carter, Vic Conant, E. Joseph Cossman, Paul and Sarah Edwards, Kenneth Feld, Mark Victor Hansen, Tom Harken, Tyler Hicks, Dan Kennedy, Cynthia Kersey, Michael Korda, Jay Conrad Levinson, Herschell Lewis, Mike Litman, Harvey MacKay, Vince McMahon Jr., Ted Nicholas, Melvin Powers, Bob Proctor, Anthony Robbins, Jim Rohn, Gene Simmons, Joe Sugarman, Fran Tarkenton, Brian Tracy, Bill Veeck, Joe "Mr. Fire" Vitale, Doug Wead, Art Williams, and Pat Williams for your friendship and/or inspiration as I completed this project.

All the employees at the Nightingale-Conant Corporation. It was a pleasure to work alongside every one of you!

My good friends Barton Blankenburg, Claude Boyks, Dana Garner, Kathy Sullivan, and the world's greatest producer of spoken word audio...Mr. John Ystrom!

All my instructors at Oakton Community College, Western Illinois University, and the BOG staff at Northeastern Illinois University! There has never been a greater honor than graduating from an institution like WIU. Go Leathernecks!

Barry Farber at the Diamond Group for being the world's best literary agent! I personally recommend you to anyone!

Ronald W. Fry, Michael Lewis, John J. O'Sullivan, Stacey Farkas, Kristen Parkes, Kirsten Beucler, Briana Rosen, Laurie Ann Kelly, and Karen Kegel at Career Press Inc. for believing in *Negotiate Your Way to Riches* and seeing this project through!

Sid Lemer (the world's greatest mentor and friend), for teaching me how to be a winner in every aspect of my life. I owe you one! No, I owe you more than that! You are tops in my book!

My wonderful parents, Stephanie and Ronald Wink, for always supporting and believing in me!

My beautiful wife, Stephanie, for all your love and inspiration.

And most of all I want to thank YOU for making this book a part of your life. I hope you benefit from it for years and years!

This book is dedicated to those special people who choose to think for themselves, try new adventures, take risks, help others, and proceed in spite of danger. This book salutes those special individuals who choose to live an extraordinary life each and every day!

Table of Contents

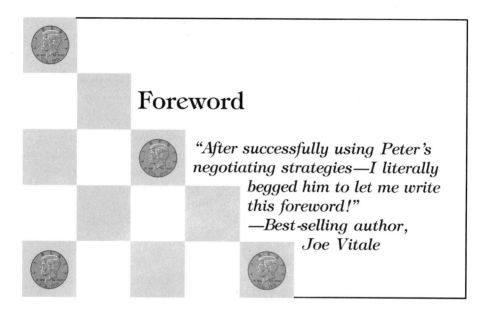

Foreword

"After successfully using Peter's negotiating strategies—I literally begged him to let me write this foreword!"
—*Best-selling author,*
Joe Vitale

Let me ask you a serious question: Is there anything in life that doesn't involve negotiating? Go through this stunning new system and you'll understand that opportunities are everywhere.

For example:

- Imagine walking into a bookstore and negotiating with the manager to *buy all the books you want by the bag-full.*

- Imagine looking at your next car purchase as a relaxed game of chess rather than an intense arm wrestling match with someone bigger than you.

These are just small examples of the kind of negotiating strategies that you'll find Peter Wink describing in *Negotiate Your Way to Riches. His system and strategies work...*take it from me!

Just recently, I used one of his techniques to close a deal worth tens of thousands of dollars—and closed it when the "other side" appeared to hold all the cards. Here's the story.

Companies and individuals always ask me to write books for them. I've co-authored books before, so these aren't unusual requests. I usually tell them my price and they say it's too much. Who hasn't heard that before? I've heard it dozens of times. I almost invariably back down and make my services available far cheaper—and I've probably lost hundreds of thousands of dollars as a result.

After going through *Negotiate Your Way to Riches*, I learned a technique that proved that I hold more cards than I once believed. I also learned how to successfully "sell myself" in a way that I can virtually name my price and get it! So, I tried it out.

A huge, well-known publisher came to me and asked me to write a new book for them. I gave them my price and then they told me it was far too high. They said they were going to have to walk away and find a different writer. And again, who hasn't heard that "line" before? As I stated, in the past I normally would've weakened. But not this time!

This time I decided to do something different. I called their bluff. I wisely realized that they needed me as much as I needed them. How did I know they needed me? Because Peter taught me how I brought something tangible to the table that the "other side" wanted and couldn't get anywhere else. They didn't just want "an author." There are thousands of authors out there who'll write a book for a very negotiable price. After all, many writers are always looking for new work.

What the publisher needed were my credentials. I'm a published author of eight books, two of them for the American Management Association. I also have an audio program with the highly respected Nightingale-Conant Corporation.

What the publisher got from working with me was more than just someone who could weave words. They also got someone with a reputation—something that would help them look good by association. That type of credibility is not an intangible—it's very real.

So I held out. I told them that if they wanted my services, they would need to pay my full fee. And they did! We closed the deal and I received my fee. The deal ended up going very smoothly.

Keep in mind that without Peter Wink's wisdom—which I got from learning his system—I would've blown the deal and lost thousands of times the investment I made in it. I wouldn't have respected my talent and credibility—and lowered the price. I might have weakened when they pushed. And I probably never would've realized that I brought more to the table than the obvious.

In fact, when I discovered Peter's strategies, I was in the process of writing a program called "The Power of Outrageous Marketing." During the writing, I had the pleasure of researching how titans, tycoons, and billionaires got rich in their own business. To my amazement, I discovered that every titan, tycoon, and billionaire cites having stellar negotiating skills as crucial to their success. And now it's your turn!

Whether you want to negotiate with a car dealer, real estate agent, tribesmen, your spouse, your kids, or Donald Trump—this system will give you all the tools you need to calmly and coolly win at the negotiating game virtually every time. And that's not a negotiable point. Just a fact!

> —Joe Vitale, best-selling author of *There's a Customer Born Every Minute, The Power of Outrageous Marketing,* and *Spiritual Marketing.*

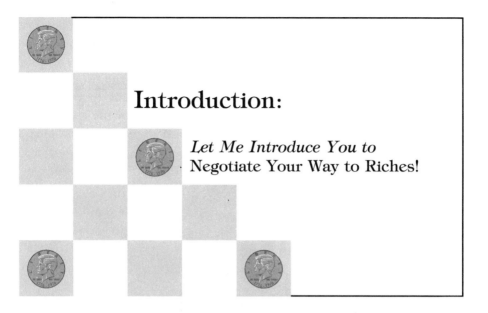

Introduction:

Let Me Introduce You to
Negotiate Your Way to Riches!

Congratulations and welcome to *Negotiate Your Way to Riches*! Why the early congratulations? Simple! You've earned it! By making an investment in yourself to learn these universal negotiating tactics, *you've put yourself in a special league*. You've moved ahead of just about everyone. You're going to be one of the few people who know how to convince others to give you just about whatever you want at substantial discounts—and in many instances FREE, with no money out of pocket. You're going to learn the same skill that's helped people such as Donald Trump, Sumner Redstone, Laurence Tisch, Madonna, John D. Rockefeller, Richard Branson, Rupert Murdoch, Ted Turner, Ross Perot, Bill Gates, P.T. Barnum, and other successful people rise to the top of their fields!

Negotiate Your Way to Riches is designed to teach you every facet of negotiating from A to Z. It's literally a step-by-step system, teaching you everything from how to develop the "negotiator's mindset" to using 36 specific negotiating tactics to close winning deals.

It makes no difference whether you're a beginner or seasoned veteran. This system is for anyone who wants to learn how to win as a deal-maker.

The title *Negotiate Your Way to Riches* makes one heck of a claim. But you can rest assured that it delivers. In fact, if you follow this system, you'll have increased your chances exponentially for success in every negotiation. Negotiating can make you very rich. *Think of all the money you can make and save over your lifetime by getting great deal after great deal.*

The money you've invested in this book will repay itself over and over again if you practice what you learn. Just think about this: in a few short hours you can learn a skill that you can benefit from for the rest of your life. You're probably asking, "What are some of the benefits to being a good strategic negotiator?" Great question!

By learning and using strategic negotiation techniques, you can:

- Save thousands (or even millions) of dollars on major purchases.
- Come out of a job interview with a fantastic salary, bonus, benefits, and other company perks.
- Distribute new products and services that may have been previously unavailable to you.
- Ask for a raise and get it with no arguments.
- Work as a negotiation consultant.
- Buy a new home for a fraction of the asking price.
- Sense liars, cheats, and other fraudulent businesspeople *before* you do business.
- Learn how to read, understand, and prepare favorable contracts.
- Obtain large discounts and say "no" to suggested retail prices.
- Walk into any car dealer or any other store and get the best possible deal.
- Convince anyone to give you just about anything on your terms.

And much more!

> *If you're still skeptical—read on to discover what one of the richest people in the world says about the value of negotiation.*

Strategic negotiation is considered one of Richard Branson's top 10 secrets to building the world-famous *Virgin* brand. By being a strategic negotiator, he's been able to convince other people to help him build companies such as *Virgin Airways*, *Virgin Atlantic*, *Virgin Megastores*, *Virgin Cola*, and countless other companies displaying the world-famous *Virgin* name. As of this writing, he has started more than 100 new ventures and is considered one of the greatest brand builders in the history of business.

How This System Works

First, you must read each section from start to finish. Go through each section word for word, in the proper sequence. Always remember that each section is designed to build on the previous one. And if you do not understand something you read, do not go any further. Go back and reread it again until the strategy or concept makes perfect sense to you. Also, if you don't know the definition of a word, immediately take out a dictionary and look it up.

Second, make sure to do all of the exercises. There aren't many so take action and do them all! Some will take minutes, and others require that you start using your new deal-making skills. It's not enough for me to put this book together, have you passively go through it, and then put it down without making any new deals. I really want you to *apply them daily*. Why? Consider the following example.

Take a moment and recall a course you've taken. First, you get stuck buying a huge (usually outdated) textbook filled with hundreds of pages of supposedly rock-solid information. You pick up that 15-pound book and say, "Wow, I'm going to be an expert when I'm done going through all this!" Will you really? By the time most people get through the end of their textbooks, they're not much further than when they started. Why? Because you have to take action and use your new skills or you won't ever be any good at deal-making. Reading is just the start; you must practice what you've learned.

Research shows that one of the main reasons people don't finish new books is because they come to a section or single word they don't understand. Then they get frustrated, put it away, never referring back to it. Then they claim the strategies and tactics don't work. I don't want this information to transmute into a paperweight. Commit to reading and understanding each and every word!

Do not, I repeat, do not skip around during your first reading. By skipping around, nothing will make proper sense to you. Give yourself the opportunity to be exposed to all of the information in the order it's presented. For instance, this book has a chapter called "The Negotiator's Mindset." If you skip it, you'll never understand how to think like a strategic negotiator. This section alone is vital to your success as a negotiator. Keep in mind that the number one reason that I've developed the *Negotiate Your Way to Riches* system is to teach you how to look at every situation from the perspective of a strategic negotiator. Even if you feel that you already possess the mindset of a strategic negotiator, read it just to reinforce yourself. Remember that repetition is the mother of skill. Therefore, go through this material and practice the tactics often!

I give you my word that my strategies won't let you down!

How This System Is Different

Before we go any further, I want to give you some background so that you understand that this isn't just another book on "negotiating."

What makes this negotiating system different from *so-called* experts' books and tapes on negotiation?

Many people ask me this question and I love them for it. In fact, the people who ask are the same people who've never had the opportunity to read this book, go through my home-study course, or see me live during one of my rare seminar appearances. Let me explain.

I'm sure you've seen countless books, videos, and seminars about negotiating and deal-making. They all have their unique *theoretical* twist. This one comes from real-life experience.

Having studied negotiation for many years, I have discovered three consistent problems with most material:

♦ They never tell you how they've personally used these skills.

♦ They give you isolated tactics, but never give you a strategy to use them in the real world.

♦ They never teach the most critical piece of the negotiation puzzle: how develop the *Negotiator's Mindset*. I suspect it's because they truly don't have one!

Some of these so-called experts are simply Ivy League students and graduates, business consultants, and researchers who have never used any of the tactics in their books and tapes. This system is different. *I've used them all and will prove it by giving you example after example.*

Negotiate Your Way to Riches has been developed for the average businessperson and consumer. This manual will show you how to use negotiation tactics for everyday purchases. Too many other books just give examples of how *Fortune* 500 executives negotiate colossal buyouts and takeovers. Some even go through hostage negotiations and other mumbo jumbo you'll never use.

The plain truth is that whether you're negotiating the purchase of a new car or a corporate buyout, the psychology and negotiation strategies all work the same way! Every negotiation is done systematically using the same tactics you're going to learn throughout this book. The variables of the deal are all that change. Remember: All great negotiators are great strategists. To be as forthright as I can, I find it hard to believe that if you follow my methods, you can possibly fail. You can make back the small investment you made in this book in only one teeny tiny deal. Now, of course, the proof is in the pudding.

Special Note: I have to ask you to please use the information you're going to learn with the highest morals and ethics. Many negotiators use systems much less powerful than mine to rob, to cheat, and to steal millions of dollars from vulnerable, unsuspecting, misinformed people. With the information you're about to learn, you can become one of the smartest, most cunning negotiators in the world—giving you a major advantage in the marketplace.

—Peter Wink

Taking the First Step on the Path to Riches!

First and absolutely foremost, I want to stop and thank you for purchasing my book. Too many authors never thank their readers and that's wrong. I'm very grateful to you for helping me become more successful as both a businessman and an author. And in return, I want to help you become as successful as you want to be as a negotiator. And now, on with the program!

Let me start by defining three terms that you'll see throughout this book. They are: *strategic negotiation*, *tactics*, and *leverage*.

▶ **Strategic negotiation is simply the act of devising and carrying out a well thought out plan to convince someone to give you something you want on your terms. Strategy is an overall, big picture plan, which includes a list of goals.**

Pretty simple, isn't it? What is it that you want? Is it a new automobile, a bigger home, or maybe a raise in your salary? Why not all three? It's not only possible, but with the strategies I'm going to teach you, it's very probable.

▶ *Tactics* **are the means by which you carry out your strategy.** They represent each step you take to achieving your strategic goal.

▶ *Leverage* **is showing that you have more to offer the other side (power, prestige, money, etc.) than they can offer you. Leverage can be real or perceived!**

The goal of *leverage* is twofold. First, it makes the other side feel as if it's a privilege to do business with you. And second, you'll make them feel that they have more to gain in the deal than you do.

Example: Think back to when you were a child. Did you ever get on a seesaw with someone heavier than you? What happened? The heavier kid always stopped at the bottom, leaving you in the air at their mercy. They basically leveraged their weight and power against yours. You're going to be a champion at leveraging your position by the time you finish this book. And the best part is that you'll know how to fully leverage your position no matter how little bargaining power you have or think you already possess.

Many negotiators will try to get you to believe they have more to offer you than they really do. Never get intimidated. By the time you've learned my techniques, you'll be able to spot liars, cheats, charlatans, and frauds from a mile away.

The goal and purpose of this program is to teach you how to convince other people to give you what you want on your own terms. Think about what I just said. By applying my negotiating strategies, other people will give you just about anything you want on your terms. And this is not being cutthroat, coercive, or threatening. *People will be happy to do business with you again and again.*

The information you learn can change your life and your bank account forever! **So let's get started learning the foundation for this entire system:** *The Negotiator's Mindset!*

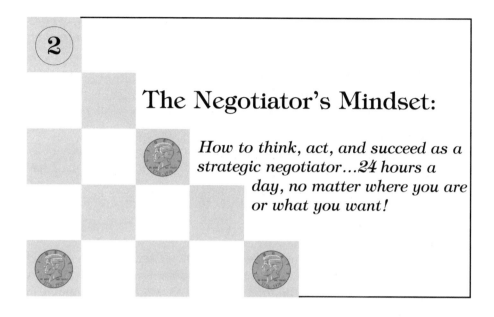

The Negotiator's Mindset:

How to think, act, and succeed as a strategic negotiator…24 hours a day, no matter where you are or what you want!

The information you're about to learn in this section is vital to your success as a negotiator! *Read it at least three times.* You absolutely, positively must know and understand it or you will not have the proper mindset to successfully implement my specialized negotiation strategies. Agreed? Good. Let's get started!

To become a skilled negotiator, you must possess what I call the *negotiator's mindset.* What do I mean by a *negotiator's mindset*? A person who possesses a negotiator's mindset has a frame of mind and thought patterns that enable him to look at every situation as a chance to negotiate and win.

Whether it's making a purchase, bartering, or convincing someone to do something for them, they're always ready to win. What's puzzling is that too many people think negotiation is only germane to product purchases or big business deals. This is a fallacy. *There are opportunities to negotiate everywhere around you—24 hours a day, seven days a week.* Did you know that every time you ask someone to do something for you, you've opened up a negotiation?

Teenagers are some of the best negotiators. I can still recall a personal example of strategic negotiation from my teen years. During my junior year of high school, I wanted my mother to extend my curfew 30 minutes on Saturday nights. At first she refused, saying that my grades would slip. I decided to negotiate with her. If she let me stay out 30 minutes later on Saturdays, I would keep my grade point average up or raise it. We both came out winners. She let me stay out later and I kept up my grade point average. Some negotiations can be that simple and some will require extreme amounts of persistence and determination.

I remember taking a memory course many years ago (no pun intended). The first thing the instructor said was that to have a good memory, I had to believe in my ability to develop it. I had to literally believe that I already possessed a perfect memory. I took his advice to heart and learned his memory program in a short amount of time. Why did I share this story?

I told you the story because most people don't see themselves as negotiators. They think that all negotiators wear a three-piece suit and work for a *Fortune* 500 company. Trust me when I say, *you'll know more about negotiating deals than 99 percent of these corporate bigwigs. It all starts with a belief in yourself and your abilities.* Most human beings have virtually the same ability to learn new skills. Did you ever set out to do something you never thought you could do? You probably attempted to do it half-heartedly and gave less than 100 percent. Why is this? By believing you can't do something, your body secretes negative chemicals in your brain, literally blocking you from thinking of ways to accomplish your goal; therefore, you feel as if you're wasting your time.

And the converse is also true. *When you have 100 percent belief in your ability to do, learn, and accomplish anything you set your mind to—you will!* Throughout my career, I've been involved in some very sophisticated negotiations, and take it from me, if you don't have 100 percent positive belief in yourself and your abilities, you're going to fail as a negotiator or anything else you try. The "other side" is sure to catch on to your weakness and beat you every time.

Discover your negotiator's mindset in only four simple steps!

The time has arrived my friend—you're now going to learn how to develop the *negotiator's mindset*. I can assure you that your life will never be the same! Ready...set...let's get started!

The following are four steps you'll have to take to develop a negotiator's mindset:

1. **Discover the vast opportunities to negotiate everywhere around you.**
2. **See yourself as a skilled negotiator.**
3. **Believe you can win every negotiation.**
4. **Practice your new negotiation skills every day.**

All four steps are vital to your development of the *negotiator's mindset*! Because these steps are so important, I'm going to take the time to talk about each one in detail.

Discover the Vast Opportunities to Negotiate Everywhere Around You

Every day you more than likely buy something. From this moment on *you must start looking at every transaction as a potential negotiation.* If you don't, you'll miss a plethora of opportunities to practice your skills. By practicing on a small scale, you'll enable yourself to see bigger opportunities to negotiate on higher priced goods and services.

Let me give you an example of how easy it is to find an opportunity to practice your negotiation skills and secure a great deal on something you already purchase regularly. For many years, I went to the same humdrum hairstylist and wore the same dull hairstyle. Finally, I got sick of the way I looked and decided to make a change. The first thing I did was fire my old stylist. Then I started going to a highly recommended, exclusive hairstylist. (Exclusive—that's just another way of saying he's extremely expensive, has degrees from several different beauty schools, serves wine, and will take you at the oddest times if necessary.)

The new stylist and I agreed on a new hairstyle and all was well. After a couple months of getting my hair styled every two weeks it dawned on me that I was spending a small fortune to keep up my look. I figured this was a great time to negotiate for a good deal!

I decided that I wanted to consistently come in every two weeks instead of once a month like I had done in the past. So one day while he was cutting my hair I asked him, "How many times a month does the average man get their hair cut?" He said, "Once." This immediately registered in my mind that I'm worth twice as much as the average male client. I also asked him how reliable the average client is. He said that most people cancel a few times a year. Again, I was special because I never canceled my appointments.

So I decided to lay it on the line and negotiate. I said, "I'd like to start coming in every other Tuesday evening at 7 p.m. if I can get a special discounted price." I explained that I would be there like clockwork and he could figure me as guaranteed cash flow twice a month. Because punctual, frequent, cash-paying customers are hard to find, he gave me a great discount and guaranteed my spot every two weeks.

We both won! He guarantees an exclusive, consistent, cash-paying customer, and I get to see the most exclusive hairstylist in the area, look terrific, and do it at a bargain price. And this is just one example you can use to build your *negotiator's mindset*. Try getting a deal with your hairstylist or mechanic.

I'll give you another example of how you can start using your negotiator's mindset. The next time you bring your car in for service, become very friendly with the mechanic. Did you know that a great deal of auto mechanics will fix you car out of their homes in their spare time? Many will fix your car for a fraction of what it costs to go back to the dealer or to a local full service car center. Most mechanics will also buy your parts at a discount and not even mark them up. It's true; all you have to do is get their phone number, call them at home, and start negotiating their hourly wage. (Remember: Many mechanics will not talk about fixing your car while they're at work. It can come off as unethical and get them fired.) I met my current mechanic in the backroom of a Pontiac dealership. This is a great way to save thousands of dollars on car repairs, so take advantage of it!

It's funny, but I've actually been practicing negotiating instinctively since I was a young child. In fact, when I first told my mother I was writing a book on negotiating, she reminded me of something I did as a youngster. You'll love this!

At the age of 13, I took advantage of a negotiation opportunity in the middle of an African jungle. Back in 1980, I was on a safari in Africa. During one of the picture taking safaris, our family jeep entered a small African village. We stopped to take pictures through our Jeep window, when suddenly we were surrounded by members of the Masai tribe, who were trying to sell arrows, knives, and various woodcarvings representing animals. The tribesmen believe that all Americans are rich and have lots of cash to spend on their woodcarvings. This was apparent because they were offering the woodcarvings at extremely high prices. By knowing and understanding the currency exchange between shillings and the dollar, I tried something interesting. I pointed to a specific tribesman who had a beautiful hunting knife I wanted. I held out an amount of shillings equal to what I thought was a bargain in U.S. dollars. Actually, it was more of a steal. He quickly rejected me. We went back and forth for a few minutes and finally he agreed on a price. I only spent an extra dollar, but to him that was a lot of money. I received the knife and he obtained extra money. A win/win negotiation resulted. I negotiated for several other pieces of artwork while I was there and got what I wanted every time.

What's even more interesting is that all of the negotiating was done using body language and facial expressions. The Masai tribe didn't speak a word of English. (You will learn how to read body language in Chapter 10.)

The point I'm making is that even in a small village in the middle of an African jungle, there was a great opportunity to practice my negotiation skills. I saved money and acquired art that would've cost my family a fortune in the United States (if you could even find it).

Now, you don't have to go to a place as obscure as Africa to find opportunities to negotiate. These opportunities are all around you—no matter where you go.

I want you to answer the following question: **What are some opportunities to negotiate that you can take advantage of today?**

Let me help you out if you're not sure. The following is a list of some common goods and services that are easily negotiated:

- **Automobiles.**
- **Salaries.**
- **Boats.**
- **Home maintenance.**
- **Chiropractic care.**
- **Educational classes.**
- **Lunches.**
- **Dinners.**
- **Hairstyling.**
- **Typing.**
- **Graphic arts.**
- **Computer programming.**

The bottom line here is that every product or service is negotiable if you're amongst decision-makers. Decision-makers are the people who can give you a discount or barter with you.

You may be saying to yourself, "There's no way that everything is negotiable." Thank you for your skepticism! You're going to learn a skill so powerful, so simple, and so available to you that you're going to see this system as worth hundreds of thousands of dollars. In fact, I'll go so far as to say millions! This skill is called *bartering*. I'll teach you how to *barter goods and services with anyone, for anything, in any place*!

Never skip over lists and exercises. You do not want to rob yourself of the opportunity to become a highly skilled negotiator. By doing all of the necessary lists and exercises, you'll become a highly skilled negotiator in no time!

As I promised, you're going to have some exercises, lists, and chances to get real negotiating experience. Here's the first of them.

It's important to recognize the vast opportunities all around you to negotiate. Take a few minutes or more and think of some negotiation opportunities that you see in your daily life. List some of these opportunities in the space provided.

Write down 20 goods and/or services that you purchase regularly:

1. _____

2. _____

3. _____

4. _____

5. _____

6. _____

7. _____

8. _____

9. _____

10. _____

11. _____

12. _____

13. _____

14. _____

15. _____

16. _____

17. _____

18. _____

19. _____

20. _____

Did you list 20 goods and/or services? Great! Good job!

Let's move on to the second step in developing a negotiator's mindset.

See Yourself as a Skilled Negotiator

To be successful at anything, you must have what's called a "positive self-concept." A "positive self-concept" is attained only when you believe you can do or accomplish anything.

Sometimes, you have to trick your mind into believing it at first. No matter what you pursue, whether it's being a skilled negotiator, doctor, waitress, or anything else, you must see and identify yourself as that person. You have to eat, sleep, and drink it. It has to become a part of you. Successful negotiators are negotiators 24 hours a day. You can't just say, "I'll only be a terrific negotiator at work." *To be a skilled negotiator at work, you must also be one when you're away from the office!* Even though I work privately for other organizations and own a couple of businesses, when people ask me what I do for a living, I always respond, "I'm a strategic negotiator."

To illustrate my point, I'm going to ask you a question. How many people can you name that study strategic negotiation? I have another question. How many people do you know who've ever spent one minute studying strategic negotiation? How many did you come up with? Did you even come up with one?

Just by starting this program and practicing what I'm teaching you, you're already becoming a more skilled negotiator. All you have to do is practice these skills each and every day to perfect them. Always have a positive self-concept in your pursuit of excellence as a strategic negotiator or anything else.

Before we go any further, I want to ask you a simple, yet revealing question. Are you a skilled negotiator? What's your answer?

If you answered an unequivocal yes, congratulations, you have 80 percent of what it takes to develop the mindset of a successful, skilled negotiator. I can assure you that if you learn all of the skills that I present in this book, you'll attain the other 20 percent in no time. If you answered no, reread the preceding section until you have a positive self-concept and identify yourself as a skilled negotiator.

Let's move on to the third step to developing the negotiator's mindset.

Believe You Can Win Every Negotiation

To learn the tactics and strategies of skilled negotiators is only one facet of becoming a strategic negotiator. To actually win a negotiation, you must believe you can win before it starts. This also has to do with having a positive self-concept. Let me explain.

Because I am from Chicago, I have the opportunity to hear a great deal of interviews with the former Chicago Bulls basketball legend, Michael Jordan. During an interview, I heard Michael answer a question that illustrates my point.

A young lady was interviewing Michael about his ability to shoot and score so many points in every game. She asked him if he could feel if a shot is going to go in or miss the basket as he releases it. I'll never forget his profound reply. He said, "I feel that every shot is going to go in or I wouldn't bother taking it." *You* have to feel the same way. *You have to feel you can win every time.* Not some of the time—*every time!*

The ability to win at the negotiating table takes a great deal of belief in yourself and your skills. Salespeople are great examples. Many salespeople take extended sales training programs. They read books, go to seminars, and attend college and continuing education programs that teach them how to prospect, present, and close the sale. So, why are so few of them successful? It's because they really don't believe they'll be able to get in the door, negotiate the deal, and close the sale.

Think of it this way. Can you imagine a surgeon graduating from school and completing all of the required training, then going into surgery feeling unsure he or she could successfully operate on the patient? What do you think the result would be? Disaster, maybe?

Too many people believe that strategic negotiating is reserved for CEOs and other executives of multi-billion dollar conglomerates. They also believe you need some genius mind or a high intelligence quotient (IQ). This is simply not the case. Anyone who follows the methods, tactics, and strategies that I'm presenting as we move through this system can negotiate with anyone, under any circumstances, and win!

Always remember that as you go through this system, you'll be learning the skills you'll need to win at strategic negotiating! The business suit isn't required or I would have provided it to you with this book.

You're doing great; let's get to the final step in developing the negotiator's mindset!

Practice Your Negotiating Skills Daily

As I stated earlier, you must look for opportunities to negotiate everywhere, all around you. Then you must use your new negotiation skills as opportunities arise.

Did you ever hear the famous phrase "use it or lose it"? Just like an unexercised muscle: if you don't negotiate regularly, you'll lose your capacity and the mental muscle it takes to strategize and win at the negotiating table. *Because strategic negotiating contains so many different elements and various deal components, you must constantly hone your skills.*

You must take advantage of the vast number of opportunities you'll have to negotiate with family members, coworkers, strangers on the street, store clerks, or anyone else, anywhere else.

 Never let a day go by without negotiating with someone over something. Regardless of your experience, you must negotiate daily, or your skills will become stale, out-of-date, and weak!

Have you ever heard the famous saying "practice makes perfect"? I have, and I want to share an important twist on it. Practice itself doesn't make perfect. You can practice skills incorrectly and never be perfect. *Practicing the correct skills is what makes perfect.* That's what you're learning here!

Quick Review

Do you feel that you now understand the four steps to developing the *negotiator's mindset*? Can you answer yes to all four of the following review questions? Let's quickly go through them.

1. **Do you now see the vast amount of goods and services you can negotiate for?**

2. **Are you a strategic negotiator?**

3. **Do you believe you can win every negotiation before you even start?**

4. **Are you practicing your new skills every day?**

If you answered yes to each of the four questions, you're ready to move on. But before we do, I'd like you to do one more simple exercise! Please take the time to write down five things that you feel you cannot obtain because they are too expensive. Don't worry about the price. As a skilled negotiator, the sky's the limit. (You'll refer to this list later in the book.)

1. _____

2. _____

3. _____

4. _____

5. _____

Whew! We've covered quite a bit of material already. Take my word that as you learn more and more, you'll see the importance of developing the *negotiator's mindset*. Keep in mind that each section will build on the notion that you're working to further develop your negotiator's mindset.

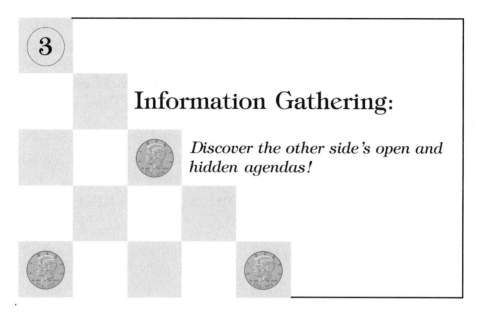

Information Gathering:

Discover the other side's open and hidden agendas!

T o win as a negotiator, you must go through a stage called *Information Gathering*. When you gather information, you learn more about yourself as well as the other side's overall position. (The other side refers to all people and/or institutions with which you will be negotiating.) By gathering information, you allow yourself to make objective moves based on a strong combination of intuition and factual research. It's always important that you never jump into any negotiation without gathering the facts and studying them very carefully.

Keep in mind that by gathering information about the other side, you're looking for both positive and negative information. As you gather information, make sure to take good notes and write everything down—no matter how miniscule it may seem. By writing down all of the facts, you allow yourself to read, reread, and evaluate the situation over and over again. In turn, you'll make better decisions and remember important details.

There are three steps in the *information gathering* process:

1. **Gather information about yourself and your own situation.**

2. **Gather information about the other side and their open or hidden agendas.**

3. **Synthesize everything and formulate an educated negotiation strategy.**

It's very important that you go through all three steps in as much detail as possible. Inexperienced negotiators take great risks by not gathering any information about the other side. And as a result, their deals fall short of their expectations or end in disaster. *By properly evaluating all of the players and their agendas in a deal, you transform a risk into an educated decision.* And this leads to more successful deal-making.

Let's go through each of the three steps of the information gathering *process in detail!*

Gather Information About Yourself and Your Own Situation

To be successful in any negotiation, you must take an objective look at where you are right now. Consider the following two-part question: What is your present situation and what is your desired outcome?

When gathering information about yourself, you must be as objective as possible and evaluate everything, including:

- **Motives:** What is driving you to do business with this person or organization and why do you need this good or service?

- **Reasoning:** What is the true, underlying reason you want to complete this deal?

- **Debts:** What are your current and future debts?

- **Capital:** What resources are available to you and what are you lacking?

- **Cash on hand:** Do you have enough available cash to finish this deal?

- **Hidden agendas:** Are you being up front with the other side or are you trying to hide something?

- **Time line:** How much time do you have to finish this deal?

- **Duress:** Do you feel pressured or are you comfortable in this situation?

- **Responsibilities:** Are you the only person representing your side? Who are all the players?

Because every deal has so many variables, I can't possibly list them all. So I'm going to give you an example of how you should gather information the next time you negotiate for a car. The next time you negotiate the price of a new car, you have to ask yourself the following 10 questions regarding your current situation:

1. **How much money can I afford to spend?**
2. **What am I willing to spend?**
3. **What are my current debts?**
4. **What new debts will I be incurring over the next year? (Then add an additional 10 percent.)**
5. **Will this purchase positively or negatively affect my lifestyle?**
6. **How's my credit?**
7. **What kind of automobile am I going to purchase?**
8. **Where do I want to purchase this automobile?**
9. **What is my level of desperation to obtain it?**
10. **Am I willing to walk away without making the purchase?**

Why must you analyze all of these questions? Let's go through them one by one as they pertain to purchasing a car!

How much money can you afford to spend on this purchase? This is simply determining the amount of money you truly have available to comfortably spend on the car. Too many people choose a maximum dollar figure they feel they can afford. However, after going through the *information gathering* process, they suddenly realize they cannot afford to spend as much as they thought.

Car dealers are notorious for trying to get you to spend more than you can afford. That's why so many people lease cars. It's usually because people can get into a car they could never dream of owning for less money. And at the end of the lease, they wind up with zilch! Always remember that salespeople are out to make the most profit they can. And rightfully so—it's their job! The challenge for you is that they're going to charge you the maximum price they feel they can get away with. That's why it's important to know the maximum amount you can afford to spend ahead of time.

How much are you willing to spend on this purchase? Just because you know you can afford to spend a certain amount of money, doesn't mean that you have to spend every cent of it. What's wrong with getting a good deal and pocketing the rest? Nothing of course! That's why you're learning how to negotiate.

Let's say you've decided the maximum amount of money you can afford to spend on a new car over the next four years is $20,000. After further *information gathering*, you may decide that you don't want to be leveraged with debt by buying an expensive car. Sometimes it's better to spend a little less on a car, and be able to save extra money for a rainy day or to buy something else.

Each and every time I buy a car, I go through this same scenario. I always figure out the maximum amount of money I can afford. And then, after going through the *information gathering* process, I realize just how much I'm willing to spend. By going through this step, you'll automatically be less susceptible to being talked into overspending by the salesperson. When you know exactly what you can and can't spend, you're in control of every negotiation.

What is the total of all your current debt? By adding up all your current debt first, you'll know before the negotiation if you have other responsibilities that must be considered. By knowing your total debt, you'll make a smarter, better-educated decision as to how much you'll spend. Again, *never let any salesperson talk you into spending more money than you can afford*. By remembering college tuition bills, landscaping charges, credit card payments, mortgages, and other debts, you'll feel confident telling the salesperson no to their inflated price.

What debts are you going to incur over the next 12 months? (Add them all up and then add an additional 10 percent.) By sitting down and thinking through all of your future debt over the next 12 months, you should be able to recall any potential expenses you didn't previously remember.

For instance, does it look like your child needs braces? Does the roof need to be replaced? Does your car need new tires? These are debts that anyone can experience at a moment's notice. Think real hard as to what amount of money you can afford to spend. If you're buying a company car, think about the next 12 months of business expenses.

Once you have your answer, add an additional 10 percent. (This is a great practice.) For instance, if your debts add up to $15,000 per year, add an additional $1,500. Why? For some reason, we seem to run into Murphy's Law at the worst possible time. Murphy's famous law says, **"If something can possibly go wrong, it will."** By adding at least a 10 percent cushion, you leave yourself room to incur some unexpected expenses. *Always expect the unexpected.*

Will this purchase affect your personal or business lifestyle? Ask yourself the following questions:

♦ **Will I have to scale back my family's lifestyle to own this product or obtain this service?**

♦ **How will my family be affected by this purchase?**

♦ **Do I like my current standard of living?**

♦ **Is it really worth it?**

♦ **Do I have to worry about paying my other bills?**

♦ **Am I risking my family's future security to pay for this item?**

♦ **Will my family disapprove of this purchase?**

♦ **Do I have another option?**

If you answered yes to any of the previous questions, you have to reevaluate your options. Take the time to analyze this situation further. If you're a risk-taker and feel you can take chances, then consider going for it. But if you're like most people, by overextending yourself financially, you may experience a lot of sleepless nights and unnecessary stress. This combination is considered very dangerous. *Always consider the long-term effects of all of your decisions on yourself, your family, and your business!*

Have you checked your credit rating? Having poor credit subjects you to paying additional percentage points on loans or even inflated prices on goods and services. Did you know that most people who try to take advantage of these "zero percent" financing deals are turned down? It's because anybody with a negative mark on their credit report can be turned down. Before making a large, expensive purchase, such as an automobile or a home, you must make sure you clear up your credit rating. Car dealers and real estate brokers love to add percentage points to your financing. For car dealers, financing represents one of their most profitable areas.

Do you know what type of automobile you're going to purchase? By knowing the exact model, year, and price that you're willing to pay, you won't subject yourself to the ruthless up-selling that many automobile salespeople are notorious for. Nowadays, with the Internet, it's so easy to find out the dealers invoice price or just about any other detail on any vehicle you could ever want. The Internet has made car dealer's jobs an absolute nightmare!

For example, I recently decided to buy a small sports car. Before I even went to the dealer, I determined the exact model, color, year, and price. I also did a lot of competitive shopping online and offline. In other words,

I went through the *information gathering* process and determined what I wanted at what price. As I predicted, the dealer tried up-selling over and over. (Up-selling is the process of convincing someone to spend more money than they were going to on a product or service.)

Always remember that *up-selling is a form of negotiation*. Salespeople will try to convince you that you can get better mileage, higher resale value, and a host of other supposed benefits. Believe me, all they want is more of your hard-earned cash! Keep in mind: All of these benefits don't mean anything if you can't afford to make the purchase in the first place!

Where are you going to purchase the vehicle? Knowing an automobile dealer or salesperson (or knowing someone who can introduce you to one) may help you get a better deal. Consider the following questions:

1. **Do you know any salespeople or dealers who can help you purchase the vehicle?**
2. **Do you know anyone who knows any salespeople or dealers?**
3. **What kind of cars do they sell?**
4. **Could they get you the car you're looking for?**
5. **Would you settle for a car they could get for you if the price is right?**

If the salesperson is close to you or your family, they may consider buying you the car using their employee discount (you'll learn more about the employee discount strategy later in this book in the Bonus Section on Employee Discounts). The bottom line is that people are the key ingredient to successful negotiations.

By searching through the newspaper, Internet, and visiting car dealers, you'll learn who charges what price and their level of disparity. And watch out! Some dealers are ridiculously overpriced! Don't forget: All major purchases are negotiable. *Both used and new car prices are easily bargained down.* I've done this successfully over and over for years.

There's a saying that birds of a feather flock together. Automobile salespeople all attend similar functions, trade shows, and networking groups. Many times, salespeople earn referral fees when they recommend each other. Seek out these golden opportunities! Just because a salesperson typically sells Cadillacs doesn't mean they don't have the Buick you want on the lot!

You also may want to take a car salesperson out to lunch. Seriously—ask a current or former salesperson to teach you the tricks of the trade when it comes to buying and selling cars. Their knowledge will prove very valuable and you can get it for the price of a burger!

Are you making this purchase out of desperation? I'll repeat this over and over again: *Never make a major purchase decision out of desperation!*

Example: Don't wait to trade in your car until it barely runs. To start, you'll have difficulty negotiating an optimal price because you're trying to sell junk. Junk has little, if any, value or leverage!

Sometimes just making a $100 repair on some part of the car can have a perceived value of thousands of dollars to the dealer or any other prospective buyer. If you fall into this category, make sure you either trade or sell your car before you experience too many problems with it. My recommendation is to *fix the car and negotiate without desperation.*

The great business guru and author of *Swim With the Sharks Without Being Eaten Alive*, Harvey MacKay, offers a great piece of advice: "Never wait until you're thirsty to dig yourself a well." If you do, it will be too late! Enough said.

By the time you've finished learning my strategies, you'll be able to negotiate and get the best price on anything you want to purchase. Just be patient with yourself!

Are you willing to walk away from the negotiation? *Walking away smiling* is the most powerful strategy you can use as a strategic negotiator. Never fall in love with a product or service because neither will love you back! You'll learn more about this strategy later in this book.

All negotiators have considered the following question at some point: "What is the worst possible thing that can happen to me if I don't do this deal?" Think about how that question plays into our automobile scenario. Is the worst-case scenario that you'll have to choose another model? Will you have to purchase a used car instead of a new car? You may even find the same car somewhere else cheaper! No big deal! Will you still have food in your mouth tomorrow? Can you still afford to keep the phone turned on? I know I sound a little flippant, but I'm trying to make a point! By playing out the worst-case scenario, you can walk into a negotiation with the personal power to *say no to a deal that isn't right for you.*

Example: One of the companies that I worked with wanted me to negotiate a deal to produce a highly complex CD-ROM that would be worth sales of at least $1 million. Development costs are usually in the neighborhood of $120,000–$500,000, depending on the features (some go into the $1 million-plus area). Normally, you need a down payment of at least 50 percent of the development costs. This company couldn't afford that kind of down payment. In fact, my goal was to give the developer a down payment of only $10,000!

Before I started negotiating, I worked through various financial scenarios and came up with an excellent agreement based on the $10,000 down payment and a royalty (an amount of money that the developer would receive for each CD-ROM we sold) to the developer. I was absolutely certain I would get what I wanted. I decided I wasn't going to budge on my parameters. I was prepared for rejection. If I had to walk away from several software developers—so be it! In the end, I'll win!

The most important decision I made was to walk away from any developers who didn't see things my way. In my head, I knew it was just a matter of time until I would find the right developer to work with. How long did it take? Not as long as I thought it would.

For three months, I approached countless developers who laughed at this deal and told me it couldn't be done. I was told the amount of the down payment was laughable, the royalty wasn't high enough, and that I had no idea what I was doing. I just kept saying "next."

As I predicted, I found a small Chicago-based software developer who was short of work and anxious to do business with us. The CD-ROM successfully sold in software stores and catalogs worldwide. And the orders well exceeded projections. Another successful deal was consummated! Why? Because I made the decision that I would rather walk away than give in. Stick to your guns—it's all a numbers game. *Be willing to laugh in the face of rejection!*

Now on to step two in the information gathering stage!

Gather Information About the Other Side!

This section is designed to teach you how to learn valuable information about the other side and their open and hidden agendas. You're probably wondering *what kind of information and for what purpose?* Excellent questions!

I'm going to start off with a quote from the world-famous philosopher/strategist Sun Tsu. He said, "If you know the enemy and know yourself, you need not fear the result of a hundred battles." What did he mean by those profound words? Think about it. If you fully understand your own situation (which I'm sure you do), you can set your agenda. Now, you must utilize a similar process and *learn everything you can about the other side.* In other words, you get to do some detective work! By knowing yourself and knowing the other side, your chances of winning the negotiation have multiplied exponentially.

The bottom line is that being successful as a negotiator requires doing some undercover detective work. You must fully investigate and analyze any available information concerning the other side and any potential agenda they may have. Once you uncover inside information, you can effectively understand the reasoning behind their every move, and then you can predict their next maneuver as if you're in a chess game. Therefore, you can strategize your counterattack and win! To say it bluntly: You have to get in their head.

To learn about the other side and their agendas, you must consider the following questions:

What kind of company culture are you going to be negotiating with?

You're probably saying, "I don't negotiate with companies, I negotiate with people." That's true—but only partially. Companies don't talk—they're invented. But keep in mind that almost anyone you negotiate with is working for, or representing, their company. Their negotiation style and agenda may not reflect their personal beliefs, ethics, values, or agenda. They reflect the company's culture. *A business is a living, breathing, socialized entity, just like you and I.* Some companies have a reputation for being honest and trustworthy. Others have a reputation of being shrewd and cutthroat. Every corporate culture is different and demands that their employees follow suit!

Some personal computer manufacturers fit the bill perfectly. Not too long ago, I approached three of the top personal computer manufacturers to get involved in a software deal I was working on. My goal was to get one of them to bundle a client's new software package on all of their new computers. All three attempts were unsuccessful.

You're probably asking yourself, "If Peter's such a great negotiating expert, why couldn't he get the deal?" Great question! Let me address it so you can understand my reasoning. It wasn't that I couldn't get a deal. It just wasn't worth our time in terms of effort and dollars. They wanted to give me pennies per unit for software that cost almost $200,000 to produce. Sure, they had excellent negotiators who promised very grandiose numbers in terms of volume. But wisely, I saw it as a smokescreen. The numbers showed that we'd lose a lot of money. I turned down each of the offers and I don't regret it!

I must admit that I did my homework in regard to the PC and software industries. I investigated all three companies and knew I was swimming in shark-infested waters. This is a prime example of a shrewd corporate culture. Their negotiators were every bit as crude as the culture! Remember the saying "know thy company!"

Who are you really negotiating with?

It's vitally important to find out as much as you can about the people you'll be negotiating with. There are several ways to do this detective work (which you'll learn later in this chapter). But for now we must learn the basics.

Consider the following questions:

1. **What is the other side's job title or position? Is he or she the president, the vice president, or a manager?**

2. **What is his or her first and last name?**

3. **How long has he or she been with the company?**

4. **Is the other side male or female?**

5. **Does he or she have a reputation for being nice and laid-back or does he or she have a reputation for being nasty and incorrigible?**

This question needs consideration for a number of reasons—mainly because each and every variable needs to be explored. As you're going to learn, everything you learn about the other side will stack the odds of winning the negotiation in your favor.

At this point, you may be wondering how to get the inside scoop! There are several things you can do.

Call the company and tell the operator or receptionist the purpose of your call. He or she will probably give you the person's name that you should be talking to. The operator will either transfer you to the person you're asking for or you can just ask the operator for the other side's full name. (I do not recommend talking to this person the first time you call.) *Write down the person's name, address, and phone number, and if you feel comfortable, ask the operator if this person is fun to work with.* (This requires being a little slick.) Believe it or not, operators will tend to answer you if you just ask! *Next, ask if he or she has an assistant.* If he or she does, you're at a major advantage. *Call and ask to speak to Mr. or Ms. X's assistant.* Once you're connected, I suggest that you turn on the charm and be very courteous, humble, and genuine.

There are certain people within an organization you need to treat with kid gloves. They can be the difference between success and failure when it comes to getting inside information. This group includes:

▶ **Phone operators:** These are the people who pick up the phone, answer questions, and transfer phone calls.

▶ **Receptionists:** Receptionists usually greet visitors, give coffee, do small administrative tasks, or otherwise entertain outside guests.

▶ **Secretaries:** Secretaries usually type letters, fax documents, send e-mail, and perform other assorted administrative tasks for their immediate supervisors.

▶ **Personal assistants:** Personal assistants usually take care of an executive's busy schedule, make travel arrangements, take notes at meetings, run errands, advise their bosses on issues, and do other miscellaneous tasks.

▶ **Gatekeepers:** A gatekeeper is a slang term for any of the above. Gatekeepers usually act as filters for their bosses. And they have the power to keep their bosses from seeing or talking to you. On the flip side: if you treat them politely, they can open doors for you.

Negotiator's Note

Treat receptionists, operators, personal assistants, and secretaries with the utmost respect. Each of them is like a file cabinet overflowing with information, just ready to give you everything you need. Mistreat any of them and you can kiss your deal goodbye. You may never even get your proposal past them, and if you do, they'll be sure to tell their bosses how rude you were to them. The boss will usually side with them. Remember to start off every relationship on a positive note!

After you've been directed to the proper person's assistant, briefly introduce yourself and tell the assistant how much you need his or her help. It's very important you don't "ask" for her help. You must tell her you "need" her help. Humbly tell her the purpose of the call and ask what the best way is for you to present your proposal to her boss. If she questions the proposal, just give her a brief explanation and then explain to her how her boss will benefit from it. From there, go on and tell her that you don't want to seem too overbearing.

Throughout my years of negotiating and meeting various gatekeepers, I haven't met one that doesn't want the reputation of being the person who brings his boss a great idea or proposal. Get chummy and gatekeepers will more than likely answer a few questions about the boss. Eventually, he will let you meet or speak to the boss.

Because their time is so precious and valuable, it's very important you know which questions to ask gatekeepers. You want to ask them questions concerning their bosses' behavior, habits, and overall demeanor.

The following are some of the questions I like to ask gatekeepers:

- Does Mr. or Ms. X like people soliciting them with proposals?
- Is Mr. or Ms. X fun to work with?
- Is Mr. or Ms. X very busy?
- Is Mr. or Ms. X hard to get a hold of?
- Does Mr. or Ms. X travel a lot?
- Is Mr. or Ms. X very nice?

Sometimes you'll come across a less than friendly gatekeeper. Have no fear because you can still get your information from various other sources. These sources are less direct, yet they're still worth investigating.

Other good information-gathering resources include:

- **Ex-employees:** Contact previous employees and ask their opinions about this person's demeanor.

- **Coworkers:** Any employee can be a great source of information. If you ask enough people, you're bound to find someone who knows information pertaining to the person you're seeking.

- **Trade journals:** Trade journals spotlight various decision-makers within different companies. Research these publications and see if you come across the person you're negotiating with.

▸ **Company annual reports:** A company's annual report always lists all the key decision-makers and their responsibilities. Annual reports are also great sources of information and employees names!

▸ **Company's vendors:** Question people who conduct business with the company.

▸ **Company's customers:** Find out who the company sells their goods and services to. Call some of them and ask about the person in question.

The bottom line is that you must *find out every detail about the individual or group—no matter how miniscule or seemingly unimportant*. Once you learn this inside information, you're going to be at a huge advantage at the negotiating table. I must tell you—even without this information, you can still win the negotiation, but you must proceed with more caution. If you follow my guidelines, I guarantee that you'll win more negotiations in less time!

What is the company or individual's agenda?

You must make a concerted effort to find out what the other side wants from you. This is vitally important! One of the major challenges that amateur negotiator's have is to stop thinking only of their own needs and wants in a negotiation. This is erroneous and dangerous strategizing. It's too one-sided—you're not completing 50 percent of the challenge! You need to know what the other side stands to gain by doing business with you.

By putting yourself in the other side's shoes and getting into their head, you can start to see the negotiation from their perspective. You must be able to accurately or fairly accurately predict what they want from you. Think about what an advantage you'd have if you could sit in on their meetings or just be a fly on the wall when they discuss their intentions. This puts you in a more intelligent bargaining position.

Let me show you how to do this. I want you to ask yourself the following question: **What does the other side want from me?**

Consider these possibilities:

♦ **Do they want a certain amount of money?**

♦ **Are they in need of something that can help with what they're working on?**

♦ **Is there a special service that you provide that they're in dire need of?**

◆ **Can they be looking to capitalize on your reputation?**

◆ **Based on their behavior, what options are the most likely?**

I personally found that one of the most effective ways to find out about the other side is to just ask. You're probably sitting there in shock. I know I was the first time someone offered me this kind of information. Many times, I've actually asked the other side, "What is the bottom line?" "What can I do for you?" More times than not, they tell me. But the key is to ask! I've had people come right out and tell me inside information they never should have.

If you ask politely, the other side may tell you:

▶ **Cost per product:** Yes, they'll tell you something as seemingly confidential as their numbers. In many instances they'll tell you the exact dollar-amount it costs to produce goods or give their service to the penny. Once you know their profit margins, you'll know what to offer to get the deal. Beware—they may be bluffing! Like I said, *do your homework!*

▶ **Financial cushion:** The other side has told me the exact amount of money they have to negotiate with. During a recent negotiation, someone actually said, "Peter, let me level with you. We run on a profit margin of 200 percent over cost, but I'm willing to do the job at 10 percent over cost, just to get the job. We're desperate!" I offered 5 percent and still closed the deal. Sound ruthless? Not at all, considering the company I was negotiating on behalf of was going bankrupt at the time.

▶ **Level of desperation:** As the previous example proved—once the other side announces how much they need your product, service, or sale, they have to play by your rules.

▶ **Willingness to lose money:** Some companies are willing to lose money on the first sale just to bring in customers to create profit during the second sale! This is typical of direct marketers and catalog retailers. My experience is that once you pay a certain price for a good or service, the price should only go down, or at least stay the same.

Of the people you attempt to deal with, 99 percent will be poor negotiators at best. This is a major advantage for you.

Next, you must consider what the other side wants from you. This can be a lot trickier. Consider the following questions:

♦ **What do I have of value that would be of interest to this person or his company?**

♦ **Do I have a product or service that can make them huge profits?**

♦ **Am I offering a service they must have to be more efficient and profitable in the future?**

♦ **Will doing business with me enhance their reputation?**

Let me illustrate this point with an example of one of my recent negotiations.

Some months ago, I was negotiating a deal to purchase a large quantity of workbooks for a famous author's home-study course. I needed to get the workbooks for cheap. Our discount needed to be much greater than normal. We knew this product was going to be a best-seller and wanted it in our catalog right away. I did my homework and researched the past price history of these workbooks through another company that had already negotiated an identical purchase.

Once I knew what the other company paid, I knew I could get our cost down another 20 percent. I learned all about the players in the deal and used our buying power and reputation to our advantage. At this point, I felt I had this deal in the bag. And because I researched the company that printed the workbooks, I found something of higher value to offer them than the initial sale.

During my research, I found the name of one of the printer's best customers. They informed me the printer was also in the lettershop business. (Lettershops sort, source, and mail letters and postcards.) Fortunately, the company I negotiated on behalf of was in the mail order business and had a vast amount of work that could be turned over to their lettershop. They would profit greatly from the additional work. It turned out that in exchange for a potential opportunity to handle some of our mailings, they gave me a better than expected deal on the workbooks. It was a win/win for everyone. The only reason I got it was because I took the time to gather information about the other side and used my imagination.

Are they reputable?

You're probably wondering why "reputation" is so relevant. Most Harvard-type business books will usually tell you not to deal with a firm that has a questionable reputation. (True, it would be much better to deal with a clean organization. And in the real world sometimes you have to take the bad with the good.) So do yourself a favor and don't buy into this kind of nonsense! Even though you have to be careful with a questionable firm, you may unfortunately still need what they're offering.

When dealing with a company that has a questionable or bad reputation (whether founded or not), *you must do extra research*. Study various trade magazines for articles or interview segments, citing reasons as to why the firm has a poor reputation and read between the lines.

Consider the following about a questionable company:

♦ **Are they known for hassling their vendors over pricing or billing?**

♦ **Have they stole money?**

♦ **Is the company manipulative?**

♦ **Do they mistreat their own or other employees?**

♦ **Have they reneged on promises?**

♦ **Do they use strong-arm tactics or subject suppliers and vendors to other forms of pressure?**

Find out any information about the other side, no matter how irrelevant it may seem. Sometimes you can spot trends or predict future challenges you're going to have to deal with. Also, make sure the information someone gives you isn't fallacious, biased, or too subjective. Some people will give you misleading information because they have a personal ax to grind. Try to separate the two.

Anyway you do it, take notes and follow up on any suspicious incidents. Always remember: Just because a company has a bad reputation, doesn't mean that you don't need their goods and services. Or for that matter, their cash!

Have you questioned people who have already done business with the other side?

Seek out people who have already done business with the firm you're proposing to deal with. This is one of the best strategies for finding inside information. (Remember the deal I told you about with the printer? I've done it over and over!) People who have previously dealt with the other side can tell you all the positive and negative aspects of dealing with them. Ask as many questions as you can regarding their past dealings. They may tell you the firm is very reputable or they may tell you how they were ripped off. This information is vital to your negotiating strategy!

Some great sources of information include:

♦ **Vendors.**

♦ **Suppliers.**

♦ **Customers.**

♦ **Employees (past and current).**

By questioning people who've already dealt with the other side, you can *get a firsthand account of what it's like to deal with this person or company.* And again, take massive amounts of notes. Someone else's fate can save you from making a foolish deal. Learn from the experiences of others.

One of the most important areas to question about any company is its financial position. Before negotiating for money, *do your homework and investigate the company's assets.* Some small companies try to throw their weight around and a novice negotiator bites—hook, line, and sinker. This can cost you a lot of money for nothing. Let me give you an example.

Some years ago, I was negotiating the purchase of thousands of videos from a very reputable video distributor. The deal went very smoothly. So smoothly that I felt a little uneasy. My hunch was correct and my upcoming celebration was a little premature. Murphy's Law came pounding on my door with a surprise I couldn't believe!

I'll never forget what happened next. A surprisingly rude lady called me on the phone, screaming at me, saying that I was purchasing a video from another vendor that only she had the right to sell. She claimed to have all the distribution rights for the Chicago area. Obviously, I had to get more information.

My first move was to call the original vendor and explain what transpired. He told me that he would investigate the matter and get back to me. About an hour or so later, my phone rang. The original vendor explained that he was new on the job and had made a horrible mistake. The original contract with me was null and void. The other distributor did indeed have an exclusive arrangement to distribute the video in Chicago. I could've been a jerk and made them stick to their agreement, but that would've led to bad feelings and a legal nightmare. After all, I wanted to do business with him again.

I decided to compromise and called the new distributor to reason with her. Right off the bat, she was loudly criticizing me about how I handled this deal. I really had to keep my composure! Believe me when I say, this one was a tough, bitter pill to swallow. Throughout the conversation, she was telling me about the hundreds of videos she exclusively handled and how I need to buy them through her if I plan on staying in this niche of the video market. I just said, "Fine!" We negotiated and struck a less than mediocre agreement and everyone was happy—except me.

I felt that it was time to do some extra investigation about this lady and her organization. I judiciously decided to call a friend of mine at a major national video distribution house. Here's what I found out.

My friend knew all about her. He warned me that she has a habit of trying to strong-arm companies into buying from her. She actually is a middleman who secured a couple of exclusive agreements with certain video producers. Lucky me, I happened to need a deal for one of them.

To make a long story short, I followed through on the deal and made sure to never buy anything from her again. I bought everything direct from the video producers, bypassing her every time. This saved our organization tens of thousands of dollars over the course of a few years. The power of information!

Whenever making a purchase, *always try to buy direct from the manufacturer and eliminate middlemen.* One easy way to find out who manufactured a product is to go a store and find the product on the shelf. Look for the name of the manufacturer on the packaging, and write down their address and phone number. Call them directly and negotiate a direct purchase with them. Some companies will agree to this and some are in legal agreements with certain distributors. If nothing else, they'll direct you to the right distributor, who can get you the best possible price.

Have you investigated the other side's financial strength?

Keep in mind that a financially weak or unstable company is generally more desperate to make a deal. Remember what we talked about previously? I said that you never want to be desperate to make a deal. A weak financial position and a less than adequate negotiator spell failure in deal-making. The one way around this is to have a negotiator that knows how to bluff well. And there are plenty! By doing your homework, you can counter any bluffing negotiator and see the value of any organization for what it really is. There are also other ways, both within and outside the organization, to get financial information.

You can find out a company's financial position from any of the following sources:

- ◆ **Annual reports.**
- ◆ **Corporate officers.**
- ◆ **Newspapers.**
- ◆ **Trade magazines.**
- ◆ **The Better Business Bureau.**

- ◆ **Lower-level employees (the mail clerk knows more than you think!).**
- ◆ **Former employees.**
- ◆ **Trade associations.**
- ◆ **Business associations.**
- ◆ **Or just ask them!**

And those are just a few!

Let me ask you a three-part question:

If the other side were to walk away from the deal, what would they lose? Did you remind them of what they'd lose? And finally, how could you have avoided the whole situation from the start?

Let's start with the first question.

If the other side were to walk away from the deal, what would they lose? Before you answer, think about it for a moment. Consider the following potential answers.

Would they lose:

- ◆ **Money?** Are they walking away from increased sales revenue or an influx of quick cash?

- ◆ **Reputation?** Could they gain prestige dealing with your organization? Is your reputation something they need?

- ◆ **Product?** Are they in need of your product? Could they purchase your product elsewhere? Are you the sole provider of your product?

- ◆ **Service?** Are they in need of your service? Is your service unique or available through other vendors? How exclusive is your service?

Example: I recently negotiated a deal for hundreds of sets of software for one of my clients. The disks contained very valuable media contact information. My client wanted to buy them inexpensively and resell them at a significant profit. I negotiated what I thought was a very acceptable offer. As a matter of fact, so did the vendor. Or so I thought! At the final hour, the vendor reneged by claiming the deal wasn't worth his while and wanted more money. He left me a voicemail saying he wanted to cancel the deal. For some reason, I had the feeling he was bluffing. Instead of calling him right back, I decided to hold off and call him back three days later. I had a feeling he was starting to sweat this one out.

How did I come to this conclusion? I considered the first question. I just asked myself, "What would he lose by walking away?" I then listed everything out. Here's what I figured he would lose:

> ▹ **Tens of thousands of dollars in initial and ongoing sales.**

> ▹ **An affiliation with a top-notch marketing company that has a great reputation.**

> ▹ **Loss of future sales revenues.**

> ▹ **Sales to more than 500 worldwide distributors.**

That was enough to convince me that I had the upper hand! Three days later, I called him back. When he heard my voice, a sigh of relief came through the telephone as loud as if he outright said, "Thank heaven you called back."

Now it's time to tackle the second part of the question.

Did you remind them of what they'd lose, if they choose to walk away? After we said the obligatory "Hi—how are you?" we finally got down to business. I asked if he thought about my previous offer. His reply was, "Yes, and I'm sure we can find some way to work this out." I agreed and immediately explained how I arrived at the price I offered. He understood my position.

Here's where I reminded him of the importance of my offer and what he'd lose.

I knew that all I had to do was sell him on one more benefit of doing business with us. The first thing I did was tell him that we'd be placing a significant order, which would bring him huge profits. He agreed. Next, I decided to hammer the point home. I reminded him of the value of an affiliation with a company that's highly respected and well known worldwide. I also made a point to let him know we wouldn't consider doing any future business with his company if he didn't accept the proposed deal on these win/win terms. And finally, I told him we'd make his software available worldwide to a network of 500 distributors. What was his final reply? Guess! Needless to say, I got the deal on my terms and he received great profits as well as all of the benefits of being affiliated with us.

Keep in mind that just because someone appears to walk away from a deal doesn't mean the deal is over. Usually the other side already knows they can lose a great deal. Sometimes they bluff, hoping for more. I know they do this because I've made a career of spotting and overcoming it!

Some of you are probably wondering why I called him back, and not the other way around. I know that some of these so-called negotiation gurus think it's detrimental to call someone back first. I've heard some of them say the first one to call loses the upper hand. That's a line of bull. As with any negotiation, the chances are 50/50.

Even though it may appear the other side is walking away permanently, there are many other reasons I haven't received a phone call or response right away.

Some of the reasons the other side seems to be stalling are:

- **People get sidetracked into other deals and become forgetful.**
- **They leave on vacation.**
- **They're afraid to make a decision.**
- **It's not their top priority.**
- **They need a little time to think about their strategy.**
- **Personal feelings were hurt.**
- **They've become intimidated.**
- **People think you don't like them.**
- **They're completely confused and afraid to make a mistake.**

The bottom line is that you can't jump the gun just because you haven't heard from someone five minutes after you call them. Sometimes you just have to be patient.

Always remember your number one priority—your own interests in the deal. Time is money, and sometimes you have to make every effort possible to keep things moving smoothly and complete the deal. Remember: *When it comes to negotiations, pride means nothing.* You can't bury it with you or deposit it in the bank. It's literally worthless! I know a plethora of people who let pride cloud their better judgment. As a result, they end up with zero. (No money and no deal.) *All that counts is the results you get.*

Did you try to keep the other side from walking away in the first place? This can be very difficult. However, you can take some precautions to stack the odds in your favor during the opening stage of the negotiation.

Here are some helpful tips to keep the other side from walking away from your deal:

1. **Remind them of the benefits of being affiliated with you.**

2. **Remind them about all future sales revenues and profits.**

3. **Refer them to others who can do business with them.**

4. **Go over all of the major terms of the deal and get them in writing as soon as possible.**

5. **Try to cover points quickly, and if possible, never let a negotiation drag on.**

6. **Make a list of what the other side has to gain and keep reminding them over and over.**

Sometimes the inevitable happens and negotiations hit an impasse. The other side decides to rethink their position. What should you do?

If negotiations hit a deadlock or impasse, you must stay calm and cool. Always remember that this happens to even the most skilled negotiators. Sometimes people just need time to think. At times you will too! That's okay. Never become discouraged, bitter, or display a negative attitude about the situation. Always stay positive and patient, and be understanding of their position.

And keep in mind that you're negotiating from the perspective of a skilled negotiator. Chances are the other side is not. Sometimes they get "freaked out" by your persistence and need to take a "time out." Let them have one. It'll just make the deal go smoother in the long run.

Have you exhausted every source you can find to gather information about this company or individual?

If you're looking for information about a company and/or individual, consider all of the following sources:

- ◆ **Annual reports.**
- ◆ **Corporate officers.**
- ◆ **Coworkers.**
- ◆ **News magazines.**
- ◆ **Library databases.**
- ◆ **Newspapers.**
- ◆ **Trade magazines.**

- ◆ **The Better Business Bureau.**
- ◆ **Credit agencies.**
- ◆ **Lower-level employees.**
- ◆ **Former employees.**
- ◆ **Trade associations.**
- ◆ **Business associations.**
- ◆ **Just ask!**

And the third and final step in the *information gathering* process is to take all of the information and formulate an action plan based on both the gathered information and your intuition.

Quick Review

Let's take a moment and review the steps you must take when going through the *information gathering* process.

When *information gathering* you must follow three steps:

1. **Gather information about yourself and your own situation.**

    When you gather information about yourself, you must consider the following questions:

    - ◆ **Motives:** What is driving you to do business with this person or organization and why do you need this good or service?
    - ◆ **Reasoning:** What is the true, underlying reason you want to complete this deal?
    - ◆ **Debts:** What are your current and future debts?
    - ◆ **Capital:** What resources are available to you and what are you lacking?

♦ **Cash on hand:** Do you have enough available cash to finish this deal?

♦ **Hidden agendas:** Are you being up front with the other side or are you trying to hide something?

♦ **Timeline:** How much time do you have to finish this deal?

♦ **Duress:** Do you feel pressured or uncomfortable in this situation?

♦ **Responsibilities:** Are you the only person representing your side? Who are all the players?

2. **Gather information about the other side's open or hidden agendas.**

When you gather information about the other side's agendas, you must evaluate the following questions:

♦ **What kind of company culture are you going to be negotiating with?**

♦ **Whom are you really negotiating with?**

♦ **What is the company or individual's agenda?**

♦ **Are they reputable?**

♦ **Have you questioned people who've done business with the other side?**

♦ **Have you investigated the other side's financial strength?**

♦ **Did you remind them of what they'd lose?**

♦ **How could you have avoided the whole situation from the start?**

♦ **If the other side were to walk away from the deal, what would they lose?**

♦ **Did you try to keep the other side from walking away in the first place?**

♦ **Have you exhausted every source you can find to gather information about this company or individual?**

3. **Put all of the information together and formulate your plan of action based on your information as well as your intuition.**

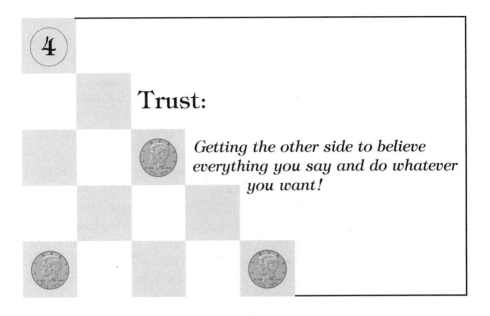

4

Trust:

Getting the other side to believe everything you say and do whatever you want!

Being trustworthy is among the top negotiation skills that you absolutely must develop. Never overlook the fact that the other side is generally going to go into a negotiation with their guard up. They'll feel (and rightfully so) that you're negotiating on your own or your organization's behalf, and not theirs. In many instances and situations, that may or may not be true. It depends on your personal agenda. I'm not here to judge you—just to help you!

Generally, you will find that most people will give you the benefit of the doubt at first. And of course, there are a few that will automatically judge you as untrustworthy, and remain overly paranoid throughout the negotiation.

There are 11 key principles you must follow to build trust during negotiations:

1. **Establish a track record.** This takes some time, but it's the most effective way to build trust. Each time you do business, or make a promise, make sure you do exactly what you say. Over a period of time, the other side will feel comfortable dealing with you on your word.

2. **Keep in touch.** When people have done something wrong or are doing other sneaky things, they have a tendency to shy away from the person

they've wronged. Always keep in contact with the "other side." Call them back and find out if there's anything else you can do for them. This will put them at ease and make them feel more comfortable in their dealings with you.

3. **Follow up.** After striking an agreement, call the other side and ask them if they're 100 percent satisfied with your product or service. People will respect you for following up on your product or service's effectiveness. This shows the other side you care about them.

4. **Go the extra mile.** When people first work with you, they believe they're taking a gamble. One of the best strategies to build trust is to make sure to go beyond what's expected of you. Maybe you've heard the expression "under promise and over deliver"? Deliver beyond their expectations and satisfy them to the point that they wouldn't even consider buying from your competition. You could even give some extra perks or concessions for doing business with you. (You'll learn more about concessions throughout this system.)

5. **Show empathy.** Always remember that the average businessperson is afraid to make a decision. Understand this major weakness and help them. Be willing to assist them in making a good decision. Show proof of what you're saying and never make them feel inferior to you. People tend to trust people who show empathy and help them when they're most vulnerable.

6. **Be trusting of others.** This can be especially tricky during your first negotiation with a new individual or organization. By showing you trust the other side, they're more than likely going to try to not only earn your trust, but also keep it! Most people have good intentions during negotiations. I'd like to share an example of how this tip could've made someone a lot of money.

Example: Some time ago, I was negotiating a partnership between a company I owned called VIP Internet and an up-and-coming magazine owner. VIP was looking at a deal to partner with the magazine owner on a Website pertaining to UFOs and other unexplainable phenomenon. The negotiations were a little slow, yet I still felt they were doable.

As the negotiations went forward, both my partner and I were starting to grow uncomfortable with the owner demeanor. He started making comments, leading us to believe he had reservations about going through with the deal. He was worried we wouldn't meet deadlines. He thought we were asking too high of a percentage of sales. And to top it off, during a teleconference with me, he made the comment, "I better not get screwed on this deal." That was the final red flag. After I hung up with him, I immediately talked with my partner and called the project off. Why? I didn't want to work with someone who, for no reason, didn't trust me. Actually, he didn't trust anyone. It's too bad he turned down such a good deal. As of this writing, he still hasn't completed the proposed Website and is losing a tremendous source of revenue. **At the same time, if a deal looks good and you feel comfortable with the players, give them a chance to prove themselves.**

Now, if you have a gut feeling that you're making a bad decision or you have some information showing that someone is not trustworthy, run the other way. You'll definitely want to take your business elsewhere. And always remember: No matter what negativity comes from a situation, never be insulting to anyone—show your class!

When I refer to giving people a chance, I'm not saying or implying that you should let down your guard. But you should give people the benefit of the doubt. And at the same time, *keep your eye on the deal and the money.*

7. **Admit when you're wrong.** If you want to build trust, admit when you've made a mistake. By admitting you're wrong, you appear trustworthy. The other side knows that when you admit to being wrong, you're demonstrating honesty and integrity.

8. **Be a team player.** Approach every negotiation as if you and the other side are on the same team. Keep in mind that the goal of every negotiation is to find a winning solution for everyone. A sense of teamwork builds friendship and camaraderie.

9. **Communicate clearly.** If you want to build trust at the negotiating table, you must be clear, articulate, and precise every time you communicate. If you're not clear or seem to be hiding information, the other side will automatically think you have a hidden agenda and start to distrust you and/or your organization.

10. **Be fair with everyone.** Being fair means treating people equally. You also need to have a genuine respect for everyone you negotiate with. Never favor one person over another or talk less than respectfully about others.

11. **Have a "can do" attitude.** Only take on tasks that you're positive you can handle. People will always want to negotiate and do business with people who believe they can get the job done without reservation. If you take on a task that you're not sure about, more than likely it will come back to haunt you. Your reputation depends on your ability to get the job done!

Quick Review

Let's take a moment and review the 11 characteristics of a trustworthy negotiator.

1. **Establish a track record.**

2. **Keep in touch.**

3. **Follow up.**

4. **Go the extra mile.**

5. **Show empathy.**

6. **Be trusting of others.**

7. **Admit when you're wrong.**

8. **Be a team player.**

9. **Communicate clearly.**

10. **Be fair with everyone.**

11. **Have a "can do" attitude.**

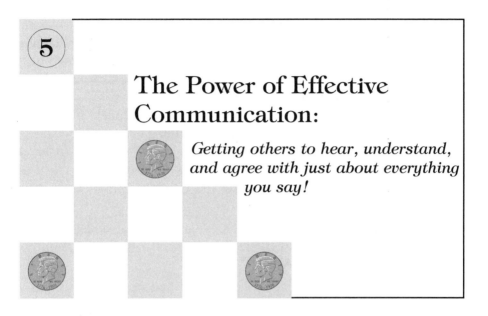

The Power of Effective Communication:

Getting others to hear, understand, and agree with just about everything you say!

In this section, I'm going to give you an overview of effective communication and how vitally important it is to being a successful negotiator. To be successful as a negotiator, you can't afford to have the other side misread your intentions or misconstrue their intentions toward you. *Accurate communication is vital to effective, successful negotiations.*

Bottom line: you must be an effective communicator to be a successful negotiator. Notice I said "successful" negotiator. Why did I call your attention to that? Because there are thousands of people who call themselves negotiators, but they never get good deals. Your goal isn't to just be a negotiator; it should be to become an "overwhelmingly successful" negotiator. Let's get started on this powerful lesson!

Early communication researchers studied the individual elements in what is called the *Communication Process Model* to determine the effect of each element on the effectiveness of the process. Ironically, most studies dealt with negotiation and persuasion as the desired outcome. For our purposes, I have developed a variation of the original Communication Process Model. I call it the *Communication/Negotiation Process Model*. For your convenience, I've created a special flowchart to delineate all of the steps involved. Let's begin!

I'll start by discussing the Communication/Negotiation Process Model and why it's vital to your success as a negotiator, and then we'll examine each step in the process. You need to know how to communicate effectively to both negotiate the best deal and protect yourself from inflated expenses, as well as potential embarrassment in the process.

What is the Communication/Negotiation Process Model? It's the system you're going to use to communicate something to another person or group during negotiations. *The communication process is the foundation for every negotiation.* Without it, you may as well talk to a wall.

These are the six main elements of the Communication/Negotiation Process:

1. **Sender:** The sender is the individual who is introducing an idea or concept and expects some sort of response or feedback from the receiver.

2. **Message:** The message is the thought that needs to be conveyed. It can be a response to a question, the introduction of a concession, the response to a query, or any other idea that needs to get to the receiver.

3. **Encoding:** Encoding is the process of putting the thought to be communicated in language the receiver can understand clearly and effectively.

4. **Channel:** The channel is the medium the sender uses to deliver the message. Examples include TV, radio, fax, e-mail, word-of-mouth, face-to-face meetings, third-party intervention, videoconferencing, the Internet, magazines, newspapers, amateur radio, short wave, citizens band, CD-ROM, or any other form of communication.

5. **Decoding:** Decoding is the receiver's process of taking the message and interpreting it based on references of both the situation and the sender. It's important you realize that the sender's credibility magnifies and amplifies the value of all the information encoded. (Also realize that the perceived status, reliability, experience, and expertise of the source add "weight" to the effectiveness of the message.)

6. **Feedback:** Feedback is the reply to the original message.

Let's examine the Communication/Negotiation flowchart:

Communication/Negotiation Process Model

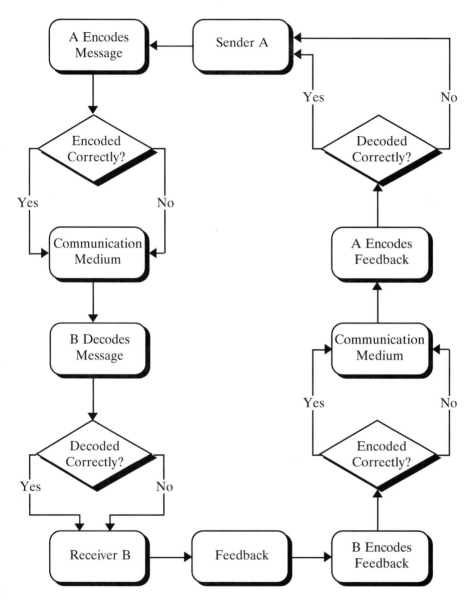

The following is a description of the original Communication Process Model based on two people we'll refer to as Sender A and Receiver B.

Example: Sender A wants to communicate a point to Receiver B. Receiver B is the receiver of the message and will have to relay his feedback back to Sender A. For this process to start out smooth, Sender A has to make sure his point is clear to Receiver B.

To start the process, Sender A must think through his message carefully, effectively, and articulately. Then, Sender A must find the most efficient and clear channel to deliver the message to Receiver B. (This could be through the telephone, face-to-face, through a third party, or utilizing technologies such as e-mail, Websites, videoconferencing, fax machines, etc.) Here, Sender A encodes the message so that it will be said or read in a certain way.

Then he delivers the message through the selected communication channel. (For our purposes, assume A and B are sitting across a table from one another negotiating verbally.) From here, Receiver B will start receiving the message. He'll attempt to decode the message based on references and then put it all together. He'll then decide how he wants to respond. Next, he'll provide feedback to Sender A by encoding his response. He'll then send it back through a channel (more than likely, the same used by Sender A). Then Sender A will start to receive the message. Sender A will attempt to decode the message based on references, which will allow him to put it all together.

This process will be repeated over and over until a deal is either struck or avoided.

Communication Breakdown

One major challenge that arises in many negotiations is called a *communication breakdown.*

Consider the following nine potential breakdowns that are common during the communication process:

1. **Noise:** *Noise* includes any distractions the receiver is experiencing during the decoding phase of the Communication/Negotiation Process. When you experience a great deal of noise, you may not properly hear or understand the communicated message. You may hear bits and pieces. By the time you try to put the divided messages together, you may not understand the message as it was intended.

Examples of noise include loud radios and televisions, people screaming in the background, ringing telephones, airplanes flying overhead, static in telephone or radio lines, and just about anything else causing you not to hear the complete message from the sender. Sometimes noise will even distort the message.

Always negotiate in a quiet atmosphere where you can properly hear everything that's being said. Also, a quiet atmosphere makes your response clearer to the "other side." Take excellent notes and repeat them back to the other side for clarity.

2. **Filtering:** *Filtering,* also called third-party negotiating, happens when someone negotiates on someone else's behalf. What happens too often is that the story is changed based upon the third party's mood, bias, interest, memory, and understanding of what was originally told to them. (If you're negotiating with a third party who's not properly informed or really doesn't understand the negotiation at hand, you'll waste time and money.)

    Example: I remember back in my college days playing a game called *What's the Scoop?* The goal of the game was to communicate a story through the filtering of five or more people. This is a classic example of how stories get misconstrued as additional sources tell it. Here's how the game works.

    First, you have at least five people sit in a line or circle next to each other. Then someone makes up a fallacious piece of gossip, writes it on a sheet of paper, and whispers what he or she wrote to the person sitting on their right. The story then gets whispered to the next person on the right and so on and so on until it gets to the last person. That last person then tells the group what the scoop is! What's the result?

    By the time the story reached the end of the circle, without exception, the story doesn't mimic, emulate, or slightly resemble the original piece of gossip. What's even more interesting is that the story is usually already exaggerated by the time it reached the second or third person.

    Examples of filtering include negotiating with any party other than the ultimate decision-maker. Classic filters include presidents, vice presidents, chief operating officers, receptionists, marketing executives, hired negotiators, secretaries, lawyers, accountants, friends, and family members.

Throughout this book, I'm going to repeat the importance of negotiating with the final decision-maker and nobody else. If you must negotiate with a third party, make sure you always repeat any valuable points, concessions, or other elements pertinent to the business at hand. Also, make sure you write everything down! Keep notes, journals, and logs of every negotiation.

3. **Clutter:** *Clutter* is all of the various messages hitting us at one time.

When you have too much clutter during a negotiation, you become too sidetracked to give the negotiation your undivided attention. To effectively negotiate, you need to strategically think through every move you make. You also need to carefully evaluate your counterattack based on the information you've received.

Examples of clutter include having an abundance of e-mail or postal mail to open and an overload of faxes to read in a short time frame. Another great example is having too many vendors pursuing you for business or having individuals place unrealistic demands on your time.

It's important for you to understand the importance of time in negotiations. Having sufficient time allows you to free your mind of daily clutter and focus your mind on the issue at hand. Too much clutter in communication is analogous to having a cluttered office, garage, or home. By viewing clutter around you, it almost screams "Do something with me!" every time you try to focus on something else. Clearing clutter out of your life will make you more effective, productive, and profitable in both your personal and professional lives.

By fully understanding the Communication/Negotiation Process, you'll communicate more articulately, effectively, concisely, timely, productively, successfully, and profitably.

4. **Technological confusion:** By being unfamiliar with the features of the technology being used (TV, radio, fax, teleconferencing, video-conferencing, Internet, e-mail, etc.) you can either transmit or receive messages incorrectly.

5. **Emotion:** When you become sad, happy, angry, upset, depressed, nervous, or anxious, you can misinterpret a situation or information based on either too positive or too negative emotions.

6. **Inconsistency between non-verbal and verbal gestures:** The way you move your body needs to match what you're saying. For instance, if you're listening to someone very intently, you should nod or lean toward the person talking. You shouldn't stare off into space or start doodling. Avoid saying or doing anything that'll send dual signals or cause inconsistency.

7. **Preconceived judgments:** Always keep an open mind when someone is trying to communicate an idea. And always wait to respond until the other side has fully explained their idea or given their side of the debate. By interrupting them, you cut off their message before they have a chance to communicate it in its entirety. Therefore, you won't have enough information to intelligently respond to what they're saying.

8. **Distrusting the sender:** If you're communicating with someone you distrust, you may as well not communicate with them at all. And if you have to communicate with them, always remember to listen very closely. In general, we tend to distort messages based on our judgments of someone we do not trust. We hear their message as we want to believe it to be. This is called *selective distortion*. When we distort a message, we don't necessarily hear the message as it was intended.

9. **Semantics:** There are certain words and phrases that send differing or inappropriate messages. Avoid using jargon, obscenities, improper language, technical terms, or any words that can have multiple meanings.

Quick Review

Let's review what you've learned about effective communication.

The following are the six main elements of the Communication/Negotiation Process model:

1. **Sender:** The sender is the individual who is introducing an idea or concept and expects some sort of response or feedback from the receiver. The sender may be you or the other side.

2. **Message:** The message is the thought that needs to be conveyed.

3. **Encoding:** Encoding is the process of putting the thought to be communicated in language the receiver can understand clearly and effectively.

4. **Channel:** The channel is the medium the sender uses to deliver the message.

5. **Decoding:** Decoding is the receiver's process of taking the message and interpreting it based on references of both the situation and the sender.

6. **Feedback:** Feedback is the reply to the original message.

The Communication/Negotiation Process is not perfect and can present a great deal of challenges. The following are nine common breakdowns during the Communication/Negotiation Process.

1. **Noise:** *Noise* includes any distractions the receiver is experiencing during the decoding phase of the Communication/Negotiation Process.

    Always negotiate in a quiet atmosphere where you can properly hear everything being said. Also, a quiet atmosphere makes your response clearer to the other side.

2. **Filtering:** *Filtering,* also called third-party negotiating, is the process of hearing a story repeated back from someone other than the original sender. What generally happens is that the story changes based on the third party's mood, bias, interest, memory, and understanding of what was originally told to them.

3. **Clutter:** *Clutter* is all of the various messages hitting us at one time.

4. **Technological confusion:** When you are unfamiliar with the features of the technology being used (TV, radio, fax, teleconferencing, videoconferencing, Internet, e-mail, etc.), you can either transmit or receive messages incorrectly.

5. **Emotion:** When you become excited, sad, happy, angry, upset, depressed, nervous, or anxious, you can misinterpret a situation or any information based on emotion.

6. **Inconsistency between non-verbal and verbal gestures:** The way you move your body needs to match what you're saying.

7. **Preconceived judgments:** Always keep an open mind when someone is trying to communicate an idea. And always wait until the other side has fully explained their idea or given their message.

8. **Distrusting the sender:** If you're communicating with someone you distrust, you may as well not communicate with him or her at all.

9. **Semantics:** There are certain words and phrases that send differing or inappropriate messages. Avoid using jargon, obscenities, improper language, technical terms, or any other words that can have multiple meanings.

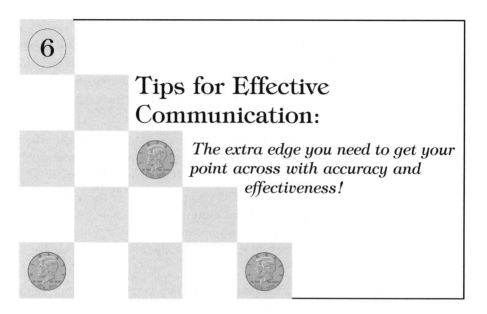

6

Tips for Effective Communication:

The extra edge you need to get your point across with accuracy and effectiveness!

Here are some more important tips on communicating effectively during negotiations:

▸ **The sender's credibility and personal characteristics affect the receiver's initial reaction and receptivity to messages.** Is the sender trusted, honest, and does he or she have a good reputation? Is he considered to be an expert in his field? Receivers will take all of these factors into consideration before agreeing to anything.

▸ **Different people receiving the same message may interpret it differently, attribute different meanings to it, and react to it in different ways.** Just because I believe my point is very valuable in the negotiation, doesn't mean you'll agree. You may have different needs and wants, as well as different references to call on.

▸ **If you wish to persuade the other side to your way of thinking, present both sides of the story and show how your way is the more effective, wiser choice.** Always consider the other side's point of view. Show them why they think a certain way and subtly show them how they can benefit by agreeing with your terms.

▶ **Anytime the other side is highly educated on a product, service, or particular market, always present both sides of the story and again show how your way of thinking is the more effective choice.** Never assume anyone is inferior or stupid! Respect their intelligence and they'll more than likely respect you! This makes for a much friendlier negotiation process.

▶ **The first part of the communication message has the greatest effect on receivers with low initial interest.** This is because anyone who doesn't care to hear what you have to say generally tunes you out fairly quickly.

▶ **The last part of the message has the greatest effect on those receivers with high initial interest.** When someone is very interested in what you have to say, they'll listen to your presentation very attentively. Best of all, they'll eagerly await your closing comments. Make your comments strong!

▶ **Using low-fear tactics and messages produce more compliance than high-fear tactics and messages.** Low-fear tactics and messages put people at ease and encourage them to believe you because they don't feel threatened by you.

▶ **High-fear tactics and messages produce defensive reactions in the receiver that lead to distortion, denial, or rejection of the message.** High-fear tactics, such as threats, make people so defensive that they become highly defiant and competitive. Even if they originally wanted your product or service, they'll battle with you, just to keep you from getting your way. These negotiations simply go nowhere!

▶ **Three factors that affect the impact of fear messages are (1) the seriousness of the subject, (2) the likelihood or probability of the feared event, and (3) the course of action.** People will always be motivated by these three factors. First, they'll evaluate just how serious a point is. If they see it as very serious, they'll analyze how likely it is that fallout in the negotiation is imminent. If they still perceive trouble, they'll start to play out different scenarios based on what they know or think you'll do next!

▶ **Communication scholars and practitioners historically have considered face-to-face communication the most direct, powerful, and preferred method for exchanging information.** It involves as few as two communicators, uses many senses, and provides immediate feedback; therefore, *saving you time and money.*

▶ **Receivers with low self-esteem and feelings of inadequacy are influenced more by persuasive messages than are people with high self-esteem and feelings of indifference toward others.** It's more difficult to persuade someone to your thinking if they're self-empowered and believe in standing up for what they think is right. However, these people are perfect candidates for reeducation regarding the benefits of your product or service over their previous or current choice. Again, proceed with caution and tact!

The *Communication/Negotiation Process Model* will prove to be one of your greatest weapons in your negotiating arsenal. Why?

By understanding and following the Communication/Negotiation Process Model, you will:

♦ Win more negotiations!

♦ Get the other side to see things from your perspective and they will want to help you.

♦ Understand the six elements of effective communication (sender, message, encoding, channel, decoding, and feedback) and become a better communicator, not only during negotiations, but anytime you need to communicate effectively with anyone.

♦ Use your negotiation strategies with confidence and clarity.

♦ Become a more effective, clear, and articulate speaker.

♦ Understand the flow of a message from sender to receiver.

♦ Know how to avoid miscommunication.

♦ Avoid the pitfalls and breakdowns that sever ties and destroy negotiations.

♦ Be able to delineate anything in concise, right to the point terminology.

♦ Keep negotiation tensions to a minimum.

♦ Establish friendly, low-pressure tactics to get your point across.

♦ Stay focused on the major issues by eliminating noise, filtering, and clutter.

♦ Use the other side's counterattacks to your advantage.

Many relationship books cite poor communication as the number one reason that people break up or end up getting divorced. Poor communication also dissolves negotiations and creates animosity. By following the Communication/Negotiation Process Model, you can now understand where your two-way communication has broken down. Then you can go back and correct it quickly and effectively!

Quick Review

The following is a recap of all of my tips for effective communication.

♦ Sender credibility and personal characteristics affect the receiver's initial reaction and receptivity to messages.

♦ Different people receiving the same message may interpret it differently, attribute different meanings to it, and react to it in different ways.

♦ If you wish to persuade the other side to your way of thinking, present both sides of the story and subtly show that your way is the more effective and wiser choice.

♦ Anytime the other side is highly educated on a product, service, or particular market, always present both sides of the story and show how your way of thinking is the more effective choice.

♦ The first part of the communication message has the greatest effect on receivers with low initial interest.

♦ The last part of the message has the greatest effect on those receivers with high initial interest.

♦ Using low-fear tactics and messages produce more compliance than do high-fear tactics and messages.

♦ High-fear tactics and messages produce defensive reactions in the receiver that lead to distortion, denial, or rejection of the message. High-fear tactics such as threats make people so defensive that they become defiant and competitive.

- Three factors that affect the impact of fear messages are:

  1. The seriousness of the subject.

  2. The likelihood or probability of the feared event.

  3. The course of action.

- Communication scholars and practitioners historically have considered face-to-face communication the most direct, powerful, and preferred method for exchanging information.

- Receivers with low self-esteem and feelings of inadequacy are influenced more by persuasive messages than are people with high self-esteem and feelings of indifference toward others.

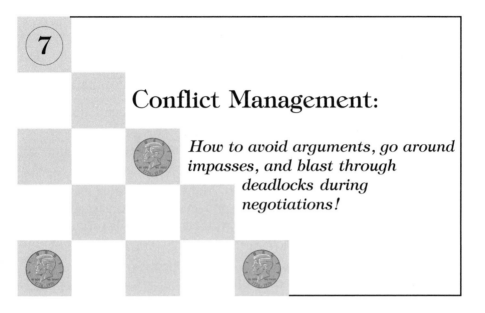

Conflict Management:

How to avoid arguments, go around impasses, and blast through deadlocks during negotiations!

To be an effective negotiator, you must be able to *keep negotiations moving along smoothly*. To do this, you must learn two important skills:

♦ **Learning how to avoid conflict.**

♦ **Resolving conflicts when they arise.**

And believe me when I say, "Conflicts will arise at the worst possible time!"

Before we go any further, I want to define *conflict* as it applies to negotiation. A conflict can be anything from a small quarrel to an all out war. In general, *a conflict is a situation that results when two or more people disagree on terms during a negotiation*. Conflicts are neither positive nor negative. They are just opportunities to meet your goals.

Conflicts usually arise due to the lack of communication by one or both parties. What usually happens is that one or both of the parties didn't understand what was said or the real intentions of the other side.

Many people feel that conflicts are negative. On the contrary! Think of the last time you had a conflict with another person. Did you have the conflict because you didn't care about the outcome? Of course not! You cared enough about the situation to try and come up with a solution. The same holds true during negotiations.

It's commonplace to experience conflict as a negotiator. It is so commonplace that you need to learn how to deal with it. You just have to make sure you don't take conflict personally. At the same time, never insult anyone personally during a negotiation. It's just business! Focus on the issues at hand and leave personal feelings out!

There are four common forms of conflict during negotiations:

1. **Conflict between two or more people.** Two or more people disagree on terms or concessions. This is common during one-on-one negotiations.

2. **Conflict between departments.** Many times, companies will experience interdepartmental problems. Many times, department members will negotiate with each other for various resources and/or power.

3. **Conflict between companies.** This is when two organizations have a conflict over competition, capital resources, people, terms, and concessions.

4. **Conflict between an individual and a group.** This happens when a person has to negotiate with a group of people. Examples are executive boards, committees, and various other teams.

 Most conflicts arise at the most unlikely times. I wish I had a dollar for every time I thought negotiations were going smoothly and all of a sudden the other side presented a challenge. Of these conflicts, 90 percent will usually fall into one of eight common causes.

8 Common Causes of Conflict During Negotiations

1. **Different perceptions:** Ever since the beginning of time, people have had different perceptions of the same issues and events. You and I could witness the same car accident, right in front of us, and I may say it was one party's fault, and you could say it was the other's. We each have different references and experiences to pull information from. Consider the following example.

Imagine that you're negotiating the purchase price of a car with a salesman. He's offering you the car at a specific price. To you, the price seems way too high. Your perception may be that he's trying to rip you off. His perception is that he's doing the best job he can, to bring in the most money for the car dealer. Is either of you wrong? Not at all! You just have different perceptions of the same situation. The car salesman may not be trying to rip you off personally. Although you see this as a personal attack, you have to remember that it's only business as usual. These types of perceptions create all sorts of personal and professional conflicts.

To avoid conflict, you always have to see the negotiation through both your own eyes as well as the other side's. Everyone looks at the deal from his or her own perspective. Don't take negotiating or it's outcome personally or you'll lose your sanity very quickly!

2. **Poor communication:** I will repeat this over and over throughout this system: *Poor communication is a deal killer.*

When you're dealing with issues as complex as those you find in negotiations, you must communicate articulately, effectively, concisely, and quickly. Both you and the other side have to be clear about what you want and have to be able to accurately communicate it as we talked about in the Communication/Negotiation Process model. Vagaries and other nebulous talk will lead to both short- and long-term conflict.

3. **Misaligned goals:** Conflict can arise from misaligned or incongruent goals between you and the other side. Both of you need to be working toward the same common goal—finishing the deal!

4. **Inconsistent values and beliefs:** Most people have been following the same values and beliefs since they were very young. In many instances, the other side may get very defensive if you violate their values or beliefs.

Let's quickly discuss both values and beliefs.

♦ **What is a value? Values are anything that you or the other side place significant importance on or hold dear.**

Let's explore the two different types.

It's very important that you understand that people have two motivations in life. They are pursuing pleasure and avoiding pain.

Success coach Anthony Robbins lists some of the most common life values in his book *Awaken the Giant Within*. He cites two different types. They are *moving-toward values* and *moving-away from values*.

Here are examples of both:

> **Moving-toward values:** These are values that people strive to achieve. They include success, love, security, intimacy, freedom, comfort, passion, health, adventure, and power. Make sure to never violate these values during negotiations. If you do, you'll more than likely hit stalls, impasses, and deadlocks.
>
> Never expect a conservative individual or company to take too many risks during negotiations. If the other side values security and you challenge it, they can get very defensive and decide to back out of the deal. You'll move them out of their comfort zone and they'll refuse to move forward.

> **Moving-away from values:** These are values that people tend to avoid at all costs. They include anger, guilt, rejection, failure, humiliation, frustration, loneliness, and depression.
>
> If you introduce any of these values into a negotiation, you're going to be doomed from the start. These values are to be avoided like the plague. To illustrate my point, consider the following question: How would you like it if someone made you feel humiliated, angry, or frustrated? Case closed!

Next, you also have to make sure that you do not violate people's *beliefs*.

♦ **What is a belief? A belief is anything that a person believes to be true about themselves, other people, or their organization.**

I didn't say it has to be true. All they have to do is believe it! Like the famous marketing expression goes—"perception is reality!" Many people feel they're superior in power, strength, service, or quality. Let them believe it and don't question them. If you question them, they may become very defensive. You have to learn to work around these opinions! In fact, by reinforcing these beliefs, you can make negotiations move much more smoothly and quickly.

5. **Incongruent personalities:** Every individual or group has a different personality. Some people will just seem to "click," or get along with you better than others, but you can't dismiss those who don't.

Again, remember that it's business and not personal. No matter what aspect of your life you're dealing with, you won't like or get along with everyone. The key is to focus on the issues, not the personality—and negotiate objectively.

6. **Contradictory expectations:** When either party of the negotiation expects to receive a concession that hasn't been provided, conflict is sure to result.

It's very important to know what the other side wants from you, and either give it to them, or subtly work around it. You'll learn how to do this later in the book.

7. **Third parties:** Third parties are people or groups asked for opinions or who are otherwise asked to participate in the negotiation. Third parties may include outside executives, managers, lawyers, consultants, accountants, friends, or family members.

I wish I had a dollar for every time I've been involved in a negotiation where the other side had to call an outside business consultant to review a contract that seemed to be complete and agreeable. The sad part is that third parties tend to stall, stymie, or deadlock negotiations. Keep in mind that it's always a good idea to have an attorney read your agreements. At the same time, don't let them keep you from pushing forward if you see a great deal! Just make sure you know what you're getting yourself and your organization into.

 When it comes to third parties, remember the old saying "Too many cooks spoil the broth." Now change it to read, "Too many negotiators spoil the deal." In other words, if you can, avoid a third party.

8. **Strong-arming:** *Strong-arming* is the act of using force or unnecessary pressure to get the other side to accept your terms.

Never try to coerce anyone into doing anything they don't feel comfortable doing. Strong-arming always comes back to haunt you. If nothing else, the other side will never do business with you again. They'll also tell every one of their friends and business associates to avoid doing business with you. You'll develop a poor reputation. No negotiation is worth that! There are *two things you never want to mess with—your credibility and your reputation.*

Never strong-arm or pressure anyone to do anything!

As I previously said, every negotiator (even the best) ends up in a conflict sooner or later. Now that you know what the basic conflicts are, you need to learn how to manage conflicts when they arise.

Tips for Resolving Conflicts

▶ **Be proactive.** Always remember that your goal is to avoid all of the common causes of conflict I shared with you. The best defense is usually a good offense; *avoid conflict from the start.* Easier said than done. Well, maybe not.

If a conflict is rising, find the source of the conflict, and do everything you can to lessen its effect before it gets out of hand. And do it quickly!

Example: I was negotiating with a prominent book publisher for more than two months. The contract went back and forth over and over again. Finally it seemed as if we negotiated a great deal, except for one small challenge. I wanted a cumulative (added from the first order) discount on some merchandise and the publisher wanted to give me a per-order (only adds the amount of the single order) discount. This seemingly small issue was enough to cause the publisher to threaten to cancel the deal. I felt this was going to become a major stumbling block.

Before we went any further, I decided to ask for a three-month cushion to reorder merchandise at the same discount rate. After all, I would've ordered everything I needed before the three months were up. The publisher agreed, and we both ended up with what we wanted. By being proactive and being responsive to the publisher's feelings, I kept a minor conflict from killing the deal, and still won!

▶ **Confront issues immediately.** By acknowledging issues and conflicts right away, you lessen their emotional effects. You also show the other side that you care about their feelings and how the outcome of the negotiation affects them. By confronting issues quickly, you demonstrate the will to find a win/win situation.

Never let conflicts drag on and on. Eventually, emotions will get the best of one of the two of you and the deal will fall through!

▶ **Communicate effectively.** If you find yourself in a conflict, make sure to ask the other side what you can do to resolve the problem. Make sure their response is very clear to you. Also, make sure you provide clear feedback to them in return.

▶ **Stay calm and cool.** Have you ever been in a room where people start yawning? What do you usually do? More than likely, you'll also start to yawn. Most people do! It's the same with emotions. If you or the other side starts to get too emotional, it tends to get everyone all worked up. By remaining calm and cool, the other side will usually do the same.

▶ **Be cooperative.** Assure the other side that it's your intention to work with them and not against them. Remember the importance of working with people and not taking advantage of them. By cooperating, you can build successful long-term relationships.

▶ **Promote a team atmosphere.** Treat the other side as if they were a strategic partner! In fact, become strategic partners. Do what you can to make them successful. In turn, they'll more than likely do what they can to make you more successful!

As the great motivational speaker Zig Ziglar says, "If you help enough people get what they want, they'll help you get what you want."

▶ **Stay open-minded.** Look at the conflict from both your and the other side's perspective and stay objective and non-judgmental. Often, they'll have valid reasons for not agreeing with you.

As you grow as a negotiator, you'll get better and better at understanding the big picture and finding solutions objectively.

♦ **Be systematic.** Come up with a process for handling various conflicts. One of the best ways is to develop several contingency plans. Play out different scenarios using different concessions and tactics. This way, when you run into a conflict, you'll know how to handle it quickly and effectively.

If you follow my principles on managing conflict during negotiations, you'll have minimal conflict and conclude deals rather smoothly. Of course, even with all of the information I've given you, it's still possible that you won't be able to resolve a conflict somewhere down the road. A deal may have been lost or a relationship may have become severed. Depending on the emotional level of the conflict and how you and the other side have handled the situation, it may or may not be possible to gain back full trust. Again, you must identify issues and solve them as quickly as possible. The longer you allow a conflict to continue, the more of a toll it takes on the relationship. But do not fear! There are many ways in which I've salvaged relationships following major conflicts.

Here are some strategies that I've used to successfully manage various conflicts during negotiations:

♦ **Communicate feelings.** If you feel you have offended someone or violated their trust, make sure to communicate with them immediately and make it known that you're sorry. That doesn't mean you have to give in to them or give extra concessions. It just means you're sorry for personally offending them and wish to reopen the relationship and negotiation.

♦ **Demonstrate strong commitment.** Stay committed to the relationship and make sure you communicate your commitment. People want to do deals with others who are committed to working with them toward a common goal and looking out for their best interest.

Also, make sure that your interests are taken care of before you enter any long-term relationships.

♦ **Remain patient.** Realize that not everyone will "let you off the hook" easily. It will take time to heal emotional wounds. Stay patient and non-emotional.

- **Make small concessions.** In some instances, *offer some small, unimportant concessions.* Just make sure that you offer concessions that are important to the other side. Many times negotiators make the mistake of getting all wrapped up in some small, meaningless concession. Then they get offended when they don't get it. Search for these small concessions and use them to your advantage.

- **Stay in touch.** Staying in touch with the other side sends a message that you care. Call them every so often and see how they're doing; even offer your services. You can also write to them if you feel more comfortable. (I don't recommend writing over calling on the phone, due to its impersonal nature.)

By closing off communications and not staying in touch, you'll demonstrate that you do not wish to carry on with the relationship.

- **Schedule a lunch or dinner meeting.** Show goodwill by offering to spend some time dining with them. This small gesture alone will show them your fervor and dedication to keeping the lines of communication open and settling the issues of the conflict. Tell them you'd like to meet for an informal lunch or dinner and start anew.

- **Send a card.** This may sound corny, but it works. Send a "we miss you" or "thinking of you" style card. This will catch their attention and show them that even in light of what's happened, you have a good sense of humor and wish to keep the lines of communication open.

Always make an attempt to salvage relationships that have gone awry. Keep in mind that we live in a small world. And everybody is just a few people away from talking to or meeting anyone. You never want anyone going around telling others that you or your organization slighted them, or are in any other way a company that should be avoided.

Quick Review

As you can see, it's very important to avoid conflicts at all cost—quickly and efficiently. The following is a review of all the main points and strategies used to *manage conflict and keep negotiations moving smoothly.*

There are four common forms of conflict during negotiations:

1. **Conflict between two or more people.** Two or more people disagree on terms or concessions.

2. **Conflict between departments.** Many times companies will experience interdepartmental problems. Often, departments will negotiate with each other for various resources and power.

3. **Conflict between companies.** This is when two organizations have a conflict over competition, capital resources, people, terms, and concessions.

4. **Conflict between an individual and a group.** This happens when a person has to negotiate with a group of people. Examples are executive boards, committees, and various other teams.

Here are the eight common causes of conflict during negotiations:

1. **Different perceptions.** Ever since the beginning of time, people have had different perceptions of the same issues and events.

2. **Poor communication.** I will repeat this over and over throughout this system. *Poor communication is a deal killer.*

   When you're dealing with issues as complex as those you find in negotiations, you must communicate articulately, effectively, concisely, and quickly. Both you and the other side have to be clear about what you want and be able to accurately communicate it to each other.

3. **Misaligned goals.** Conflict can arise from misaligned or incongruent goals between you and the "other side." Both of you need to be working toward the same common goal—to finish the deal!

4. **Inconsistent values and beliefs.** Most people have been following the same values and beliefs since they were very young. In many instances, the other side may get very defensive if you violate their beliefs or goals.

What is a value? Values are anything that you or the other side place significant importance on or hold dear.

Let's define the two different types of values:

A. **Moving-toward values:** These values include success, love, security, intimacy, freedom, comfort, passion, health, adventure, and power.

B. **Moving-away from values:** These values include anger, guilt, rejection, failure, humiliation, frustration, loneliness, and depression.

Next, you have to make sure not to violate people's beliefs.

What is a belief? A belief is anything that a person believes to be true about themselves, other people, their organization, or anything else.

5. **Incongruent personalities.** Every individual or group has a different personality. Some people will just seem to "click," or get along with you better than others, but you can't dismiss those who don't.

6. **Contradictory expectations.** When either party of the negotiation expects to receive a concession that hasn't been provided, conflict is sure to result.

7. **Third parties.** Third parties are people or groups asked for opinions or who are otherwise asked to participate in the negotiation. Third parties may include outside executives, managers, lawyers, consultants, accountants, friends, or family members.

8. **Strong-arming.** Strong-arming is the act of using force or unnecessary pressure to get the other side to accept your terms.

The following are some of the successful strategies that you can use to resolve conflicts during negotiations:

♦ **Be proactive.** Always remember that your goal is to avoid all of the common causes of conflict previously listed.

If you feel a conflict arising, find the source of the conflict, and do everything you can to lessen its effect—before it gets out of hand. And I mean quickly!

♦ **Confront issues immediately.** By acknowledging issues and conflicts right away, you lessen the emotional effects of the conflict. You also show the other side how much you care about their feelings and how the outcome of the negotiation affects them.

♦ **Communicate effectively.** If you find yourself in a conflict, make sure to ask the other side what the problem is. Make sure they're articulate and not leaving out any details. Also in return, make sure you provide them with clear feedback.

♦ **Stay calm and cool.** If either party starts to get emotional, it tends to get everyone all worked up. When you remain calm and cool, everyone will usually do the same.

♦ **Be cooperative.** Assure them that it's your intention to work with them and not against them. Remember the importance of working with people and not trying to take advantage of them. By cooperating, you can *build successful long-term relationships*.

♦ **Promote a team atmosphere.** Treat them as if they are strategic partners! In fact, *become strategic partners*! Do what you can to make them successful. In turn, they'll more than likely do what they can to make you more successful!

♦ **Stay open-minded.** Look at the conflict from both perspectives and stay objective and non-judgmental.

♦ **Be systematic.** Come up with a process for handling various conflicts. One of the best ways is to develop several contingency plans. Play out different scenarios using different concessions and tactics. This way, when you run into a conflict, you'll know how to handle it quickly and effectively.

Many times I've dealt with conflicts that temporarily severed relationships. There are many ways in which I've salvaged relationships following major conflicts. Here are some strategies that I've used to successfully manage various conflicts during negotiations:

♦ **Communicate feelings.** If you feel that you've offended someone or violated their trust, make sure to communicate with them immediately and make it known that you are sorry.

♦ **Show strong commitment.** Stay committed to the relationship and make sure that you communicate it to the other side.

- **Remain patient.** Understand that not everyone will "let you off the hook" easily. It will take time to heal emotional wounds. Stay patient and non-emotional.

- **Make small concessions.** Offer some small, unimportant concessions to the other side. Just make sure that these concessions are more important to them than to you.

- **Stay in touch.** Staying in touch with the other side demonstrates how much you care about the relationship. Call them every so often and see how they're doing; even offer your services.

- **Schedule a lunch or dinner meeting.** Show goodwill by offering to spend some time dining with the other side.

- **Send a card.** Send a "we miss you" or "thinking of you" style card. Always make an attempt to salvage relationships that have gone awry.

Wow—you've come a long way! Let's move right into the next chapter, where you'll learn the *11 characteristics of successful negotiators*!

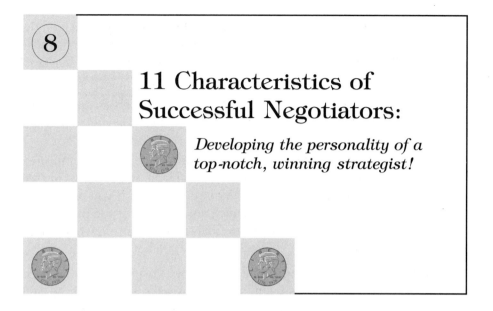

11 Characteristics of Successful Negotiators:

Developing the personality of a top-notch, winning strategist!

This chapter focuses on the 11 key characteristics of top strategic negotiators. These characteristics are based on my personal experience as a negotiator, as well as years of research on negotiators, including the likes of P.T. Barnum, Donald Trump, Ted Turner, and hundreds of others in both small and large businesses.

One of the primary goals of *Negotiate Your Way to Riches* is to help you adopt all 11 characteristics. So, if you see a characteristic that is not your strong point, do not fear. By the end of this chapter, you'll know what you have to do so that you can develop each one.

Characteristics of Successful Negotiators

Successful negotiators are:

1. **"No limit" thinkers.** Top negotiators go into every negotiation believing that no matter what the circumstance, situation, or terms of the deal, they can get exactly what they want! They look at every deal and say, "Why not?" or "I'm going for it all."

When I negotiate, I believe I'm invincible. I'm ready to take on the best! If you go in with reservations, low self-confidence, or feel the slightest bit inferior, the other side will pick up on it and use it against you. In a nutshell—you'll lose!

2. **Intuitive.** Negotiators are great at feeling out situations and making decisions based on the emotional tone of the deal. They are also great at predicting outcomes.

    Think of the last time a situation made you feel uneasy or unsure. You may have not even had solid proof you were in danger or at risk, but somehow you just knew something wasn't right. If you based your decision on your intuition and instinct, you probably made the best decision and kept yourself from harm. The same holds true when you're negotiating a deal.

3. **Goal setters.** Goal-setting is one of the keys to success as a negotiator. You absolutely, positively, must *know what you're after*. You'll also have to develop new goals as the deal progresses. It's very important to have clear goals before starting a negotiation. If you don't, you're like a ship without a rudder—you won't have any direction and you'll lose sight of your destination and get lost.

    Before I start the negotiation process, I make a list of the terms and concessions that I expect to attain. I know where I'm going to be flexible, as well as where I have to stand firm. I also keep a goal list in front of me during the negotiation as a reminder of what I must pursue. My goal list acts as a scorecard!

4. **Strategic thinkers.** Top negotiators map out their whole strategy before the negotiation begins. They generally have three or more plans of attack. For example, they may have Plan A, Plan B, and Plan C. Plan A represents the plan they start the negotiation with. Plan A usually represents the best-case scenario. Plans B and C are contingency plans based on variances in the agreement.

    It's very important that you plan for several scenarios. Based on how the negotiation is going, you need to have the ability to quickly implement strategies that will enable you to make the best decisions. I pride myself on having the ability to plan every move. Every time I sit down to negotiate, my strategy has been planned from start to finish. I've taken all of the details of the deal into account and have thought through different scenarios. Only on a rare occasion do I have to do a

180-degree turn in my strategy. This only happens when the other side makes unreasonable demands or asks for concessions they're not entitled to.

What always amazes me is the lack of planning most negotiators demonstrate. Most are disorganized, unreasonable, selfish, and unsure of the value of their product and/or service. What really gets me more than anything is how many only think of themselves or their organizations. Believe me when I say, a successful, organized negotiator can spot a weak, unprepared negotiator a mile away.

5. **Decisive.** All successful negotiators are very decisive. They know what they're after and are relentless in its pursuit. They've laid the battle plans and are ready for war. They also realize that wavering during a negotiation can weaken their position to the point of wasting their time.

   I've also developed the habit of sticking to my guns. I decide what I want and where I'm going. All of my decisions are made with precision and thought. You need to do the same!

6. **Visionaries.** Negotiators have vision and foresight. They see the negotiation as successfully completed before they even begin.

   Every skilled negotiator that I've had the opportunity to work with or study, pictures the negotiation in their mind prior to every negotiation. They picture themselves giving their presentation and getting positive feedback from the "other side." They see the room, hear the sounds, feel the demeanor, and picture the body language. This is called creative visualization. Learning to use this skill can change every aspect of your life both personally and professionally. I use creative visualization before every negotiation. In fact, I just used it recently to handle an exceptionally good negotiator. Let me explain the scenario.

Example: A colleague came to me very distressed. He told me he'd just negotiated a deal with a major publisher. The result was fruitless and unfavorable. He was given an unreasonable discount and unfavorable terms. He went to his boss with the bad news and the boss rejected the terms of the contract. Tensions were high between the two companies. He went on to explain that the other side, who happened to be the president of the other company, is a jerk, unfriendly, and unwilling to budge on his position. I smelled a major opportunity!

Right away I asked if I could have the opportunity to reconfigure the deal and make a new proposal. He said, "Okay, but you'll be sorry. You'll never get anywhere. He's too tough." Right away I was able to tell why my colleague failed. He had no confidence in himself, and the other side picked up on it! I was ready to show him how to close the deal!

Here's how I used *creative visualization* to close the winning deal: I closed my eyes and put everything out of my mind for 10 minutes. Next, I drew a picture in my mind of what the other side would look like. I pictured him looking professional, smiling, and being very friendly. Then I then pictured how he would sound—low tone, moderate rate of speech, very articulate, and having a friendly rate of inflexion. Next, I pictured myself asking this gentleman for the terms and concessions needed to complete the deal. And at the same time, I pictured how he'd look and sound as he gave his positive feedback to all of my requests. And finally, I pictured the desired outcome. *Now you're probably wondering what happened.*

He was friendly from the very beginning. He responded very similarly to what I'd pictured in my mind's eye. I received all but one concession I asked for. That particular concession was just a *red herring* (you'll learn about red herrings in Chapter 12) and not very important anyway. My colleague was more than amazed.

7. **Firm yet flexible.** Successful negotiators always stand firm on their convictions and their ability to attain them. At the same time, they also realize that new details and hidden information pop up constantly. Therefore, a successful negotiator adapts to the new environment without missing a beat.

   I've been in countless negotiations where new information is presented at the most inopportune times. Sometimes it changes the whole course of a deal and I have to quickly reevaluate the situation. My ability to remain flexible has led me to success over and over again.

8. **Calm and cool.** Top negotiators never crack under pressure. Even in the face of adversity, they remain mentally stable and secure in their position.

   Many times during negotiations, I've felt uneasy or uncomfortable. Did I ever crack? Not on your life! What I do is delay the negotiation and take a quick break. I usually make up a great excuse while I go and rethink my position. Cracking under pressure or starting tirades will never help you. Always stay calm and cool!

9. **Master persuaders.** To become successful at negotiating, you must learn how to become a master persuader. I'm not going to spend much time explaining this at this point because you'll be learning how to do this as you go through this system.

   The bottom line is to persuade the other side to see things from your perspective. You must leverage all of your power and explain the importance of doing business with you. Also, remind them of all of the things you can do for them. By the time you reach the end of this book, you'll be an expert at persuading the other side to help you accomplish your goals. And I mean that in a positive way!

10. **Focused on people.** Top negotiators are focused on forming good, solid, long-term relationships with all of their vendors, suppliers, and customers. Later, in Chapter 17, you will learn all of the fundamental people skills you'll need to develop to close more favorable deals.

    My ability to become a "people person" and form long-term relationships has been my secret to success during negotiations. All business is about people. *You need to have people working with you instead of against you!* This rule always holds true!

11. **Detail-oriented.** Your ability to understand details will have a direct impact on your ability to strategize. As you'll learn, you need to be able to synthesize all of the elements and details of a deal into an action plan.

Quick Review

Let's quickly review the 11 characteristics of successful negotiators. Successful negotiators are:

1. **"No limit" thinkers.** Top negotiators go into every negotiation believing that no matter what the circumstances or the terms of the deal, they can get exactly what they want.

2. **Intuitive.** Negotiators are great at feeling out situations and making decisions based on the emotional tone of the deal.

3. **Goal setters.** It's very important to know your goal before going into any negotiation. If you don't, you're like a ship without a rudder—you'll lose sight of your destination and get lost.

4. **Strategic thinkers.** Top negotiators map out their whole strategy before the negotiation starts. They have three or more plans of attack. *It's very important that you plan for several scenarios.*

5. **Decisive.** All successful negotiators are very decisive. They know what it is they're after and are relentless in its pursuit.

6. **Visionaries.** Negotiators have vision and foresight. They see the negotiation as successfully completed before they even begin. And they use *creative visualization* to help them achieve their goals.

7. **Firm yet flexible.** Successful negotiators always stand firm on their convictions and their ability to attain them. At the same time, they also realize that new details and hidden information pop up constantly. Therefore, a successful negotiator adapts to the new environment without missing a beat.

8. **Calm and cool.** Top negotiators never crack under pressure. Even in the face of adversity, they remain mentally stable and secure in their position.

9. **Master persuaders.** To become successful at negotiating, you must learn how to become a master persuader.

10. **Focused on people.** Top negotiators are focused on forming good, solid, long-term relationships with all of their vendors, suppliers, and customers.

11. **Detail-oriented.** Your ability to understand details will have a direct impact on your ability to strategize. You need to be able to synthesize all of the elements and details of a deal into an action plan.

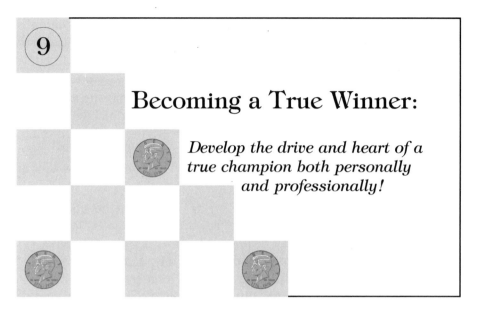

Becoming a True Winner:

Develop the drive and heart of a true champion both personally and professionally!

U p until this chapter, we have discussed the basics of the *negotiator's mindset* and the other preliminary skills you'll need to understand and develop to get through the rest of this system. Soon, you'll be ready to get your hands dirty and dig into negotiating strategies. So before I take you into the meat and potatoes of this system, we have just a few more subjects to discuss. First we're going to discuss becoming a winner!

I'm not a motivational speaker, prophet, or some other guru thinking he has all of the answers, but I do know the importance of becoming a winner and its effect on all negotiations. We need to get you in the right "winning" mindset to be able to negotiate effectively. I'd like to offer some suggestions as to why a winning attitude is crucial to success in negotiating. And then I'll briefly explain why a "losing" attitude will almost invariably lead to disaster during your negotiations.

First, I want to talk about winners. Some so-called noble beings think that losing is a virtue and the pursuit of victory is a sign of greed. Let me go on the record by telling you that if you do not play to win, then negotiating is not a skill you'll ever master. You'll always feel guilty asking for whatever you want. This is pure nonsense! *You have a given right to ask for and pursue* *anything you want in your business and personal life.* (One admonition is that you don't want to do anything that hurts another person physically, or is immoral or unethical.) In some ways it's unfortunate that most people have a losing mentality, but it works in your favor.

To be a successful negotiator, you have to see deal-making as a game. Remember when you were a child and played Monopoly or Life? Did you play to lose? Did you like to lose? Of course not! It's the same when you're going head-to-head with another individual or group. (You'll understand this better after you learn this entire system and accumulate a few wins at the bargaining table.)

We've all heard the saying "its not whether you win or lose, its how you play the game." Remember that one? I truly believe that whoever made that point was an absolute loser! Does anyone remember who *lost* the last Super Bowl or World Series? Does anyone care? It's your right to win big!

In order to be a winner, you must commit to a principle that success coach Tony Robbins calls *CANI*. *CANI* is an acronym for Constant And Never-ending Improvement. *CANI* means that each and every day, you make a commitment to better yourself in both your personal and professional lives.

To become a "winner" at the negotiating table, you must:

- ♦ **Read every book you can get your hands on that were written by *experienced negotiators*.**

- ♦ **Seek out and attend local negotiating seminars given by *experienced negotiators*.**

- ♦ **Purchase any negotiating audiocassettes, videos, compact discs, CD-ROMS, DVDs, etc.**

- ♦ **Read books on negotiating skills and positive thinking.**

- ♦ **Attend negotiating classes given at local colleges.**

- ♦ **Seek out every opportunity to practice *CANI* and your success as a negotiator is virtually guaranteed.**

- ♦ **Commit today to be a winner in everything that you do.**

Now I want to talk about losers. Every day we meet people who look, act, and think like everyone else. They all wear the same type of clothes, lease cars to impress their friends, and are afraid to voice their opinions or think for themselves. They never seek out seminars, books, tapes, CDs, classes, or training videos to improve their careers. They're too busy watching television, gossiping, and making the same excuses that brought them nowhere to begin with. Don't let this be you!

The typical loser's day goes something like this: They get up 20 minutes late, drink a pot of coffee, and eat a couple of doughnuts. Next, they scream upstairs to wake their children, who are also running late. They put on the same work clothes they wore two days ago, dash out of the driveway like Mario Andretti, and start swearing at every driver in their way. They park, make a mad dash to their desk, and work a half-hearted day at the office. Two hours are spent working and six hours are split between eating lunch and gossiping about their coworkers. When 5 p.m. rolls around, they dash home, eat an oversized dinner, and plop themselves in front of the boob tube and laugh about people like you and I who attend seminars, read books, listen to audiocassettes, and attend night classes to better ourselves.

You have to commit to being different, standing out in the crowd, humbly tooting your own horn, and bettering yourself. Enough said! Practice *CANI* daily!

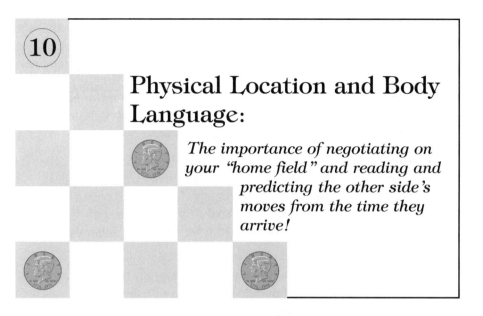

10

Physical Location and Body Language:

The importance of negotiating on your "home field" and reading and predicting the other side's moves from the time they arrive!

Congratulations, you've survived boot camp!

I want to start this chapter with two very important tips:

1. **Whenever possible, negotiate at your place of business.** Sports teams always want the "home field advantage." Why do you think that is? I'll tell you. It's because teams tend to play better and win more games when they're played in their own home stadium. The same holds true when negotiating.

   By hosting the negotiation, you automatically put yourself at ease by being in familiar surroundings. It's always easier to negotiate in familiar surroundings, as well as have supportive coworkers to back you at any time.

   Quite a few years ago, when I was very inexperienced, I was involved in the worst negotiation ever. It was so horrible that I remember it as if it happened yesterday! A business partner and I visited a major Japanese electronic parts manufacturer to discuss taking over the development of their Website. The manufacturer's representatives wanted us to meet them at their local headquarters. We really needed the work and enthusiastically agreed. On the phone, we were told that we would be meeting with only two people—the consultant who was hiring us and the vice president of marketing. When we arrived, we were ushered into their boardroom. Inside there were 12 Japanese people, including eight who couldn't speak a word of English. This situation was so intimidating that we would have said almost anything to get out in one piece. I firmly believe they did that purposely, and it paid off for them. They ended up with a great deal.

When you're hosting the negotiation, it forces the other party to tell you the names of all the dealmakers they'll be bringing. This enables you to know who's who. They have to provide you with the information so you can have proper accommodations in place.

What happened to us was simple. We had no Plan B to fall back on. We only planned on how we were going to handle the two people we were originally meeting. As soon as we saw 10 additional people, we were scared beyond description.

2. **When the other side arrives, you need to seat them together on one side of the table or side-by-side in your plain view.**

    Many negotiators may disagree with me on this one. They'll say this seating arrangement creates a "me versus you" or "us versus them" negotiating environment. And technically it is! At the same time, there's a valid, proven reason for using this strategic seating arrangement: Doing so gives you the opportunity to read the other side's body language in plain view. By encouraging them to sit according to this seating arrangement, you'll be able to read all of their facial expressions and body language, both individually and as a team. If you keep a close eye on them, you'll notice that their body language speaks louder than their words. And once you get good at this, you'll be able to see if they're telling the truth or lying.

Body Language

Someone once told me that the body can't lie. Supposedly, if you look hard enough, liars will give themselves away in some subtle or obvious way. I've found this to be true. Just keep in mind that some people have turned lying into a science. Therefore, *you must know how to read people's body language and facial expressions.*

Let's go over the negotiating environment, personal space, and body language.

The ideal negotiating environment

In order to create the ideal negotiating environment, you must use the environment and personal space to your advantage.

Use environment to your advantage

One of the most overlooked aspects of strategic negotiating is the negotiating environment. I have always tried to keep people a little uncomfortable in order to keep negotiations moving quickly. And the quick pace almost always works in my favor.

Let's discuss the ideal negotiating environment:

+ **Chairs:** Chairs that are a little rigid, stationary, or hard on the bottom tend to work well in negotiations. People sitting in these chairs become a little uncomfortable and anxious to get done with business.

+ **Writing utensils:** Keep these out of view, and have them ready if anyone needs them. Any time the other side asks you for anything, you're psychologically helping them feel more trusting of you. What's even better is that they subconsciously believe they owe you something. Don't ask me why this works—it just does.

+ **Tables:** Always have adequate space for writing. Also, make sure there's enough room for everyone. It's still to your advantage to keep the size of the table to a minimum. If the other side feels too comfortable, they may drag negotiations out too long.

+ **Lighting:** Make sure you have adequate lighting for writing. At the same time, dim light may help the other side feel sleepy and drop their defenses.

+ **Temperature:** Heat makes people sleepy, sweaty, anxious, and somewhat irritated. Frigid air conditioning keeps people alert and somewhat uncomfortable. I feel that the more heat, the better!

+ **Driving or flying distance:** The general rule is that whoever travels the farthest has the least leverage. That means if you're doing the traveling, you're starting out at a major disadvantage. The more distance, the worse it gets.

Example: Let's say you have to travel 150 or 200 miles. You fly in, get to your hotel, drive to the negotiation, and meet for whatever length of time. This is time-consuming and very unnerving. Wouldn't you be more anxious to get this deal over with, without having to come back? Absolutely! The more anxious you are, the worse judgment you'll demonstrate.

Example: A company asked me to help them find a new computer programmer to do their Internet development. As usual, they had a small budget. My goal was to find an inexpensive, yet highly skilled programmer.

I contacted a friend in the computer department at Northeastern Illinois University and explained the requirements for the position. She arranged for me to meet with someone perfect for the position.

At the time, I had a very spacious office with comfortable chairs, pleasing lighting, good mood music, and one heck of an air conditioning system. This wasn't going to help! So I decided I was going to make this gentleman somewhat physically uncomfortable and end the negotiation quickly. How did I do this?

I decided to meet with the gentleman in an upstairs conference room that could've doubled as an interrogation room for the Chicago Police. The room had bright lights, uncomfortable chairs, no music, no decorations, and terrible ventilation. I strategically asked him to sit down directly across the conference table. We stared at each other for about 15 seconds. We discussed his past experience for about 20 minutes and then I explained the opportunity I had available. He became very enthusiastic.

As we started talking money, he loosened his collar and started to sweat and fidget in his chair. I had him right where I wanted him. I could tell from his body language that he was asking for more money than he ever made before. Every time he told me how much he wanted, I immediately rejected him. Finally, I named an amount I felt comfortable with and he accepted the offer and breathed a sigh of relief.

Think about the last time you attended a meeting or event where you felt totally or semi-uncomfortable. What did you want to do? You probably wanted to get done with business and get out! And remember: The strategy isn't designed to give them a backache, just to wear them down.

I'm not encouraging you to do anything that'll cause the other side pain or stimulate a totally unpleasant experience. You must *always be professional.* If you make them too comfortable, you'll slow down the negotiation process. *Use your best discretion when eliciting this psychological strategy.*

Utilize personal space to your advantage

It's always been my experience that in order to negotiate effectively, you have to keep as little space as possible between the sides. I'm not telling you to sit on their lap or cram six people into a space suitable for four. But if you're negotiating on your "home field," it's wise to make them uncomfortable enough to want to finish business and get out. Some of you are probably saying, "This Wink guy is a real jerk." On the contrary! It's not in your best interest to turn your business meeting into a social gathering. You can socialize after the negotiation!

Has someone ever told you that you're invading their personal space? If they have, they're telling you in a nice way that you're getting too close and to back off. Most people have a specific comfort zone when it comes to negotiating. Let's discuss how to use distance as an advantage during negotiations.

There are four zones of distance:

1. **Intimate distance (touching to 18 inches):** *Intimate distance is reserved for family, friends, loved ones, and lovers.* You should never get this close in any business negotiation. If for some reason you do, be careful! This distance is very threatening and can be easily misconstrued. Also, if you're in someone's intimate distance, they'll more than likely get very defensive with you.

    Intimate distance can be considered making actual physical contact or being within 18 inches of someone. Generally, men will try to keep greater distances from each other. Therefore, if you're a man negotiating with another man, you'll want to stay at least a foot or two away. Why? If you're too close to a man in a negotiation, they'll become doubly defensive.

First, they'll automatically be a little defensive due to the nature of your negotiating relationship. And second, they'll be defensive about you violating their personal space. Many men seem to have a complex about being too close to other men. And that's fine.

Now, if you're a man negotiating with a woman, you have a different set of rules to follow. Men and women accept each other easier in a closer setting. And at the same time, if you get too close to a woman during a negotiation, you may be considered to be violating their space in a sexual or intimate way. Keep a safe distance so the member of the opposite sex doesn't mistake your intentions or become uncomfortable. Always focus on the negotiation, not surrounding factors that are sure to become distractions.

If you're a woman negotiating with a man, the rules play in your favor. In general, a woman can benefit from moving into the personal space of a man. Men tend to find the closeness complementary. However, this isn't always the case. Some men don't care for overly aggressive women, and will back away or simply become uncomfortable. Every situation is different; therefore, *read the situation and use your best judgment.*

2. **Personal distance (18 inches to 4 feet):** *Personal distance is typically visited by good friends and business colleagues.* This space is typical of employees when they stand and talk to each other. You'll often find yourself next to or across the table from the other side during negotiations. In many instances, you'll find yourself within their personal distance.

    My recommendation is to stay farther away. Stay at least three feet away. You never, ever want to start a negotiation with someone on the defensive. At the same time, if you feel the urge to push them and make them feel uncomfortable, then stand or talk to them at three feet away or less. Just be very careful!

3. **Social/work distance (4 to 12 feet):** *Social/work distance represents the typical negotiating distance.* By staying within this range, you'll be received as considerate and non-intrusive.

4. **Public distance (12 or more feet away):** Public distance is maintained at presentations and other large gatherings. Many times you'll negotiate at a large table where you can be 12 or more feet away from the person with whom you're speaking. Avoid this distance if possible. The greater the distance you are from the other side, the harder it is to communicate accurately and articulately. You may need to use a microphone if you're too far apart from the other side.

Understand and read facial expressions

We've all heard the expression "watch their poker face." You know the type—always rigid, never smile, glassy eyes, and say very little. They are plotting, scheming, and getting ready to do whatever it takes to get you to give them whatever they want. They will lie, cheat, steal, and rob you blind if you let them. Keep in mind, they're good at it.

Let's take a moment and discuss the meanings of certain facial expressions. Here are some guidelines to reading the other side's body language:

1. **If someone stares at you intensely, look away.** Chances are, they're trying to intimidate you. By staring at you, they're trying to exert psychological power over you.

    One counterstrategy I use over and over is to ask them if they're married or some other unrelated question. You're probably wondering why I do that. Simple! I want to break their level of intensity and cause what's called a *behavior pattern interrupt*. In other words, I broke their concentration and made it difficult for them to regain their thought pattern by asking a seemingly absurd question.

2. **Watch people's facial expressions when they're giving you information. Look for signs of lying or deceit.**

    Signs of potential lying or deceit happen when the other side:

    ⏵ **Smiles too much or too little.** The first sign that someone is lying to you is when they're trying to keep from smiling when they talk to you. Liars can't usually go a couple of minutes without giving themselves away. Look for smirks, smiles, or outright laughing. The reason people tend to laugh at this point is because they get too excited and overcome with anxiety about lying to you. They tend to crack at the beginning or toward the end of the lie. One counterstrategy you can use is to make constant movements or ask the person to look at something you've written on a piece of paper. This will break their concentration.

> **Constantly looks away from you.** Another way people show they might be lying is when they keep from looking you straight in the eye for more than a few seconds. Most people give a momentary glance at the person they're communicating with. They do this to make sure they're paying attention and listening.

The reason most people can't look you in the eye when they're lying to you is that they're afraid to face you. It's because *they know they're doing something wrong.* In general, most people have good intentions and want to do the right thing. However, some want to impress the boss, collect a big fat bonus, or prove they can one-up you.

One counterstrategy I use is to do whatever I can to get them to look up at me. When you speak to the other side, use hypnotic visual words. While you're speaking to them, use words and phrases such as "look," "see it from this perspective," "picture this," "couldn't you see it?" and so forth. Notice the visual words in each phrase (*look, picture, see*). Some people say this is unethical. It's simply called being prepared and getting to the truth.

Keep in mind that there are always exceptions to every rule. *Some people won't look you in the eye because they're outright shy.* As you negotiate with more eclectic, different types of people, you'll get better at picking out who's sincere and who isn't.

One sure sign of a smart, cunning negotiator is one who exhibits the following characteristics: they are tight-lipped, wide-eyed, straight-faced, and talk very little. They're usually thinking and strategizing of how they can either counter what you're going to say, or simply use your offer to their advantage. Watch them very closely and learn from them.

Facial expressions are just one area of body language that you need to understand. Whenever you negotiate, you also want to be very perceptive of their physical posture and subtle body movements.

Watch the other side's posture and body movements

Always arrive at the negotiation first. Why? By arriving first, you can gauge the other side's emotional state by simply watching them as they approach the negotiating table.

The following are some typical scenarios and how you can read the other side's posture and body movements. Consider the following nine questions when reading the other side:

1. **When they entered the room, did they walk with a positive, reassuring strut?** If so, they may have an ace up their sleeve or are at least trying to be perceived as such. Watch for the bluff!

2. **Are they smiling or frowning? A healthy smile can mean that they're coming in goodwill for a clean negotiation.** An over-confident smirk may be their way of trying to intimidate you. Or they may feel they have a distinct advantage over you and/ or your organization.

   A frown may be a sign of inferiority. The other side may feel they don't bring enough to the table to make it worth your while or they may be just plain scared to death. In some instances, they may be planning on bluffing and feel nervous about pulling it off. Remember that negotiating is not for everyone. Many people are put in powerful positions to negotiate for goods and services, who would rather leave the negotiating to someone else.

3. **Do they seem intense or nervous?** If they're too intense or too nervous, this is a sign of weakness. Use this to your advantage.

4. **Are they walking slowly with their head facing down?** Quite possibly, they're inexperienced, intimidated, and just praying you don't notice.

5. **Did they shake your hand first or simply sit down and get started?** If they shake your hand and smile, this may be a sign that they're very relaxed and hoping to come to a "win/win" negotiation. If not, they mean business!

6. **If someone is steepling their hands when they talk, they're more than likely trying to exercise control over you.** They may also be analyzing you. Look for an intense look in their eyes. If they're demonstrating intense feelings, they're probably being analytical and strategizing, so prepare to give a quick response.

7. **Watch the other side's posture while they're seated.** If they're leaning forward, they're more than likely trying to invade your space to intimidate you. They're more than likely listening to every word you're saying. If they're doing the talking, they're trying to get you to see things from their perspective. If you're talking, they probably aren't listening very much and counting the seconds until they can jump in with their opinion.

8. **Keep your eye out for defensive signals.** When people become defensive, they tend to get real intense—almost to the point of anger. Some early warnings that people are becoming defensive include folded arms, clenched fists, and more than likely they'll be looking away from you. The clenched fist seems to reinforce the folded arm. It's a sign that they're ready for physical or emotional battle. Be very careful.

   Many times, when people are starting to get defensive, they'll either raise their voice or stop talking altogether.

9. **Check to see if their hands are on their hips.** This type of body language is almost always viewed as defiant or authoritarian. (Again, in a few instances, there are exceptions to the rule—they could be just resting their hands.)

Quick Review

Always remember these two tips:

1. **Whenever possible, negotiate in *your* place of business.**

2. **When the other side arrives, seat them together on one side of the table or side-by-side in your plain view.**

Do you remember how to read people's body language and what it may be telling you? The following is a quick review of the main points you learned in this section.

▶ **Understand how to use environment to your advantage when negotiating.**
Some elements of environment include:

◆ **Chairs:** Chairs that are a little rigid, stationary, or hard on the bottom tend to work well in negotiations.

◆ **Writing utensils:** Keep these out of view, but have them ready if anyone needs them. By having the other side ask for them, you are psychologically helping them to be more trusting of you. Also, they subconsciously believe they owe you something.

◆ **Tables:** Always have adequate space for writing.

◆ **Lighting:** Make sure you have adequate lighting for writing. At the same time, dim lighting may help the other side feel sleepy or less defensive.

◆ **Temperature:** High heat makes people sleepy, sweaty, anxious, and irritated. Frigid air conditioning keeps people alert and somewhat uncomfortable.

◆ **Driving or flying distance:** The general rule is whoever travels the farthest has the least leverage.

▶ **Maximize the use of personal space.**
There are four zones of distance:

1. **Intimate distance (Touching to 18 inches):** Intimate distance is reserved for family, friends, loved ones, and lovers.

2. **Personal distance (18 inches to 4 feet):** Personal distance is typically visited by good friends and business colleagues.

3. **Social/work distance (4 to 12 feet):** Social/work distance represents the typical negotiating distance. *Whenever possible, try to stay in this range.*

4. **Public distance (12 or more feet away):** Public distance is maintained at presentations and other large gatherings. Avoid this distance if possible.

▶ **Understand and read facial expressions.**
Here are some tips on reading body language:

1. **If someone stares at you intensely, look away quickly. Chances are that the other side is trying to intimidate you. By staring at you, they're trying to exert psychological power over you.**

2. **Watch people's facial expressions when they're giving you valuable information.**

    Two "red flags" are when the other side:

    ▷ **Smiles too much or too little.** The first sign the other side is lying is when they try to keep from smiling when they're talking to you.

    ▷ **Constantly looks away from you.** Another way that people show they're lying is when they can't look you straight in the eye for more than a few seconds.

    One sure sign of a smart, cunning negotiator is one who is usually tight-lipped, wide-eyed, straight-faced, and who talks very little.

    Facial expressions are just one area of body language you need to understand. Whenever you negotiate, you also want to be very perceptive of the other side's posture and movements.

▶ **Watch the other side's posture and body movements.**

    Position yourself to arrive at the negotiation first. Why? By arriving first, you can gauge the emotional state of the other side by simply watching them as they approach the negotiation table.

    Consider the following nine questions when trying to read the other side:

    1. **When they entered the room, did they walk with a positive, reassuring strut?**

    2. **Are they smiling or frowning?**

    3. **Do they seem intense or nervous?**

    4. **Are they walking slowly with their head down?**

    5. **Did they shake your hand or simply sit down and get started?**

    6. **Are they steepling their hands when talking to you?**

    7. **What kind of posture are they exhibiting when seated?**

    8. **Are there any defensive signals?**

    9. **Are their hands on their hips?**

Now that you know all about language, I want to start discussing what you have to offer the other side instead of money!

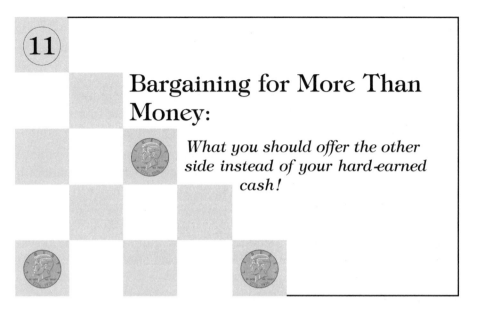

11

Bargaining for More Than Money:

What you should offer the other side instead of your hard-earned cash!

You may not believe it just yet, but people are interested in negotiating on issues other than just price.

It's true: Money is just one aspect of negotiations!

Too many people are under the impression that all that counts during a negotiation is price. This is false information given by people who haven't truly played the negotiating game.

Think of it this way: If the statement held true that "money is the most important element of the buying decision," shoppers wouldn't shadow the doorways of stores such as Bloomingdale's, Neiman Marcus, Lord & Taylor, Nordstrom, or Gucci. People would never buy a Rolls Royce, Ferrari, or Lotus. Nobody would be paying premium prices for any goods and services. But they do!

In this section, we're going to focus on 15 deal elements that are every bit as important as money. In fact, some people put money far down on their list. They want more from their buying experience than a discount.

The 15 Crucial Deal Elements (Excluding Money)

1. **Assembly:** Many companies sell products that require assembly. Examples are model cars, playground equipment, and outdoor gazebos. Do your competitors offer to come and put it together or set it up for free? If you do, tell your prospect. This is a great negotiating gambit.

2. **Attitude:** Are you happy, cheerful, and knowledgeable? Do you have an aura of professionalism when your prospect comes to negotiate with you? Too many stores that I've shopped in employ boisterous teens or angry, bitter adults who act as if serving customers is an imposition. A good attitude and awesome shopping experience for the customer will make negotiations go very smoothly. A good attitude is so rare nowadays; you won't even have to tell the prospect about yours. You'll just stand out instantly.

3. **Credit:** The United States is the credit capital of the world! That's why our personal credit is one of the most valuable assets we possess. So in turn, people and businesses want to use it more than ever. Therefore, to be competitive, you not only need to offer it, you need to have a better credit policy to offer the "other side."

    Consider the following questions relating to credit:

    ♦ **Can the other side make longer payments?**

    ♦ **Do you accept all major credit cards?**

    ♦ **Do you take both personal and business checks?**

    ♦ **Can they defer their first payment for a couple of months?**

    ♦ **Do you offer in-house credit?**

    ♦ **Can they pay with a smaller down payment than your competitors offer?**

    ♦ **Can you give zero percent financing?**

    All of these will make you stand out from the competition.

4. **Delivery:** Quite a few product distributors and manufacturers offer different types of delivery.

    Consider the following questions relating to delivery:

♦ **What are your competitors offering?**

♦ **How will you stand out when negotiating with your prospect?**

♦ **Will you offer free delivery?**

♦ **Next-day or second-day delivery?**

♦ **How about same-day delivery?**

Whatever the competition offers, you must go the extra mile for your customers and remind them you did!

5. **Expertise:** Most people want to purchase from someone who possesses uncommon expertise. If you're trying to sell someone a Rolls Royce at a premium price, you'd better know the car inside and out. You must know all of the features; including options, fabrics, paint, history, and everything else that differentiates it from competitors such as Maserati, Ferrari, or Lamborghini. Negotiate on the merits of these unique features, and then *sell them on the benefits*!

6. **Guarantee:** These days, everyone expects a rock-solid, ironclad guarantee that you'll refund money on products and services. So how can you differentiate yourself from the crowd?

Consider the following questions relating to guarantees:

♦ **Can you offer an unconditional guarantee?**

♦ **If someone isn't satisfied with the quality of your product or service, can you offer a no-questions-asked refund guarantee?**

♦ **Do you offer lifetime guarantees?**

♦ **Can you offer to guarantee double or triple the value if they're not satisfied?**

The point is that when you're negotiating similar products, you need to have a better than expected guarantee. You have to have an edge! This is a great negotiating gambit.

7. **Honest solutions:** If you want to stand head and shoulders above the competition, you must *offer the people a solution to their problems*. People want to buy products and services from someone who genuinely cares about their needs. That means you should never sell anything to anyone that they don't need. Always offer a product, service, or any other options that you know are beneficial to them.

Also, if your product or service doesn't match their needs, tell them where they can get a product or service that will. They'll feel obligated to buy from you in the future or tell friends and acquaintances about your honesty and fervor. This makes future negotiations very easy for you!

8. **Payment terms:** Quite often, *people will purchase an item because of the attractive payment terms that are offered.* (Do not confuse payment terms with actual price.) Ask any car dealer and they'll tell you that special finance rates help drive automobile sales. Most people never really consider the full price they're paying over the life of a loan. What they're more concerned with are the finance rate, number of payments, and the payment amounts. Explain to your customer how your payment terms are different and more beneficial than your competitor's.

9. **Partnerships:** Show the other side that you're on the same team. Act more like a strategic partner with their best interests at heart. People tend to do business with people that have long-term relationship potential.

    Consider the following questions relating to partnerships:

    ♦ **Does the other side consider you just another vendor offering an average product or service?**

    ♦ **Do they think of you as a strategic partner with their interests in mind?**

    ♦ **Do you go the extra mile every time you see them?**

    ♦ **Are you easily accessible?**

10. **Quality:** Why do some people purchase a Seiko watch instead of a Timex, or a Pontiac instead of a Hyundai? In many cases, people are paying for the perceived quality of the item. I'm not going to judge the actual quality of any of these items. I will say that the majority of people I sampled felt that Pontiac and Seiko were of higher quality than the respective competitors I listed. Even so, you better be able to tell the customer why!

11. **Reliability:** In today's buying environment, people are becoming more and more skeptical of salespeople. To negotiate effectively, you must assure them that you stand behind your product 100 percent. You have to prove to them that it's in their best interests to do business with you because they can count on you. And then you must always stand by your word!

12. **Return privileges:** Astute prospects know the value of return privileges. This means that you've given them the right to return used or unused products at any time, under any condition. Most companies don't automatically grant return privileges (especially wholesalers and distributors). By allowing your prospects full return privileges, you can differentiate yourself from your competitors. Another good option is to trade unused products for new ones. Sometimes your distributor cannot sell a certain product, but maybe they can sell another. Return privileges show goodwill on your part and eliminate any risk on the buyer.

13. **Service:** Because of the vast competition for every product and service, good customer service is more than just expected—it's become a rule! As expected as good customer service is, it's rarely practiced. In fact, if you provide good customer service, you will stand out in the top 5 percent of businesses. How can you differentiate yourself as a service champion?

    Consider the following questions relating to service:

    ◆ **Are your phones answered 24 hours a day?**

    ◆ **Does a live person answer the phone or is it an impersonal machine?**

    ◆ **Do you pick up the phone before the second ring?**

    ◆ **Do you load packages in someone's car for free?**

    ◆ **If someone has a major problem with a major appliance they bought from you, do you service it right away?**

    ◆ **Do you fix your products with no questions asked?**

    ◆ **Is your service guaranteed for life?**

    ◆ **Do you have one of those annoying automated answering systems that ask question after question and give option after option? Customers hate these!**

    To stand out, you really have to become a service champion!

14. **Warranty:** To survive in business and have an advantage during negotiations, you must carry warranties on all of your products. And if they break down, you not only have to replace the faulty product, you must do it quickly.

Consider the following questions relating to warranties:

♦ **Will you pick up the faulty product and replace it with a new one the same day?**

♦ **Are you willing to fix the product at the customer's home or business?**

♦ **Will you fix it the same day?**

♦ **Is the product fixed at your office or at least locally?**

♦ **Do you have lifetime warranties?**

These are very important considerations when you try to base your negotiation on a better than average warranty.

15. **Word-of-mouth:** By establishing yourself as a caring, trustworthy, friendly, ethical, and reliable businessperson, people will tell their friends about you, and they'll tell their friends, and so on and so on. When people see you as the expert who truly cares about them, the negotiation will take care of itself. Why? *Because people want to buy from people that have a reputation for caring about their customers.* By having strong, positive, friendly, word-of-mouth advertising, you'll have more sales than you can ever negotiate!

By implementing the practices listed previously, you'll win more negotiations and increase your sales. You'll also keep more customers and establish long-term relationships. By offering these options, you'll stand out from your competitors. Therefore, 80 percent of your negotiating task is already done. The key is that you have to tell your customer how you're different from your competitors. Remind them over and over. Educate them over and over. And most important, if you say that you'll do something—do it! Or your competitors will!

Let's take a moment and review what you've learned.

Quick Review

By negotiating on non-price issues, you put yourself at a major advantage over your competitors. The following is a quick review of what you can offer the other side instead of money.

The 15 crucial deal elements (excluding money):

1. **Assembly:** Many companies sell products that require assembly. If you do, you must offer an assembly service.

2. **Attitude:** You must be happy, cheerful, and knowledgeable. You also must possess an aura of professionalism when your prospects come to negotiate purchases with you.

3. **Credit:** The United States is the credit capital of the world! To be competitive, you not only need to offer it, you need to have a better credit policy than your competition.

4. **Delivery:** Quite a few product distributors and manufacturers offer delivery. You must offer an array of delivery options such as same day, next day, and second day.

5. **Expertise:** To be successful, you must possess uncommon expertise in your field. You must know more about your product and/or service than your competition.

6. **Guarantee:** Offer a rock-solid, ironclad guarantee. Always refund money on products and services—no questions asked.

7. **Honest solutions:** If you want to stand head and shoulders above the competition, you must offer the other side an honest solution to their problems.

8. **Payment terms:** Offer the most attractive payment terms in your industry.

9. **Partnerships:** Act more like a strategic partner than a salesperson.

10. **Quality:** You must only sell products and services of the utmost quality.

11. **Reliability:** In today's buying environment, people are becoming more and more incredulous and less trusting of sellers when making purchases. To negotiate effectively, you must assure people you stand behind your product or service 100 percent.

12. **Return privileges:** Astute prospects know the value of return privileges. This simply means that you give the other side the right to return used or unused products at any time, under any condition.

13. **Service:** You have to give better than expected customer service. **And you must become a service champion!**

14. **Warranty:** To have an advantage over your competitors, you must carry no-questions-asked warranties on everything you sell.

15. **Word-of-mouth:** When people know you as a caring, trustworthy, friendly, ethical, and reliable businessperson, they'll tell their friends about you, and they'll tell their friends, and so on and so on.

Congratulations! You've made it! It's now time to learn the 36 specialized negotiating tactics. After learning these strategies, you'll be able to negotiate with anyone, anyplace, at anytime to win big! So without further delay—let's get started!

36 Specialized Negotiation Tactics:

Skills and strategies you can use today to convince people to give you almost anything you want!

By mastering the following 36 negotiation tactics, you can convince more and more people to give you what you want on your terms.

Before we go any further, I want to dispel a myth here and now. Using my 36 tactics is not unethical, deceptive, or unscrupulous, as some may want you to believe. Learning these 36 strategies simply gives you the edge. An edge that enables you to get what you want, when you want it. And if you follow my strategies correctly, the other side will be glad to give you what you want on your own terms.

Now keep in mind as you learn these 36 strategies that there's nothing wrong with being competitive. You have to play to win. I want you to *use these tactics every day*. And always remember to read through all the counterattacks simply because sooner or later, they'll be used against you.

Before I go into the first negotiating tactic, I want to define a term that you'll see repeated throughout the rest of this book. The term is *concession*. **A *concession* is something that you or the other side gives up during the negotiation.** The key is for you to get as many concessions from the other side as you can and give up very few.

Take the time to learn each of the following 36 negotiation strategies in detail!

1. The Final Decision-Maker

The *final decision-maker* is an unseen party who supposedly finalizes your deal. Final decision-maker is one of the most used negotiation tactics. In fact, many negotiators use it to make themselves look like a good guy. Generally, the final decision-maker is the boss—a hard-nosed bad guy! He's the one who supposedly won't approve the sale or deal at the price the other side is offering.

If you're going to use the final decision-maker strategy during negotiations, I strongly recommend making the final decision-maker a committee, review board, executive staff, board of directors, or some other group. There are two immediate benefits to doing this. First, you never have to reveal their name. And second, you never have to worry about the other side asking to see them one-on-one. And remember: Never let the other side play your ego by getting you to admit that you're the final decision-maker. Leave your ego at the door when you come to work and never bring it to the bargaining table.

Some of the benefits you get by using the final decision-maker strategy are:

♦ **The other side grows frustrated and weaker because they can't get to the final decision-maker.**

♦ **You can put off the final decision by telling the other side that the board takes quite some time to reach decisions.**

♦ **At this point, you can tell the other side they have to raise their offer or the board will not approve the deal.**

♦ **You automatically gain extra power because the other side knows they have to impress you before the final decision-maker.**

♦ **You're in a position to tell them you're going to get opposing bids.**

Example: After carefully analyzing advertising prices in a local magazine, I decided to call the publisher and negotiate for a much lower cost.

The negotiation was definitely going very well; however, their bottom line price was still a few percentage points off my target. I told the publisher that my boss (the final decision-maker) already refused to budget any more money than my original offer. I told the publisher that if the last price he gave me was the best he could do, we'd have to go to a review committee and see if they would accept this price. (In fact, to make this look more realistic, I told him I would be meeting with the review committee in three days and would have to get back to him.) A few days later, I called the publisher back and said, "My boss and the review committee have rejected your offer and we've chosen to advertise in another publication. Not wanting to lose the sale and give his competition a sale, he agreed to my price. As it turned out, we both profited. To this day, we continue to have a great business relationship.

Always ask the other side the following two questions before you start the negotiation process:

◆ **Do you have the authority to make the final decision?**

◆ **If I present you an acceptable offer, will you be able to make a buying decision today?**

These questions will save you a great deal of work. If they answer them honestly, you'll know how much work you'll have to go through to end the negotiation successfully.

How to counteract the *final decision-maker* strategy

The following are counterattack strategies for you to use if someone uses the final decision-maker strategy against you:

◆ **Immediately say you also have to answer to a final decision-maker before you can make a move. Again, use a committee or some other group. Make sure to remind the other side of how long a process it is!**

◆ **Ask them who the final decision-maker is.**

◆ **Put them on the spot whenever possible by asking specific questions about the final decision-maker.**

◆ **See if you can meet the final decision-maker and ask them what it will take to finish the deal.**

No matter how problematic a situation feels, *never lose your cool!* To negotiate strategically, you need to keep your mind clear. I understand that when someone uses a negotiating tactic on you, you may feel the urge to become frustrated, defensive, or even lash out. You just have to ask the right questions and weather the storm as best as you can. With practice, you'll emerge victorious.

2. Ultimatums

When you use the *ultimatum*, you're basically telling the other side to "take it or leave it." You usually arrive at this point when you've reached the end of your comfort level.

Some negotiations seem to go on and on with no end in sight. Finally, you get to the end of your rope. You hit your bottom line offer and have no room to budge. This means that every concession is starting to cost you more time and money. The law of diminishing returns has set in and the deal is starting to look less attractive. Many times, you'll even consider backing out of the agreement. That's when you present an ultimatum.

Example: I was assigned the task of negotiating with a top-notch local designer to do some layouts for a direct mail campaign. I asked the designer to meet with me at my office. During this meeting, I talked about the project at hand. Next, I discussed the immediate benefits of doing business with my company. I also reminded him of the long-term dollar value of the relationship. Then I went into greater detail about the project. I asked him his rate and told him to send me a written estimate. He promptly faxed me an estimate that was more than I was willing to pay.

I called him and countered their offer. He asked if we could meet half way and split the difference in price. I refused! We went back and forth for about half an hour and I finally used an ultimatum.

I said, "Either meet my offer or I'm going to seek another designer. I've offered you everything I have budgeted for this project." At this point, I was prepared to walk away. I wasn't very surprised when he suddenly agreed to my more than generous offer. *Many times you need to use the ultimatum strategy to finish a deal quickly, efficiently, and profitably.*

In many ways, ultimatums can be considered "the point of no return." Before you give someone an *ultimatum*, you'd better be darn sure the other side is going to accept it. If they reject you, and you decide you want to renegotiate, you'll lose all of your power. You'll end up with a less than satisfactory deal, if any deal at all!

How to counteract the *ultimatum*

First and foremost, never be intimidated by an ultimatum. Ultimatums are easy to counterattack. Here's how!

If someone gives you an ultimatum, your first consideration is to figure out who has the most to lose if the deal doesn't go through. Generally, someone will give you an ultimatum as a bluff or a warning that you've hit the bottom line amount that they can afford.

Notice their attitude when they give you an ultimatum. If they seem cocky, reassured, or nervous, you're probably being tested. They more than likely want to see if they can get more out of you or give you less than you're asking for. If they're coming across as fervent and genuine, they may have given all that they can. Your intuition will play a big part in your next move.

If you're presented with an ultimatum, you can:

♦ **Accept the ultimatum and give in if it's a good deal for you.**

♦ **Bluff and let them walk away.**

♦ **Remind them of the cost of walking away from the deal, as well as the benefits of working with you.**

Using the ultimatum strategy can be a very effective way to settle negotiations that have come to a deadlock or impasse. Sometimes it takes one of the parties involved to put the pressure on the other to make a final decision.

3. Nibbling

Nibbling **is waiting until late in a negotiation to ask for at least one more concession from the other side.**

Example: Whenever I buy a car, I wait until just before I sign the agreement to ask for some extra goodies. I've received discounts on the price, car mats, rust proofing, extended warranties, cleaning supplies, poly coating, and a host of other services. You're probably wondering why this works so well. Consider the following.

For more than two hours I was negotiating the price of a new Ford Mustang. The salesman had me to the point of signing on the dotted line. I grabbed my pen and just before I signed I put it down and said, "I'm sure you wouldn't mind throwing in a new set of mats. After all, you wouldn't want to see me wreck my carpeting." He agreed. Next I said, "You wouldn't mind having the guys in back shoot a little undercoating on the car to prevent rust would you?" By the time I left, I had him throw in six items that weren't part of the original deal. And one of the items was an extended warranty worth $500! Now you know how to do the same!

Why does nibbling work? Late in a negotiation, most rookie negotiators start getting tired and become anxious to get the deal over with. Many times they're worried that you'll drop the deal and never come back. They figure they'll secure the deal by giving you some extra perks that are fairly inexpensive to them.

Nibbling is becoming a very popular negotiation strategy. Therefore, I want to go extensively into counterattack strategies.

How to counteract *nibbling*

To prevent someone from nibbling, you must do the following:

♦ **Tell them you don't have the authority to give any more.** Remind them of the extra time and cost to them to finish the deal. Use the final decision-maker strategy!

♦ **Threaten to renegotiate the entire deal.** Tell them that if they want more concessions, you'll have to reexamine the entire deal because it's costing you too much already. Make sure to remind them of the long process and inflated costs involved in renegotiating.

♦ **Start *nibbling* them right back.** Say, "Now that I think about it, I'd like some extras myself." This alone will throw them out of sync and make them rethink about trying to nibble you for more.

Many times the other party will start nibbling after the deal is completed. In my opinion, this is borderline unethical. Regardless of what I think, it happens all the time! But there are ways to get around it!

The following are several reasons why people start nibbling after the deal is completed:

♦ **Buyer's remorse.** A fair amount of buyers start questioning their purchase decision for a variety of reasons. In many of these instances, it comes down to two things: (1) they think they could've bought it cheaper, and (2) they never really wanted it in the first place.

♦ **They realized the deal wasn't as good as they thought.** A good amount of buyers start questioning their deal-making skills and feel they could've done better.

♦ **Pressure from a senior employee.** Many times, executives, bosses, and managers aren't satisfied with a specific deal and make their employees renegotiate based on the final decision-maker strategy.

♦ **Just to test you.** Occasionally someone will ask for a concession just to see if you'll say yes.

♦ **To practice their negotiation skills.** Practicing negotiators always push the envelope and try to attain more and more from every deal. Expect them to nibble you to the bone!

♦ **They become disgruntled with the person they made the deal with.** Every so often a deal becomes personal. It becomes "me" versus "you." This is probably the most problematic way to negotiate. If someone becomes disgruntled, they may disagree with you and waste a lot of your time. In many instances, you have to have a third party step in and finish the deal for you.

To prevent nibbling, you need to:

♦ **Let the other side think they've negotiated a great deal for themselves.**

♦ **Negotiate all of the terms up front and put everything in writing.**

♦ **Go over the terms over and over again.**

♦ **Have the agreement drawn up and signed as quickly as possible.**

Make a list of extra items you'd like to add to the deal. Call this your *Nibble List*. Just before you sign the agreement, examine this list carefully and start asking for these items. A warning: Do not let a good deal get away by asking for too many concessions. **Don't lose sight of the goal of the negotiation!**

4. Put-Aside for Now Strategy

This is when you take a large issue that has come to a deadlock and put it aside while you build momentum agreeing on smaller issues.

Example: A business partner and I were bidding on a job with a potential client. The potential client was in need of many of the Internet services our company provided. They needed Website development, Web hosting services, e-mail accounts, and a service agreement for monthly maintenance. We couldn't come to an agreement on the price of the Web development, so we decided to put it aside and turned our attention to the three other issues. I said, "Let's come back to Web development shortly. Let's discuss hosting, e-mail, and your service agreement." In a relatively short amount of time, we came to three agreements on the other issues and built huge momentum. When we revisited the Web development price issue, we rode the current momentum, and we were able to break the deadlock and come to four win/win agreements.

How to counteract the *put aside for now* strategy

Many negotiators will try to divert your attention from the major issue. Don't let this happen to you. Whoever has the momentum moving in their favor usually wins the negotiation. Why? Because psychologically they're building up wins every time they get a concession.

If someone starts to use the put-aside for now strategy, you need to:

- ♦ **Bring the focus back to the main issue.** Explain to them that you don't want to deal with other issues until you solve the major issue at hand.

- ♦ **Tell them you're not in a position to cover the other issues.** Refer to a final decision-maker.

- ♦ **If they insist on negotiating small issues, tell them you'd like to take some time and think them over.**

5. Surprised Look

Here's how it works. Just seconds after the other side gives you an opening offer or counteroffer, immediately use body language to show that you're shocked, surprised, insulted, or even very upset.

Sometimes this strategy is known as "flinching." The reason that I don't use that outdated term is because as an effective negotiator, you don't want to limit yourself to a simple flinch.

After the other side gives you an offer, you automatically do one or a combination of the following:

♦ **Raise your eyebrows and look shocked.**

♦ **Sit silent and open your mouth wide in disbelief.**

♦ **Shift your head back and shake your head "no."**

♦ **Say, "Huh, are you serious?" or "Come on; you've got to be kidding."**

♦ **Act short of breath.**

♦ **Act upset or sad.**

For this strategy to work you need to act totally displeased with their offer. *The more offended or shocked you look, the better.* Right away, you'll throw them for a loop. When you look surprised or unhappy, the other side knows they have some work ahead of them and may have to make extra concessions.

Example: I walked into a showroom at a local car dealer. As usual, I was greeted by a typical, fast-talking, smooth salesman. We exchanged the usual pleasantries and I proceeded to tell him that I was interested in purchasing a mid-sized car. He showed me several models and we eventually found a car I liked. I knew I was interested, but I didn't tell him that. We started talking price. And when he gave me his opening price I could've won an Oscar! I stopped dead in my tracks, opened my eyes wide, and then I said with a stern look on my face, "Tom you've got to be kidding me." His immediate reaction was to say, "Don't worry Peter, I'm sure we can work with the price. Let me check with my boss." (Sound like the final decision-maker strategy?) He walked away for about 10 minutes and then he returned. We negotiated back and forth for more than 90 minutes. How did I do?

By the end of the negotiation I bought the car for $2,000 dollars less than the asking price. How did I make out so well? By using the surprised look strategy, I confused him into thinking that either I couldn't afford the car, felt it wasn't worth it, or wasn't really all that interested in it. He desperately needed to make the sale, and he did. As a result, we both got what we wanted!

How to counteract the *surprised look* strategy

The surprised look is a widely used negotiation tactic. Most people use it without even realizing it. Some are overly dramatic. Unfortunately, you can *expect the other side to use this strategy on you in at least 50 percent of your face-to-face negotiations.*

When someone gives you a surprised look, you must:

♦ **Act surprised that they look surprised.** This psychologically will make them think they may have offended you.

♦ **Say, "What could you possibly not be happy with?"** Address their concerns.

♦ **Ask, "Did I say something to offend you?"**

♦ **Reaffirm the benefits of your product or service.**

♦ **Tell them how your product or service is superior to your competitors.**

♦ **Explain that they've negotiated a great deal for themselves.**

♦ **Show them proof that you're giving them better than competitive terms.**

The main thing is that the other side's challenges are counterattacked quickly and effectively. Don't get nervous because they're confronting you. They usually just need more information, so they can make an educated decision. Sometimes they'll just be testing you!

Never feel intimidated by car salesmen. Believe me when I say that as the customer, you hold all of the cards. More than likely, the salesperson you're dealing with lives on commission and realizes that if he doesn't give you the lowest price, dealer B down the street will. Automobile dealerships are some of the most dog-eat-dog businesses in the country. Use this to your advantage!

6. Good Guy/Bad Guy

The strategy is to have two people work together as a team. One seems friendly and the other seems unreasonable. This is a favorite strategy among automobile dealers and TV police shows. How does it work?

Example: There are two people (Negotiators A and B) negotiating over the purchase of a washer and dryer set at a local appliance store. Negotiator A is the saleswoman and Negotiator B is the customer. The customer wants a discount. What happens is that Negotiator A will agree with Negotiator B that the price is a little steep. Negotiator A will say, "I have to go in the back and speak to my manager and see what I can do to get you a better price." Negotiator A is acting like a good guy (or girl), supposedly trying to help you secure a better price. What she's really doing is getting ready to introduce you to Negotiator C, the manager (the bad guy).

Next, Negotiator C will walk out and give you a plethora of reasons why they can't lower the price. Chances are better than you think that Negotiator C will say, "I'll tell you what. If you buy this washer and dryer right now, I'll give you $150 off and that's our final offer." Most customers will say they have to think about it for a minute. At this point, Negotiator C walks away and turns the sale back over to Negotiator A. Negotiator A, acting as the good guy says, "Wow! I can't believe she gave you such a great deal. This is unheard of. I'd take it while she's in a good mood. She's normally hard to deal with."

At this point, you feel that you obtained a great deal, but you were really a victim of the good guy/bad guy strategy.

Sometimes Negotiator C (the manager) will:

 - **Refuse to lower the price or give any concessions.**
 - **Give you a small tradeoff or discount.**
 - **Be nasty and try to intimidate you.**
 - **Refer you back to Negotiator A.**

Example: The good guy/bad guy strategy can also work in favor of the customer. Let me explain.

I went with a young lady to purchase a new automobile. We picked out a car the night before and met with a salesman the next day. He was trying to give her the runaround about the dealer's cost for the car. My role as the bad guy was to start acting impatient. Every time the salesman mentioned the price, I acted surprised and kept telling him the price was far too high and that we'd be forced to purchase the car elsewhere. Finally, I told the salesman how much we were willing to pay and not a penny more (the ultimatum strategy). At that point, the young lady purposely asked me to leave the room, and I left in a huff.

After I left the office, the salesman asked if he could deal with her directly. She agreed and he ended up giving her the car at the price we offered to pay. We used the good guy/bad guy strategy to perfection and saved $5,000 as a result.

How to counteract the *good guy/bad guy* strategy

Good guy/bad guy is widely used due to its exposure on television cop shows. Therefore, you must understand how to counterattack it.

If somebody uses the good guy/bad guy strategy on you, you can:

- ♦ **Create your own bad guy.** Explain that you'd like to comply with the agreement but Mr. or Ms. X has to approve it first. You then tell them that it's highly unlikely they'll go along with a new deal.

- ♦ **Never be intimidated by attorneys.** Attorneys are usually brought into negotiations to act as a bad guy. Explain to them that they can drop the bad guy facade. The goal is to consummate the deal.

- ♦ **Let the bad guy put their foot in their mouth.** Because most bad guys are not directly involved with the issue at hand, they'll usually say things you can exploit. Listen for those things very closely.

- ♦ **Go straight to the final decision-maker strategy.** Tell the other side's superior what the other two are trying to do to you and explain that you're trying to finish the deal and don't have time for games or any other shenanigans.

- ♦ **Call their bluff.** Sometimes you can say to them, "Look, I know the whole good guy/bad guy routine. Knock it off or I'll take my business elsewhere." Or you can say, "Look, I know the whole good guy/bad guy strategy, let's drop the whole thing and finish the deal without playing games." Many times they'll feel a little intimidated or embarrassed that they were caught and retreat from using this strategy.

If you plan on using the good guy/bad guy strategy, try to do everything in your power to keep the other party from asking to see the bad guy face-to-face. Once you bring the bad guy into the picture, you lose some of your negotiating strength.

7. Walk Away Smiling

This is the negotiator's best weapon. Here's how it works. **If the negotiation falls short of what you're willing to pay, get up and start to leave.** Say, "Thanks for everything, but I'm not interested in the terms of this agreement. This deal is not for me or my organization." With a fervent, sincere smile on your face, get up, shake their hands, and wish them the best.

Remember: *Never ever, ever, fall in love with a product or service.* You must always be willing to walk away from a negotiation. By staying emotionally detached from a deal, you can make smarter, more rational decisions.

There's a reason this strategy is called *walk away smiling*. It's because you not only want to walk away, you want to do it in a way that doesn't close you off to future deals with the "other side." I recommend that you always smile as you leave. And I don't mean in a cocky sort of way. Walk away smiling means that you're walking away with a positive attitude and not becoming bitter. If you walk away bitter or display a negative attitude, the other side may not want to counter or ever revisit the deal.

I've heard it said that *the individual who holds the most power in any relationship is the individual who cares the least.* The same rule holds true for the two parties involved in a negotiation.

Example: An opportunity came up to work solely for an up and coming organization that knew of my reputation as a negotiator and direct marketer. The president of the company and I decided to meet over lunch to discuss the opportunity. Quite honestly, I was only lukewarm to the idea, but figured, what the heck. It only took about 10 minutes for me to realize the opportunity wasn't anything I desired. The president then made me an offer that included a whopping salary and several major perks. I thanked him and told him I had no interest in the position. I then got up to leave. Naturally, he figured the reason I was leaving was because I wanted more money. He literally stopped me in my tracks and made a higher offer. Again, I refused. He did this twice and I kept telling him I wasn't interested. Finally, he got the message. What's the relevance?

This example proves the effectiveness of using the walk away smiling strategy. If I fell in love with the position, I wouldn't have had the willpower to walk away smiling from the first offer. By walking away with a positive attitude, I received several counteroffers with higher salaries. Had I not used the walk away smiling strategy, I would've settled for the first offer and lost a great deal of money!

How to counterattack the *walk away smiling* strategy

Having someone walk away from a negotiation is pretty rare. For the most part, only highly skilled negotiators use the walk away smiling strategy effectively.

If someone walks away smiling, you can:

+ **Let them go and wait for a better deal.** Say, "I'm sorry you feel that way, but we have given you our final offer, I'm sorry it didn't work out."

+ **Call them back and remind them of what it'll cost them in time and money.** Then try to renegotiate. Ask, "I want you to keep in mind that we've already gone to great expense to finish this deal, why don't we cut costs on future meetings and sign this agreement right now?"

+ **Ask them what it'll take for them to be happy with this deal (make them commit to a starting amount).** Ask them, "What do you feel is fair?" or "What is it you're looking for?"

+ **Give them an ultimatum to respond to your offer.** Exclaim, "I understand your reason for walking away; however, we'll give you only seven more days to make your decision or we'll be forced to pursue other vendors."

Many times you'll come across deals that aren't right for you no matter how good the negotiation seems to go. Some will be for financial reasons and others may be for personal reasons. That's okay! Let those types of offers go. Consider these wins and move on to the next deal.

8. Never Take the First Offer or Counteroffer

This is refusing to accept the other side's first offer or counteroffer.

First, you have to realize that *most companies build a huge profit into products and services.* They figure that there will still be room to bargain if a savvy buyer approaches them. Let's use contractors as an example.

Anytime you get a bid on construction work, you can be assured that the contractor purposely built in a heavy profit margin. When you refuse their first bid, 99 percent of the time they quickly come back with another. Never accept this bid either. Say, "That isn't within our budget" or "At that price, we're forced to request further bids from other companies." Test them and see if they come at you with another counteroffer. Most of the time, you'll get at least one counteroffer. They won't admit it, but believe me when I say that they want your business every bit as much as you need them to do the work!

Example: On one occasion, I was negotiating with a major software manufacturer for a product upgrade. They made an offer to do the upgrade in an unacceptable way and I turned it down. They countered by offering to do a new version, and again I turned them down and told them what needed to be done. The third offer was the magic one. They agreed to do exactly what I needed.

Always turn down unacceptable counteroffers!

How to counteract the *never take the first offer or counteroffer* strategy

Always remember:

♦ **The first person that makes an offer takes the risk of being rejected and helps the other side establish their negotiation strategy.** You're going to hear me repeat this throughout this book: *Never make the first offer.* If you follow my advice, you never have to worry about the other side refusing your first offer.

♦ **You must remind the customer that your offer is better than the competition.** Say, "You can bid this work out and I think you'll find that we're priced below our competitors."

 People are going to constantly test your limits (especially during the first negotiation). Stick to your guns! Make the other side give the first offer! In the long run, this is invariably the best strategy.

9. Red Herring

The *red herring* is introducing what seems to be an important issue, with the intent of withdrawing it for another concession. If you're successful, you'll distract the other side from the major issue and sway them into giving you what you originally wanted. This is a famous strategy and is pretty common in the negotiating arena.

Example: Red herring is a strategy that I use successfully over and over again! I used this strategy when I·purchased a sports car. One night after the dealer closed, I cased the lot and found the exact car and model I was looking for. While I was there, I noticed something peculiar—every model was black or red. My true intent was to purchase a black or dark blue model, but I remained somewhat flexible. I picked out the car I wanted to buy and went back to the dealer early the next morning. The car was a little pricey, so I decided to go for a major discount. I decided to use the red herring strategy.

I told the salesman that I was only interested in purchasing the car in dark blue (the color was the red herring). The salesman said he could order me a new, dark blue model and have it delivered to the dealership within two weeks. I told him I would search for the car elsewhere. He said, "That won't be necessary, if you're willing to purchase a black or red one. I'll give you a super deal." Of course, I acted faintly interested. But I started listening.

We negotiated for a few hours and I eventually drove the car home at an acceptable price. *I saved $5,000 by doing a few hours of work.* Quite a savings! By introducing a red herring (the color), I distracted the salesman from the real issue (the price). I withdrew the red herring in return for a reduction in the price. You can successfully do it too!

How to counteract the *red herring* strategy

As a skilled negotiator, you'll undoubtedly be involved in various types of negotiations. Therefore, you'll have red herrings thrown at you at various times. The following are strategies to counteract red herrings and get to the real issues.

If someone introduces a red herring, you can:

♦ **Tell the other side you have to clear it with a final decision-maker.** Also make sure that you tell them that the final decision-maker would never approve the concession.

♦ **Stick to the main issues at hand.** Say, "First, I'd like to settle the most important issues, and we'll deal with the smaller points later."

♦ **Play hardball and refuse to negotiate the red herring.** Remind them of the value and benefits of your product or service. (This strategy can be feast or famine.) Sometimes it works like a charm and sometimes it blows up in your face. Use your better discretion.

10. Act Stupid/Negotiate Brilliant

This strategy is implemented when you walk into a negotiation and act inferior to the other side. The rule here is to never let them know you're a skilled negotiator. You'll be surprised at the amount of confidential information they'll give you. Let me give you a fun example to prove my point.

Did you ever watch the TV detective series *Columbo*? If you haven't, I urge you to keep your eye out for it. The Columbo character is a brilliant master negotiator. You're probably wondering what's special about him. He's a private detective that comes off as clumsy, unsure, and a bit dim in the head. As he questions suspects, he always asks them in a way that'll lead the suspect to believe that he's on the wrong track. The suspect always slips up and gives him a little too much of an explanation and bingo— "Columbo has 'em!"

Example: Recently, I talked with the president of a company that specializes in audiocassette learning programs. His company is a major competitor of our organization. I needed some important information and decided to try to squeeze it out of him. So I decided to use the act stupid/negotiate brilliant strategy. It worked great!

At the time this all went down, we were thinking of purchasing a large quantity of this gentleman's audiocassettes. Of course, I didn't tell him that, but it was my latent plan. Instead, I told him we were planning to launch a similar type of program and I asked him how his results were. To discourage me, he not only gave me his results, he explained his company's whole strategy for selling them. I told him that he talked me out of producing the program. I never placed the order with his company, and he recently told me the product was an absolute bomb. As a result, we saved thousands of dollars when we purchased the audiocassettes.

How to counteract the *act stupid/negotiate brilliant* strategy

Skilled negotiators will use this strategy to try to frustrate you. Ultimately, they'll try to use it to get you to reveal important information without you even knowing it.

If someone uses the act stupid/negotiate brilliant strategy:

♦ **Act stupid in response and try to frustrate them.**

♦ **Threaten to renegotiate the deal.**

♦ **Start to reexplain every clause, paragraph, amendment, and addendum of the deal just to irritate them.**

The key is for you to act stupid/negotiate brilliant and frustrate them back into reality.

The most valuable commodity is information. Having the right information in a negotiation is invariably the difference between success and failure. Listen to everything people say. With the right approach, people will tell you everything you need to know!

Which leads us to another of my favorite negotiation skills!

11. Listen, Listen, Listen

When negotiating, do very little talking and a whole lot of listening. Some pundits have said we have two ears and one mouth for a reason. We're supposed to talk half as much as we listen. When we listen, we learn. And when we learn, we earn!

Whenever you're talking to the other side, you must listen carefully for all of the most pertinent information they give about their product or service. As a rule, never interrupt them when they're giving you information. I can't tell you how many times someone has slipped and said something they shouldn't have. *If you're talking, you can't listen effectively.* How have I made this work for me?

> **Example:** I was recently talking with an author of a well-known home-study course on getting rich. Our company was going to purchase the program directly from him to resell to our customers. As we talked, we grew friendlier and friendlier. Before the negotiation started, I purposely opened up a discussion about the increase in my company's product costs. As we were both complaining, he mistakenly said how his product cost went from $8.95 to $10.50. He gave me his product cost to the penny (never do this). I acted as if I never heard him. And I believe to this day that he thinks I never heard him. When it came time to negotiate, I knew that anything I offered him over $10.50 per piece would give him a profit. I offered $11 per piece and he bit—hook, line, and sinker. This negotiation went very smoothly because I let him keep talking and talking. All I did was listen very carefully!

How to counteract the *listen, listen, listen* strategy

Every good negotiator listens extremely attentively. When you're negotiating a deal, say as little as possible.

If you find yourself in a negotiation with a good, strategic listener, make sure to:

♦ **Say as little as possible.**

♦ **Talk slowly—never get ahead of your self.**

♦ **Think about the possible ramifications of everything you say.**

♦ **Never be verbally judgmental about the other side.**

♦ **Say little about your prices or costs.**

♦ **Talk sparingly about competitors.**

♦ **Make every word count—disclose as little as possible (only what you have to).**

When you're listening attentively, you put yourself in a position to take excellent mental notes of everything being said. Early in my career, I took a memory course that helped me learn how to do this effectively. There are many good memory courses available. I recommend Kevin Trudeau's *Mega Memory* or any books by Harry Lorayne. **A good memory is invaluable to a skilled negotiator.**

12. Third Party

During deadlocks, you or the other side solicits a neutral *third party* to settle the dispute. The key is to provide a third party mediator you feel will side with you and your organization.

Example: Whenever I have a challenge with a good negotiator who doesn't see things from my point of view, I ask for a third party to come in and objectively settle the dispute. Usually it's my own attorney.

On one occasion, I was negotiating with one of my business partners about expanding into a new business venture. He was understandably reluctant, yet he was open to hearing more. Instead of giving him more of my opinion, I arranged a conference call with a third party who saw things from a more objective perspective. After talking with this third party, my partner not only agreed to go into this new venture, he became so excited that he's become very proactive in seeing to it that everything goes smoothly.

Always use a third party who has nothing to gain and thinks as you do.

How to counteract the *third party* strategy

Third parties are every effective at helping settle disputes and aiding in the decision-making process. Sometimes the other side will provide their own third-party mediator. As always, it's important that you know how to work with them.

To counter third-party experts you can:

♦ **Ask for their credentials.** Ask, "What makes you an expert in this specific area?" or "What interest do you have in this deal?"

♦ **Refuse to use them or any other sort of mediator.** Say, "I'm not comfortable knowing a third party has access to secret information; therefore, I'd like to settle the agreement between us."

♦ **Challenge the third party's responses and ask for in-depth analysis as to why they made their decision.** Ask the third party questions such as, "Why do you feel that way?" or "Has this been your experience in the past?"

♦ **Look for agendas.** Question what they have to gain.

13. Give and Take

Every time you give something to the other side, ask for something in return.

If the other side asks you to buy a high volume of merchandise, automatically ask for a much lower price. With few exceptions, negotiations will have various tradeoffs for both sides. Sometimes you can trade off on price, quantity, or even billing terms. (Refer to Chapter 11.)

Example: Book publishers are notorious for giving poor discounts to small distributors. Recently, I represented a small distributor involved in a large book deal. They wanted to buy a couple thousand copies of a certain book at a large discount. (A couple thousand copies is a small quantity by a major book publisher's standards.)

We negotiated until we finally came to a good agreement. I didn't feel the deal was great—just good. I decided to ask for a trade-off. I decided to ask for a trade on the discount and payment terms. Originally, the publisher offered a per-order discount (this means that our discount is only applicable to the number of books purchased in a single order) on 30-day billing terms, with no returns on unsold merchandise. I wanted more. I asked for a cumulative discount (that means that all of our orders are added together and accumulated over the year, which is considered the total volume purchased), 60-day billing terms, and full return privileges on unsold merchandise.

All of my demands were met and my client sold all of the books before the invoice was even due. *We didn't have to put out one red cent.* Those terms were not only very profitable, but we financed the deal without using any of our own money.

How to counteract the *give and take* strategy

If the other side asks for new concessions, you can:

♦ **Immediately ask for more concessions.** By asking for more concessions, you'll alert the other side that before you give you want something in return. In most cases, they'll want to cut their losses immediately.

♦ **Say, "Sure, we can give you $39.95 for each blender, in return we'd like 60-day billing and full return privileges."** Always *ask for something in return right away*!

♦ **Act as if the concession will cost too much.** Use the surprised look strategy to show that you're not going to passively agree to any concessions. Ask, "How can you expect us to do that? We're already cutting too far into our profits to make it worthwhile."

♦ **Give in to their concessions and change the terms.** It's okay to give a concession if the deal is right for you. However, you don't want to become a welcome mat for future concessions. In exchange for any concession, ask for some change in the terms that reflect in your favor.

♦ **Turn the trade-off into a larger concession for yourself later in the negotiation process.** By giving a small concession, you may be able to use it as a gesture of goodwill to get something more valuable later on.

14. The Old Squeeze Play

This is when you put pressure on the other side to see things your way. If someone gives you an offer or counteroffer that's unacceptable, tell them that if they cannot do better, you'll go elsewhere. You may also want to tell them that their offer isn't even doable. Go for more! *Always squeeze everything you can out of every deal.*

Example: I like the toothpaste analogy. For some reason, people seem to have a habit of trying to drain every drop out of a tube of toothpaste. Go into someone's bathroom and chances are you'll find a flattened, twisted, or otherwise deformed, 99.9 percent empty tube of toothpaste. Most people seem compelled to get every last cents' worth out of a tube of toothpaste, yet they won't squeeze salespeople or business executives for every last concession. It's funny, toothpaste is only worth a couple of dollars and deal concessions can be worth hundreds or thousands of dollars over time, and few people ask for them. This has always been an enigma to me!

How to counteract the *old squeeze play* strategy

If you ever experience a negotiator using the old squeeze play strategy, ask them how much better you'll have to do to make the deal work. By doing this you'll make them feel a little uneasy, because they now have the spotlight on them.

I remember meeting with an appliance salesman who gave me a price and terms that I couldn't afford at the time. Being honest, I told the salesman I really wanted to buy the stove, but he'd have to do better on the price (I was convinced that this salesman was desperate for a sale). I kept telling him, over and over, that he'd have to do better. I was noticing a pattern: the price kept coming down. This went on for six hours. We finally agreed on a price, hundreds less than the original. I also got it delivered the same day.

Keep telling the other side, "You have to do better." Do it over and over. This strategy works great when combined with the walk away smiling strategy.

This is a great place to remind you that many of these negotiation strategies are used in concert with each other. Don't be afraid to combine strategies! In almost every negotiation, I *use a combination of four or more strategies.*

15. Puppy Dog

This technique is used by millions of salespeople and other negotiators worldwide. **What you do is get the purchaser to try the product (or take it home), so that they get emotionally involved with it.** I truly believe that if you can get a prospect to try your product or service, then 90 percent of your job as a negotiator is complete.

Car dealers are now letting qualified buyers take cars home overnight for test-drives. Why? Because statistics show that they'll fall in love with the car and buy it. There is no better way to sell someone than on emotion!

Record and book clubs are other great examples. These clubs automatically send their subscribers a monthly selection to try out. Invariably, a certain percentage will automatically love the selection or just be too lazy to send it back. This is the easiest close there is!

Think of how much easier your job is as a negotiator if the other side has already sold themselves on your product or service.

Have you ever noticed all of the different fast food and quick service restaurants that allow you to sample food? Take Krispy Kreme doughnuts, for example. The first thing that happens when you enter a store is one of their employees hands you one those irresistible Original Glazed Doughnuts. One bite and people are automatically emotionally hooked. The product then sells itself. Many companies are now doing the same thing.

Example: One of the companies I used to consult with sent all of its motivational audiocassette programs to qualified buyers FREE for 30 days. They do this because they realize the easiest way to close the sale is to simply let the customer reap the product's benefits, FREE for 30 days. The law of numbers also says that a certain percentage of people will purchase the program and never return it. I have spent a great deal of time studying their strategy and have found this success formula to repeat itself over and over. It's all a numbers game!

How to counteract the *puppy dog* strategy

If the other side tries to use the puppy dog strategy, you can:

♦ **Automatically withdraw emotional feelings for the product or service.** As I've said throughout this book, never, ever fall in love with a product or service. Strong emotions can temporarily cloud your judgment. The puppy dog is a strategy that preys on your emotional attachment to the product or service. *Refuse to get emotional when trying out new products and services.* Keep in mind that you can probably purchase the product or service cheaper from somewhere else!

- **Refuse to take a car home for an overnight or weekend test drive.** If you aren't sure you want the car at first, chances are it isn't the right car for you.

- **Be firm with the "other side."** If they see you caving in, they'll prey on your emotions until they reach your breaking point.

16. Show It in Writing

One way to convince the other side to see things from your perspective is to show them something in print. People tend to believe what they see in print from an objective third party!

If you're trying to negotiate with someone who's reluctant to commit to a deal with you, show them that your prices and/or benefits are either in line with, or better than, your competitors. Pull out competitor's catalogs or price sheets, and show your customer the difference. These make strong, lasting visuals. I believe that you should negotiate on non-price issues, but sometimes it comes back down to the almighty buck. No problem! *A competitor's written literature can be your best friend.*

You can even use third-party reviews of your product to show an even stronger point of view.

Example: One of my clients owned a major catalog house that sold software to the public. They decided to open up negotiations with a large software producer for one of their most popular software programs. Negotiations were going poorly and I was called into the deal-making process. I did some homework on this and similar products. I then asked the producer for what I thought was an acceptable discount rate. I was immediately denied. They told me the rate that I was asking for wasn't realistic for the industry. I told them their competitors were giving similar rates for similar software products. They said that if I would present them with proof, they would beat the competitor's rate. I said, "Absolutely." I faxed them a competitor's most recent ad. They immediately called me back and honored the discount.

The *show it in writing* strategy works very well. Use it often.

Always check the validity of printed materials. There is a great deal of false information circulating among salespeople.

How to counteract the *show it in writing* strategy

If someone presents you with written proof of any kind, you should:

♦ **Check the credentials of the person who's making the written claim.** Call the phone number of the individual and ask them for signed proof that the document is valid.

♦ **Show proof to the contrary.** The other side may show you a price for a new or used car using the blue book value. In response, pull out an ad for the same car at ABC Auto, showing the price at a discount. Say, "Will you beat this price?"

♦ **Make sure their proof isn't handwritten or unprofessionally typed.** These are dead giveaways that you're being conned.

♦ **Tell the other side you don't believe their information and try to negotiate around it.**

Whenever possible, present backup material. Many times the other side hasn't a clue as to what the item they're selling is really worth in the marketplace. For instance, many people try to sell their homes without using a qualified, licensed, real estate broker. They attempt to sell their property based on their emotions and personal attachment to the property. They have no concept of a realistic selling price and tend to overvalue their property. If you bring written materials showing comparable properties in the area, at a certain price, they're more apt to come back down to earth and sell the property to you at a reasonable price.

17. Ask for Everything, Including the Kitchen Sink

Whenever you start negotiating with someone, make it a rule to always ask for much more than you expect to receive. This is similar to the old squeeze play strategy.

The key here is not to overdo it! Many times negotiations are stalled because the other side thinks what you're asking for is out of their comfort level.

Asking for more than you expect to receive works for you in three ways:

♦ **You may get a simple "yes" and get everything you want.**

♦ **The other side automatically realizes they're going to have to start the negotiation off by offering you more than they had originally expected.**

♦ **The perception of the value of what you have to offer goes up dramatically.**

Example: I opened one negotiation by asking the president of a large company for the price of their product. His price was ridiculous! Nearly insulting! In return I not only asked for a dirt-cheap price for his product, but I wanted free packaging. (I never expected to get the free packaging.) By asking for more than I expected to receive, I ended up with a dirt-cheap price and a minimal charge for the packaging.

Had I asked for just a good price, I would've received a decent price and paid full price for the packaging.

Always ask for more than you expect to receive! **No exceptions to this rule!**

How to counteract someone *asking for everything, including the kitchen sink*

Any halfway decent negotiator is going to ask for everything they can get. Many start to get a little unrealistic. There are many ways to counterattack these individuals before they get out of hand.

To counteract someone who tries asking for too much, you can:

♦ **Respond with the final decision-maker strategy.** Tell them you're not authorized to give anything else away. Also mention that the *final decision-maker* would never approve of the requested concessions. Say, "I'd love to give it to you, however, my boss would flip and I'd probably end up getting fired."

♦ **As soon as they start asking you for too much, use the surprised look strategy.** Once they see the surprised look, they'll generally stop asking for more concessions. This is strictly a psychological way of telling the other side they've gone too far.

♦ **Stand tough and tell them what they've asked for is out of the question.** This will instantly change their attitude or kill the deal. As risky as this strategy may sound, it's only on rare occasion that anyone will just walk away from the deal. Say, "There's no way I can provide that to you."

♦ **Tell them you're willing to give them what they want if they give you what you want!** If they can ask for everything including the kitchen sink—so can you! Say, "Oh you want me to give you A? That's fine, but in return, I want B."

♦ **Ask them to justify all of the concessions.** Many times, people will ask for more than they expect to get. Ask, "How can you expect me to do that?"

♦ **To call their bluff regarding the value of what they're negotiating for versus what you're getting from the deal.**

♦ **Tell them what they're asking for is too expensive.** For most negotiators, money is a hard subject to counterattack.

18. Cry Poor

This is telling the other side you don't have the money to buy their product or service at their price. *Cry poor* is one of the best negotiating strategies because it's hard for the other side to prove you wrong.

Many years ago, I was counseling a client who was buying her first house. She needed all sorts of advice on how to purchase the house for a small down payment. I advised her to play hardball. I told her to tell the seller that she didn't have enough money for the down payment. This strategy was so successful, she not only obtained the house for a phenomenal price, but she also managed to get the sellers to finance the down payment themselves.

Cry poor is a hit or miss strategy because once you use it, you've closed the door! In a sense, it's similar to the ultimatum strategy, with one major difference. In cry poor, the only reason that you use for giving an ultimatum is that you just don't have the money.

How to counteract the *cry poor* strategy

If someone uses the cry poor strategy, you can:

♦ **Ask them how much they can afford.** This will elicit a commitment as to the amount they're willing to spend. You may find that they simply aren't qualified to buy your product or service. Therefore, you save yourself wasted time.

♦ **Try to get them to make installment payments.** Many times prospects cannot afford to spend large or even small sums of money all at once. And just like when they use credit cards, mortgages, and car payments, they can afford to buy it over several months or years. Ask them, "Can you afford to pay for the item over one or two years?"

♦ **Remind them of the benefits of your product or service.** This may cause them to break down and stretch themselves to come up with the money. Say, "Our product is guaranteed to make your back feel better within seven days. Our competitor's products can't. Isn't that alone worth the price of this item?"

♦ **Ask them if they've considered budgeting elsewhere.** Many times you have to remind the other side they may be able to cut unnecessary costs elsewhere to purchase what you're selling. It's always important to be subtle when asking someone to budget. If said wrong, this can come off as intrusive!

19. Never Show Your Hand

Think of a poker game. What would happen if one of the other players knew what cards you were holding in your hand? Right—you would lose every time! The same is true during negotiations. **Never tell anyone what strategy you plan to use. Also, never act as if you have an ace up your sleeve.**

Furthermore, *no matter how much you want to make the deal, always act as if it's not that important to you.* If you put too much emphasis and excitement on the deal, the other side will catch on and prey on your enthusiasm.

Example: One of my clients asked me to get a best-selling author to record their book on tape so they could resell it to the public. The author was pretty shrewd and decided to hold out for a great deal of money. We talked and I discussed his contract with him in detail. I was very sensitive to him and at the same time made him aware that we had a list of other popular authors who wanted to do deals with us. I was subtle yet firm in telling him that if he refused to agree to our generous terms within two days, we would withdraw our offer. This is a combination of the ultimatum and walk away smiling techniques. (Deep down I really wanted to work with him, but I wasn't about to let him know it.)

Judging from the tone of his voice, we ended our conversation on a downer. As I anticipated, he called me back the next afternoon and accepted the deal. As soon as he realized he wasn't the only fish in the sea and that he may blow the deal, he changed his attitude. This was a win/win situation for both of us. Had I told him how much I needed his services, he would have held out for a lot more money.

How to counteract the *never show your hand* strategy

If somebody acts as if doing business with you is not very important, you have several options at your disposal to bring truth to the surface.

Try the following:

♦ **Bluff and walk away smiling as if the deal is meaningless to you.** Walking away is pretty risky. However, if the other party is committed to working with you, chances are that they won't let you go for too long, if at all! They may pull you back right away or call you a day later. This strategy takes patience.

♦ **Ask valuable questions consistently and strategically.** Keep asking questions such as, "What did you have in mind?" or "Can you tell me more about that?" or "Why do you feel reluctant to do this deal?" or even "Did I offend you?" The more questions you ask, the better the pieces fall in place. Therefore, you can figure out their negotiation strategy.

♦ **Play on their emotions.** Keep in mind that even the most strategic negotiators are only human. Act distraught or offended in a sympathetic tone. Never get confrontational or angry. The challenge is to get the other side to show signs that they really want to work with you.

20. Draw up the Agreement

Absolutely, positively, no ifs, ands, or buts about it—spend the money to have the contract drawn up by your team. Always have your contract administrator and lawyer draw up the contract on your behalf.

Make sure you go over every clause, paragraph, addendum, and each and every sentence in the agreement. Explain to your lawyer and administrator all of the terms of the contract, including the key players and organizations.

You're probably wondering why I'm so adamant about this. Consider the following:

Having the other side draw up the agreement puts you at two major disadvantages:

♦ **First, the other side (if they're smart), will start to reexamine the contract and possibly second-guess some of the major deal components they agreed to.** This may cause the renegotiation of what you thought was a very beneficial contract.

♦ **Second, you never know what surprises will be added or omitted from the agreement when you get it back.**

On the flip side, drawing up the agreement yourself gives you two major advantages:

♦ **First, by reexamining the terms before you draw up the agreement, you now have the advantage of rethinking any parts of the agreement.** If you decide to make changes, you would be wise to bring them to the other side's attention or immediately call them by phone and verbally renegotiate the parts of the agreement you're not comfortable with. This is not the place to be sly or clandestine!

♦ **You have the opportunity to make changes in the agreement or contract.**

Example: I had the pleasure of negotiating with one of the largest infomercial companies in the world. I was attempting to purchase a high volume of health and fitness programs at both a reasonable cost and reasonable terms. Our negotiation dragged on and on for a week. At the end, we both felt we reached an agreeable deal. Here's the only challenge we faced: They wanted to draw up the agreement. We reluctantly agreed and asked them to draw it up within three business days.

(This is a good place to warn you that when you give the other side the power to draw up an agreement, you also give up control of the time it will take to receive a signed agreement. This could delay the deal endlessly.)

As luck would have it, the agreement took three weeks to arrive. Upon reading their agreement, I found that they made several changes without my consent. They changed clauses concerning shipping, inventory, indemnity, and duration. When I brought this to their attention, they said that after thinking about these terms, they found them to be unacceptable. Instead of calling us and giving us the chance to renegotiate, they went ahead and changed the agreement. This negotiation went on for two more weeks until I gave them an ultimatum. I told them they had to stick to the original agreement or we were canceling the order and buying from one of their competitors.

They stuck to the original offer. But bad luck showed its face again. They sent their product to us a month late, and as a result, many of our customers canceled their orders. Needless to say (even though I'm going to say it), we fulfilled all remaining backorders and then decided to discontinue offering it. We have never dealt with that company again!

How to counteract anyone who wants to *draw up the agreement*

For some reason, I tend to find that most people I negotiate with aren't interested in writing up the agreement. However, there are a few that insist on handling the contract.

If the other side insists on writing the agreement, you can:

♦ **Play the hero by offering to take care of the contract and all of the associated legal expenses**. Keep reminding them of the huge legal expense in drawing up the agreement themselves.

- **Present them with an agreement that's already filled out.** Many times, this will encourage them just to sign it or have their lawyer briefly look at it. *If you have a standard template, you can expedite the process.*

- **Tell them that you're afraid that if they write the contract, your legal department will start nitpicking, waste valuable time, or possibly kill the entire deal.** Remind them how some lawyers tend to slow deals down and create legal headaches (no offense to any lawyers reading this!).

- **Play hardball and insist that if your organization does not write the agreement, you'll walk away from the deal.** This is utilizing the ultimatum strategy. Most of the time, the other side will back off and agree to let you handle all of the legal details. However, you may face someone who refuses to give in. Say, "It's nothing personal; it's just our company policy."

- **Give in if the deal is a good one.** At the same time, make sure that when you get the contract, you and your lawyer read through everything and check to make sure there are no extra clauses, addendums, or paragraphs.

If the other side insists on writing the agreement and it's a great deal for you, make sure you seek proper legal counsel before committing to it. Try to avoid signing documents marked "subject to attorney's approval." Save time and get the attorney's approval first!

21. Read Everything

Always read every word of every agreement no matter how large or small. Furthermore, make sure the person signing the agreement is authorized to do so. Also, have legal counsel with you or make notes for them read through on your behalf. (Always make sure they explain every part of the agreement to you). *You must understand what you're signing your name to.*

I can't even begin to tell you how many people are ripped off because they didn't understand the agreement they signed. This goes for all contracts, warranties, and guarantees.

Example: I had the opportunity to save the day for a client. A contract had arrived that was supposed to secure a major deal. The first person who read the agreement gave it a quick glance and assumed all was well and handed it off to their contract administrator, who looked it over and found a vague clause. She called me in to go over all the details. Upon investigation, I noticed that a clause was added. This clause granted a non-exclusive agreement to a party who promised us an exclusive deal. In other words, under this new clause, if we did not attain a certain amount in gross sales, we would lose our exclusivity to the product. This would cost us thousands of dollars. By reading every word, we were able to avoid what would have turned out to be a legal nightmare.

Always read every word of the contract! Case closed!

Never counteract this strategy!

Always encourage the other side to read through the agreement. If you're ethical and honest, you should have no problem with the other side checking your work. If you're trying to hide something from someone, you'll more than likely get caught. This can cost you the deal and your relationship with the "other side." Sometimes people end up in jail or pay major fines! Don't let this happen to you or your organization.

Always remember that a contract signed by authorized parties will be legally binding in a court of law. As the saying goes, "if you snooze, you lose." And sometimes the losses are really valuable! Check everything!

22. Reluctant Seller

Never seem anxious to sell your product or service. By acting reluctant to sell your product or service, the other side will feel obligated to increase their offer to get you to consider making the sale.

For instance, if you're selling a collectible to someone, you have to tell the buyer about the sentimental value you place on the item and how hard it will be to let it go. To go one step further, tell them how you're reconsidering even selling the item. This will make a serious buyer start to sweat!

Example: I am an avid collector of rare records. One item in my collection is an uncommon album that I happened to buy from a collector many years ago. I purchased it at a bargain price. I mentioned this record to a friend. He asked me how much I wanted for it. I gave him a high dollar figure, figuring he'd automatically turn it down. To my surprise, he said that if I wanted to sell it, he'd have the money that afternoon. I then told him I really didn't want to sell it. He doubled his offer to try to convince me to make the sale. The offer was so good that I finally gave in and said yes.

If I didn't seem reluctant to sell, I would have received much less for the album. Using the reluctant seller strategy, I obtained double the original offer.

How to counterattack a *reluctant seller*

I wish I had a dollar for every time a seller lost his will to sell me a product at the last minute. If a seller thinks you're easy bait, they'll hold out for more and more money.

If someone assumes the role of reluctant seller, you can:

♦ **Act very stoic and unemotional.** Act as if the product or service is not that important to you. Start to act as if you're walking away from the deal, never to return. At this point, gauge their reaction and then play your hand very carefully. Say, "I'm sorry, but you're asking too high a price. I would suggest that if that item is so important to you, you should just keep it."

♦ **When they ask for more money and concessions, tell them you don't have the authority to give them.** Also, make sure to mention that the final decision-maker won't approve any other offers, and is sure to make you walk away from the deal.

♦ **Ask them what amount they want to sell the product or service for.** Make them give you a figure that you can work with. Ask them, "What is your final offer?" and close the deal on the spot!

♦ **If they're unreasonable, walk away from the deal!** There's no sense getting taken for a ride and ripped off.

♦ **Work the seller with an associate.** Use the good guy/bad guy strategy. Act as if you want to pay a higher amount, but your friend insists that you don't. Make sure your friend assumes the role of the bad guy.

As I've said before, never accept anyone's first offer or counteroffer. This will motivate the other side to increase their offer.

23. Reluctant Buyer

Whenever you're buying something, you never want to seem anxious to make the purchase.

Example: When it comes to making major purchases, everyone has a different level of comfort. I start becoming more reluctant when an item is more than $100. A salesperson will have to work hard to sell me.

Two of my favorite places to use the *reluctant buyer* strategy are at flea markets and clearance sales. For instance, I was at a local flea market where I met a couple who were selling off their music video collection. Thirty classics! I asked them how much they wanted for the entire collection. They said they wanted $140. I immediately used the *surprised look* strategy and said "thank you," as if I were shocked. I then started to act reluctant and disinterested and started walking away from their booth. As I was leaving, the wife said, "Come on back, maybe we can work something out." I knew at that point, the videos would be mine for whatever I offered. I told her I was just curious how much she wanted, but not interested in the slightest at buying them for $140. She asked me how much I thought they were worth. I pulled out $20 figuring she'd say no. To my surprise, she actually accepted my offer!

I wasn't taking advantage of her—I really was reluctant to spend a lot of money on the tapes. It ended up being a win/win situation. She sold some old music videos that she would never watch again, and I added to my collection.

How to counteract a *reluctant buyer*

People will constantly try to use the reluctant buyer negotiation strategy on you. If they didn't, they couldn't possibly negotiate with you at all.

When someone acts reluctant, you can:

♦ **Ask them questions.** Find out what's holding them back. Ask, "Is the price too high?" "Is this the product you're looking for?" "Do you have the authority to make the purchase?" "Do you need financing?" Dig deeper and deeper and eventually you'll find out the underlying cause.

♦ **Try to get the other side to commit to an offer.** You can say, "If $100 is too much to spend, then what do you think is a fair amount?" It's important to *work the product or service's benefits into your negotiation.* By reminding them of the benefits, they'll weaken to your way of thinking. If you do this effectively, you'll establish a range in which to start the negotiation. Many times they'll commit to an acceptable amount and you can close the offer on the spot.

♦ **Reject their offer.** Try playing a little hardball. See if they're willing to walk away from the deal. Test them. If worse comes to worse, you can bargain with them. However, by bargaining, you can lose a lot of your negotiating strength and leverage.

♦ **Walk away smiling.** If they're too reluctant, they may not have wanted the product or service in the first place. By trying to force them to buy, you'll make them defensive, and at best you create buyer's remorse.

Flea markets, rummage sales, garage sales, clearance sales, and going out of business sales are great places to practice your negotiating techniques. All items are easily negotiated! Not to mention, you can find some unbelievable deals on great stuff!

Always remember that it's important that you buy at the right time of the day. Generally, *if you wait until the end of the business day, you'll get better deals.* Why? People are tired and their defenses are down. Also remember that these people don't want to pack up their merchandise and bring it back home. This is wasted time and effort in their minds. Take advantage of it.

Traditionally, weekend sales start Friday night and run through Sunday afternoon. One of my favorite strategies is to attend these sales late on Sunday. Again, the salespeople are tired and willing to take just about anything for their merchandise. The only challenge is that if you wait until late on Sunday, many of the best and least expensive goods will already have been purchased.

24. Hot Potato

The *hot potato* strategy takes place when you dump a real or perceived problem on the other party.

Example: One of the vendors I was dealing with sold me a flawed software product. The software was supposed to contain a list of all the major media people in the United States (reporters, newspaper columnists, talk show hosts, etc.).

After I resold hundreds of these disks to the public, it was brought to my attention that listings from about half the states were never included. Complaints were pouring in from angry customers.

I went back to the vendor and explained the problem to him. He said that if we wanted new disks we would have to pay extra for them. Here's where I used the hot potato. I immediately told him we'd refuse to pay his invoice and would never order from him again if he didn't correct the problem immediately. I basically threw the problem back at him.

As I predicted, he not only corrected the problem and sent new disks, he also included updated packaging. The hot potato is very effective.

Some typical phrases you can use that exemplify the hot potato include:

- ♦ **"We don't have it in the budget."**
- ♦ **"My spouse would never allow me to spend that much money."**
- ♦ **"We don't have enough room for it."**
- ♦ **"I'm not authorized by my company to spend more than $500."**

How to counteract the *hot potato* strategy

To counteract the hot potato, you must:

♦ **Test the other side to see if the problem is even valid.** Use questions such as, "Are you sure you can't come up with any more money?" or "If I give you better terms, will you buy it?"

♦ **Walk away smiling from the deal and see if they try to renegotiate.** If they do, you know they were lying and their hot potato strategy was really a bluff.

Anytime somebody tries to pass their problem to you, immediately throw it back to them and test its validity.

25. Lowest Common Denominator

When dealing with prices, always use strategic phrasing to give the illusion the dollar amount is much smaller.

You may see an ad on TV asking you to sponsor a young, poverty-stricken child in a foreign country. The council won't come out and ask you for the $30 per month they're really seeking. They'll say, "For less than the price of a cup of coffee per day, you can save the life of a young child." Or have you ever heard the phrase: "For less than $1 per day, you can have a brand new TV entertainment center"? It's all the same strategy.

Example: One deal I was working with required that I tell the owner of a small company that he was risking a deal worth tens of thousands of dollars because he wouldn't discount his product by less than five cents per piece. Our order alone was large enough that he could beat last year's total sales. When he weighed the miniscule few cents per unit versus the lifetime value of our order, he immediately asked us to send the purchase order and agreed to all of our terms. All that was gained from *simply paraphrasing the deal*!

How to counteract the *lowest common denominator* strategy

Smart negotiators will always try to get you to give more than you perceive. There is a great deal of verbal trickery used by the top negotiators, so you must have a strategy to deal with them.

If someone tries to hide the true amount of a purchase:

- **Ask good questions.** Questions such as, "What is the exact dollar amount that I'll be paying?" and "How much does that translate to?" The strategy is to force the other side to remain clear in their verbiage and give you the exact dollar amount you'll be spending.

- **Every time the other party refers to a dollar amount in some other context, ask them to clarify what they're saying.** Eventually they'll stop using the strategy. The other side will figure that it's ineffective.

- **When the other side refers to a vague or unclear amount, act as if you have no idea what they're talking about.** Make them clarify what they're saying. Say, "Excuse me, I don't understand, could you repeat that for me?"

Be wary of anyone using this strategy on you. Chances are great that they're hiding something or trying to put one over on you. Never fall for this trick! *Always make sure that the other side talks in total dollars and cents.*

26. Meet Me Halfway

This is when you ask the other side to meet halfway between differing prices.

As I said earlier, you must always ask for more than you expect to get. Let's say you're negotiating the price of a new car. The dealer offers you the car for $14,000, and you want the car for $12,000. Following the *meet me halfway* strategy, you simply offer the dealer $10,000 for the car. At $10,000, the dealer should refuse your offer. They'll likely say, "We'll go down to $13,500." At this point, say, "why don't we meet halfway?" (By offering only $10,000, you've established that $14,000 is too high. Therefore, you'll meet halfway between $14,000 and $10,000. And here is where you get your $12,000 price.) Many times they'll agree (if the prices are realistic) and the deal is done at half the difference in opposing prices.

Example: Many years ago I was negotiating my salary with a potential employer. We were $6,000 away from an agreement. We went back and forth, and I said, "Give me $3,000 and we'll call it even." After deliberations, they finally agreed to pay me half the difference.

How to counteract someone who wants to *meet you halfway*

This tactic isn't as popular as you'd imagine. Most people, if they negotiate at all, never think of meeting halfway on differing prices. Occasionally you'll run into a pretty savvy negotiator who tries to get you to deduct half the difference. Don't do it! If someone tries to use the meet me halfway strategy, you can:

- ♦ **Ask the other side why they feel the price you offered is unfair or unreasonable.** Say, "Why doesn't my price seem fair to you?" Many times, if you have a good explanation and remind them about the benefits of your product or service, they'll realize they're getting a good deal and give in.

- ♦ **Tell the other side the price you offered is the final price and give them an ultimatum.** You can say, "Take it or leave it." Many times, the price you're asking is as low as you can go. Don't take a less than favorable price just to settle negotiations.

- ♦ **Negotiate down in intervals of 5 percent or less.** Instead of coming down and meeting the difference in price at the halfway point, *only concede a small amount at a time.* Let's say the two of you have a difference in price of $5,000. Instead of conceding $2,500, you offer to come down $200. Say, "Okay, you got me, I'll come down another $200, but I can't afford a penny more!" By bringing the price down in miniscule increments, you'll frustrate them, make them restless, and make them extremely eager to settle the deal. It'll become painfully obvious that you're not going to settle for half the difference.

Never give unnecessary concessions to anyone. Meet me halfway is really a cutthroat strategy. Remember the example above is only for a $5,000 difference in price. Many negotiations have differences in price of $100,000 or more. Would you be so eager to sacrifice $50,000? I didn't think so! Case closed!

27. Let Me Sleep on It

This is telling the other side that you want to give yourself at least one full day to think your decision through. By telling them you want to sleep on your decision, you're subconsciously telling them you're not satisfied with the deal, and you're going to prolong it. This strategy is designed to get the other side to give in at the last minute.

Example: Allison hired me to negotiate as much of a discount as possible on a car she wanted. The salesman and I negotiated back and forth for a few hours. He gave his final price, saying, "This is my final offer." He was still $450 too high. I told him that Allison wanted to sleep on her decision.

What do you think went through the salesman's head? He probably figured she didn't like the deal and would buy the car elsewhere or we would possibly put off the buying decision entirely. Just as we were leaving, he said, "Okay, you can have the car for another $450 off." This is an all-time classic strategy.

How to counteract someone who wants to *sleep on it*

Let me sleep on it is one of the most overused cop-outs in the history of deal-making. This strategy is usually a euphemism for someone telling you that a deal is off or not likely. On occasion, savvy negotiators will use this strategy to sort out the details and restrategize their position.

Occasionally, people really do need extra time to think a decision through. For whatever reason, many people feel too pressured to make a buying decision on the spot. Some people are naturally slow buyers. In time, you'll be able to spot these people instantaneously.

If someone tries to use the let me sleep on it strategy, you can:

♦ **Find out why they want to put off their buying decision.** Ask terrific questions such as, "What is making you feel that way?" "Is there some reason we cannot finish the deal right now?" "Are you disappointed with the terms of the deal?" "How can I make you happy?" Be subtle and empathetic. Most people are at a very fragile point when they come to this stage of a negotiation.

♦ **Play hardball and try to get the deal settled on the spot.** Say, "I see no reason to carry the negotiation any further. You've been given the best possible price, I'm sorry but I cannot help you." (Extreme—but very effective in many cases.)

♦ **Say, "I can understand why you feel this way, but sleeping on it will just prolong the decision-making process."** Give them stories about past and present clients and customers who made the decision to buy and how happy they were after they bought.

♦ **Use "time pressure" to seal the deal.** This is a great strategy for salespeople selling one-of-a-kind or hard-to-get items. Use phrases such as, "Another guy came in here and seemed pretty interested. He went home to talk it over with his wife and said he'd be back in a couple of hours." "I can't hold the product overnight—our policy is first come, first served." "I can't guarantee it will stay on the shelf very long. Every time they come in, they sell out right away." "We only have a limited supply—when they're gone, they're gone for good." "The special is over today." Get the point? *Remind the prospect of the importance of taking the product home or buying the service the same day.*

♦ **Let them take the product home with them.** (Otherwise known as the puppy dog strategy.) This will form a psychological advantage in your favor. The customer will be reminded of your product and how much they enjoy having it at their home.

♦ **Agree to resume negotiations the next day.** Some people are just plain nervous and will get defensive if you don't give them some space. The goal is to give them as little space as possible. Get a firm commitment to resume the negotiation.

Negotiator's Note

The goal of every negotiation is to get it done quickly, effectively, and profitably. By letting someone use the let me sleep on it strategy, you are in essence letting the other side walk away from the deal. **If the deal is well in your favor, close it as soon as possible!**

28. Focus on the Big Picture

Always make sure you don't lose a major deal by holding out for a minor concession. Never nickel and dime yourself out of a good deal.

Far too often, people demand minor concessions, which end up becoming deal stoppers. *Always keep your eye on the major issues.* People lose relationships with vendors and suppliers by being too nitpicky over small concessions and unreasonable demands. Losing these relationships can be very costly.

Example: I once found myself in a heated negotiation with one of my suppliers. We both knew that the product in question was extremely cheap for her to produce (and I mean literally pennies per piece). She tried to grind every last cent out of me, to the point that I was sick of dealing with her and ready to go elsewhere.

Not wanting to go elsewhere, I kept reminding her that if her product proved successful, she'd have ongoing business worth hundreds of thousands of dollars over the next 10 years. She would hear nothing of it. I explained to her that I was going to use another supplier. She thought I was bluffing.

What was the result? I'm now using another supplier for this product. The new supplier is making thousands and thousands of dollars and we have even purchased a few of their other products. Think of it this way: The former supplier gave up 10 years of business, tens of thousands of dollars in future sales, all for trying to squeeze an extra $3,500 out of me.

The following are four reasons you must maintain a big picture focus:

♦ **You may lose the lifetime dollar value of a customer, supplier, or vendor.** For instance, if you're now making $15,000 per year from one of your customers, you must multiply that amount by the number of years they'll buy from you. Over five years, this same customer is worth $75,000. Now add in inflation and the potential for increased orders, and you may lose a $100,000 customer.

♦ **Finding new suppliers costs money and takes a great deal of time.** If you lose suppliers and vendors in a negotiation, you'll be forced to spend time and money finding new ones.

♦ **You'll develop a reputation as a petty negotiator.** You never want to have the reputation of being a "nickel and dimer." Other companies will hear about you and avoid you and your organization like the plague!

♦ **Finding solutions to these challenges will make you a better negotiator.** It's easier to become a quick thinker and an excellent problem-solver. This alone will make you more money.

The goal is to keep the big picture in mind. The big picture is to develop a profitable, long-term relationship that is mutually beneficial to both sides.

It costs between five and 10 times as much money to find a new customer than to resell to an existing one. The same goes for finding new suppliers and vendors.

29. Non-Confrontational Negotiation

Never start off a negotiation with an "I'm going to stomp them in the ground" mentality. Always try to avoid negative confrontations!

Try to start off every negotiation with a win/win solution in mind. If the other side thinks you're only looking out for yourself, chances are that they'll walk away from the negotiation and never do business with you again. Neither side will get anywhere!

And remember: If you go into a negotiation being confrontational, the other party will become defensive and hard, if not impossible, to deal with.

Example: I remember a time that I really shot myself in the foot. A personnel manager was interviewing me for a sales position. I acted like I was the greatest salesperson who ever lived. Man oh man was I cocky! I told him that if he wanted to hire me, he would have to fork over twice the salary he was offering. He sensed my confrontational attitude and said, "I'm sorry Mr. Wink, I don't think that you working for XYZ corporation would work out." Then he got up and proceeded to show me the door. There was no chance to renegotiate! I learned quickly not to get confrontational with anyone.

Always be humble and avoid having a confrontational attitude at all cost.

30. I'm Going to Shop Around

Tell the other side you're going to check their competitor's prices. This puts you in a much more powerful position.

This strategy is meant to be a psychological ploy. As with the let me sleep on it strategy, the salesperson is going to feel like he needs to give you a better deal or you're going to walk out and never return. He knows that the chances of you coming back are close to zero.

> **Example:** This strategy worked great when I was negotiating with a local printer. We were throwing numbers back and forth until he gave me his final offer. (Keep in mind that I understand printing costs fairly well.) I said, "I'm sorry that you don't want to accept my offer, but I'll guarantee one of your competitors will." I proceeded to hang up the phone and no longer than 20 minutes later he called me back and gave in.

Unless you get a super deal up front, always threaten to shop their competitors!

How to counteract someone wanting to *shop around*

The majority of people who'll use this strategy against you are very price-conscious. And good news is on the way! There are several strategies that you may use to counter it!

If someone tries to use the I'm going to shop around strategy, you can:

♦ **Try to find out why they're going elsewhere to purchase the product or service.**

Ask good questions such as:

▷ "Do you know of a store offering better prices?"

▷ "Are you satisfied with the warranty?"

▷ "Do you feel we have competitive quality?"

▷ "Is there some reason that we can't finish the deal right now?"

▷ "Are you disappointed with the terms of the deal?"

♦ **Play hardball and try to get the deal settled on the spot.** Use an *ultimatum*! Say, "I see no reason to carry the negotiation any further. I've given you the best price possible and cannot go any lower."

♦ **Assure the other side your prices are the best in town.** Then make them a special offer. Tell them you'll beat anyone else's prices and guarantee. How can they turn you down?

♦ **Tell the other side you can understand their concerns and want to do everything you can to satisfy them.** Do whatever it takes (within reason) to make the prospect a happy, paying customer. Tell them stories about past and present customers who made the decision to buy, and how happy they were to make the decision to buy from you. Say, "I understand your feelings. I just sold this same product to Mrs. X. She was also very skeptical. But once she tried the product, she was convinced she made a good choice." If possible, provide a happy customer's name and phone number.

♦ **Use "time pressure" to seal the deal.** This is a great negotiating strategy for salespeople selling one-of-a-kind or hard-to-get items.

Use these types of phrases where applicable:

▷ "Another guy came in here and seemed pretty interested. He went home to talk it over with his wife and said he'd be back later today."

▷ "I can't hold the product for anyone—our policy is first come, first served."

- ‣ "I can't guarantee that this product will stay on the shelf very long—every time we get one, someone buys it."
- ‣ "We only have a limited supply—when they're gone, they're gone for good."
- ‣ "The special is over today." (Remind the prospect of the importance of taking the product home the same day.)

- ♦ **Use the puppy dog strategy and let them take the product home.** This will form a psychological advantage in your favor.

- ♦ **Agree to resume negotiations the next day.** Some people are just plain nervous to make a choice. This is especially challenging when it comes to high-value purchases. Give them some space: Just make sure to *give them as little space as possible.* Get a firm commitment to resume negotiations as soon as possible.

31. Let Them Save Face

This is simply making it easy for the other side to agree to your terms without seeming as if they've given in to you.

Example: Always present your side of the deal as a great choice. Never dwell on why there side of the debate is a bad or inferior choice for them. Let the other side convince themselves your way is in their best interests. Leave it up to them. If you're presentation was convincing, they'll make the choice themselves.

When negotiating, *always make sure to give the other party the chance to make the final decision on their own.* People do not like being coerced into a buying decision. Sometimes you simply have to reframe the situation to make it more attractive. I refer to this as *strategic persuasion.*

32. Monopoly Cash

This is when you describe your price in terms other than dollars and cents.

If you were trying to sell someone a new computer system for $1,000, you would have to describe it in a way that doesn't call out the fact they'll be shelling out $1,000. For most people, a thousand dollars is big bucks. Instead, you would tell them that for the price of a couple good dinners a month, they could own a state-of-the-art computer in less than a year. Think about it. What's easier to part with: two good dinners a month over one year or $1,000?

The point is to use terminology that circumnavigates the cash value.

Example: Back in my telemarketing days, I used to cold call people, trying to sell them motivational and inspirational audio programs. I was much more successful than any of my coworkers and set company records for one reason only. While my coworkers would be giving customers pricing strictly in terms of dollars and cents, I would be reshaping the pitch in a way that showed them how they could rebudget their money in a way where they could have the benefits of our program without interrupting their lifestyle. Not only that, but I also used phrases such as, "What's more important, an audio program that teaches you the secrets of the wealthy or an extra cup of coffee a day at the local café? Use our programs and you could own the café yourself!" It was truly that simple!

How to counteract the *monopoly cash* strategy

If someone tries to use the monopoly cash strategy on you:

+ **Make sure you ask the other side to clarify what they're saying.** Ask good, concise, focused questions over and over again. Questions such as, "What is the exact dollar amount I'll be paying?" "How much does that translate to in dollars and cents?" The strategy is to *force them to remain clear in their verbiage.*

+ **Every time the other side tries to circumnavigate around the true price, ask them to clarify and specify the exact dollar amount.**

+ **When they refer to a vague or unclear amount, act as if you have no idea what they're talking about. Then ask for a discount!**

+ **Look at them like they're crazy.** Use the *surprised look* strategy. Use phrases such as, "What are you talking about" or "Could you say that in plain English?"

Always get the other side to describe prices in terms of dollars and cents. This is not an area to fool around with. Many deals have been incorrectly agreed to because some swift negotiator used fancy verbiage and fooled someone less than savvy.

33. Negotiate Now, Perform Later

Always negotiate terms and receive payment before rendering any service to anyone. Why? Because once you fulfill a service, the motivation for the other side to pay you in a timely fashion will dramatically decrease.

Example: An executive in one of my former companies decided to trust a new client. He waved our standard 50 percent deposit and finished the client's project. To add insult to injury, he turned the finished project over to him. What happened? When we tried to collect our fee, the client claimed to have all sorts of financial difficulties. We never collected that fee!

Had we decided to collect our 50 percent deposit, we would've at least covered our costs.

How to counteract the *negotiate now, perform later* strategy

Never let the other side convince you to perform services until they've paid their bill in full or have given you at least a 50 percent down payment.

If someone tries to get you to perform services before they pay, you can:

♦ **Ask for full payment and see if they go for it.** There's nothing better than collecting 100 percent of your money up-front.

♦ **Refuse to perform any services and act as if you're going to walk away smiling.** By not performing the service, you create a sense of urgency on the other side's part. They'll feel pressured to pay you, knowing you won't render the needed services without it.

♦ **Refuse to work without a down payment.** A down payment is an agreed upon percentage of the total dollar value of the work order. It is standard in many types of service businesses to receive a 50 percent down payment and receive the rest of the monies owed after the work is completed. Down payments usually range from 25 to 75 percent of the total bill.

I don't care who you are or what you sell—the value of your service diminishes after it's performed. There are no exceptions. I refuse to work for free and so should you! Even if the customer is your best friend, you must protect yourself!

34. Wavering Concessions

When making any sort of concessions to the other side, always make sure you change the increments of value for each concession. In other words, *never show a consistent pattern.* Consider the following.

Let's suppose you're offering a prospective buyer a new BMW for $34,000. Their counteroffer is $30,000. At this point, you need to decide your next move. Let's say that you ultimately decided you would accept $32,000. You now have a $4,000 disparity. (At this point, you have to figure that your prospect is probably figuring that you're going to counter, and has left some negotiating space for themselves.)

When you counter an offer, always change the increment of the concession. Remember, if you always make $200 or $1,000 concessions, the other side will pick up on it and expect $200 or $1,000 off the price each and every time you counter an offer. One time you may come down $100, next time $140, etc.

> **Example:** Each time I negotiate, I take a look at the difference in the price that I'm willing to offer as opposed to what the other side is willing to accept. Let's say that we have a difference of $1,500. If I cannot settle the negotiation on a non-price issue, I will start the process of concessions. Usually I will offer $150 extra, then maybe $75, then maybe $20. The bottom line is to keep them guessing and do your best to frustrate them into completing the deal.

How to counteract the *wavering concessions* strategy

Wavering concessions is a pretty rare tactic. Ninety percent or more of the people you negotiate with will never use it. And out of those who do, just about everyone will use it incorrectly.

When the other side tries to waver concessions, you can:

- **Remind them they're already getting a really good deal.** The best strategy is to get them to agree to forget about the proposed concession and remind them of the benefits and value of your product or service. This way they can feel good about going with your offer. Say, "This washer and dryer set is considered the finest around. The amount of time, water, and money you'll save is incredible."

- **Immediately refuse to negotiate concessions any further.** This can bring a sense of urgency to close the deal. Say, "I don't have time for games. I'd really love to complete this agreement with you, but I can only afford to make this purchase at this amount."

- **Refer to the final decision-maker strategy.** Tell them you don't have the authority to make any concessions. Also, mention that the final decision-maker is likely to reject any further concessions.

- **Ask them a simple question: "If you get what you asked for, will you agree to close the deal?"** This puts them on the spot to show their hand. If they say yes, you can either reject the concession or close the deal if it's in your best interest. If they say no, then you know their agenda was to push for more and more.

I always recommend using a decreasing concession cycle because the other side usually gets worried that you will offer them less and less. They'll get the feeling that they better accept your final offer before it goes down even further.

35. Get a Commitment From the Other Side First

Never commit to anything when you start a negotiation. Let the other side open the negotiation. Don't give a starting price, terms, or anything else that's relevant to an agreement. Why? Because many times you'll find that by letting them talk first, they'll give you clues as to a good starting ground.

Many times, the other side will open negotiations with a dollar figure or terms that are better than you would've even asked for!

The following are benefits to you when you let the other side open the negotiation:

♦ **They'll give you information that forms a basis for the whole negotiation.** This gives you an opening number to start with. Therefore, you can strategically plan a realistic counteroffer.

♦ **The other side may offer you a better deal than you ever would've asked for.** In fact, you may find them offering you terms that are far superior to any terms you could've ever imagined.

Here's how I would go about negotiating for a discount on a new stereo system. First, I'd locate and visit a discount store specializing in electronic equipment. I'd take an hour or so and study all of the various systems.

When a salesman catches up with me and asks if he can be of assistance, I'd indifferently say, "Sure, could you show me various systems." When he comes to the one I'm interested in, I'd inquire about it, look at the sticker price and use the surprised look technique we discussed earlier. This is the cue to the salesman that I'm semi-interested, yet shocked at the price. He'll more than likely ask me what I consider a fair price. I'd play stupid and ask him what he's willing to sell it for. Then I'll let the salesman give me his counteroffer. This will set the pace for the rest of the negotiation.

Now, had I given an immediate counteroffer, I may have offered him more money than he would have asked for. These days, salespeople will give you rock bottom prices to clear out unsold inventory. After all, they need to live on their commissions and make quotas.

Example: One Christmas I was out shopping at one of my favorite bookstores. This particular bookstore is used by major booksellers and publishers as a dumping ground to clear out overstocked items. Everything is discounted 50 to 90 percent from the standard retail price.

While I was browsing the aisles, I had an idea. I walked up to the night manager and asked, "Does the store give volume discounts for large purchases?" He replied, "We don't have a set policy. What did you have in mind?" I asked him if I could buy books by the grocery bag. He looked surprised and thought about it some more. To my surprise, he said, "Sure, how much will you give me per bag?" (At this point, I was thinking about offering $30 per bag.) I said, "I'm not sure, you're the boss, you tell me." To my absolute astonishment, he said, "Ten dollars." I brought in several bags and bought 86 books.

The point I'm trying to make is that if I committed to a price first, I would've paid three times as much per bag. By letting him give the first offer I saved 66 percent.

Always let the other side commit to the deal first. You never can tell when the next great offer will come along!

How to counteract a *negotiator who's not willing to commit first*

Even though most negotiators will never require you to open the negotiation—SOME WILL! Never let the other side get you to commit to an opening price.

When someone tries to get you to commit to an opening price, you can:

♦ **Play stupid and act as if you have no idea what the real value is.** This is the simplest of all strategies because you have an out. Say, "I'm not sure what a fair price is, what do you think?"

♦ **Act as if you're getting irritated that they're nagging you for an offer.** You may get them to back off and open the negotiation.

♦ **Immediately ask them, "What do you think its worth?" or "What do comparable items go for?"**

♦ **Immediately put pressure on them by asking, "Why won't you give me an answer first?"** This will definitely throw them a curve. Say, "I want to try to close this deal as soon as possible and make you happy, why don't you tell me what you're willing to pay."

♦ **Give a ridiculously low offer.** This will get a response you can benchmark against. Make sure the price is low enough to get a response, but not low enough to be considered embarrassing or offensive.

36. Never Gloat

After you get what you want in a negotiation, be courteous to the "other side." Never gloat or make light of anyone that you convince to give you what you want.

It's important that you do not gloat for at least six reasons:

♦ **It's outright rude and unprofessional to put people down.**

♦ **You may be blacklisted in your industry.**

♦ **What goes around comes around.**

♦ **You may want to do business with them again.**

♦ **You avoid them having buyer's remorse and returning your product for a refund.**

♦ **And probably the most important reason is that by making others feel good about themselves, you'll feel terrific about yourself.**

My suggestion is to *congratulate the other side for doing a great job negotiating with you.* Remind them of the benefits of your product or service and how excited you are to work with them in the future. Compliment them on how honored you feel to be working with their organization.

Consider your victories to be gifts! Remember: The other side is putting their faith in their dealings with you!

 After one of my negotiations, the president of the company said, "Peter, you're the toughest negotiator I've ever dealt with, you've grinded me down to the bone!" Instead of gloating or being elitist, I said, "Jim, you were excellent yourself. You obtained the best deal I could offer and I'm looking forward to working with you in the future." You could hear it in his voice—his self-esteem escalated. We've worked together ever since!

Quick Review

Do you feel that you fully understand all 36 tactics? If not, go back and reread any that don't make sense to you.

The following is a summary of all 36 negotiating tactics:

1. *The Final Decision-Maker*: The final decision-maker is an unseen individual who supposedly will make the final decision.

2. *Ultimatums*: When you use ultimatums, you're basically saying, "Take it or leave it."

3. *Nibbling*: *Nibbling* is waiting until late in a negotiation to ask for at least one more thing.

4. *Put Aside for Now*: This is when you take a large issue that's come to a deadlock and put it aside while you build momentum agreeing on smaller issues.

5. *Surprised Look*: The surprised look takes place the second after the other side gives you their offer or counteroffer.

6. *Good Guy/Bad Guy*: The idea is to have one reasonable and one unreasonable person work together as a team to psych out the other side.

7. *Walk Away Smiling*: If the negotiation falls short of what you're willing to pay, get up, smile, shake hands, and start to leave.

8. *Never Take the First Offer or Counteroffer*: This is the act of refusing to accept the other side's first or second offer.

9. *Red Herring*: The red herring raises what seems to be an important issue, with the intent of withdrawing it for another concession.

10. *Act Stupid/Negotiate Brilliant*: This is when you walk into a negotiation and act inferior to the other side.

11. *Listen, Listen, Listen*: When negotiating, do very little talking and a whole lot of listening. When you listen, you learn. And when you learn, you earn!

12. *Third Party*: During a deadlock, you or the other side brings in a neutral third party to settle the dispute.

13. *Give and Take*: Every time you give something to the "other side," right away, you have to ask for something in return.

14. *The Old Squeeze Play*: Put pressure on the other side to see things your way and squeeze everything out of them.

15. *Puppy Dog*: Get the purchaser to try the product so they get emotionally involved with it.

16. *Show It in Writing*: One way to convince the other side to see things from your perspective is to show them something in print.

17. *Ask for Everything Including the Kitchen Sink*: Always ask for much more than you expect to receive.

18. *Cry Poor*: Tell the other side you just don't have the money to buy their product or service for the price they're asking.

19. *Never Show Your Hand*: No matter how much you want to make the deal, always act like it's not that important to you.

20. *Draw up the Agreement*: Absolutely, positively, no ifs, ands, or buts about it—spend the money to have the contract or agreement drawn up by your own team.

21. *Read Everything*: Always read every word of every agreement no matter how large or small the contract is.

22. *Reluctant Seller*: Whenever you're selling something, you never want to seem anxious to make the sale.

23. *Reluctant Buyer*: Whenever you're buying something, you never want to seem anxious to make the purchase.

24. *Hot Potato*: The *hot potato* strategy is the act of dumping a real or perceived problem on the other side.

25. *Lowest Common Denominator*: When dealing with prices, always use strategic phrasing to give the illusion that the total price is much smaller.

26. *Meet Me Halfway*: This is when you ask the other side to meet halfway between differing prices.

27. *Let Me Sleep On It*: This is telling the other side that you want to give your self at least one full day to think your decision through.

28. *Focus on the Big Picture*: Always make sure that you do not lose a major deal by holding out for an unimportant concession.

29. *Non-Confrontational Negotiation*: Never start off a negotiation with an "I'm going to stomp them into the ground" mentality.

30. *I'm Going to Shop Around*: Tell the salesman you're going to check their competitor's prices.

31. *Let Them Save Face*: This is simply changing the perspective and making it easy for the other side to agree to your terms without seeming as if they've given in to you.

32. *Monopoly Cash*: Take the actual dollar figure and describe it in simpler terms.

33. *Negotiate Now, Perform Later*: Always negotiate terms and collect a down payment before rendering any service to anyone.

34. *Wavering Concessions*: When making any sort of concessions to the other side, always make sure you change the increments of value to throw them off.

35. *Get a Commitment From the Other Side First*: Let the other side make the first offer.

36. *Never Gloat*: After you get what you want in a negotiation, be courteous to the other side.

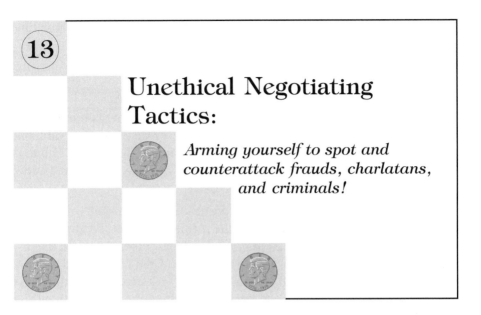

13

Unethical Negotiating Tactics:

Arming yourself to spot and counterattack frauds, charlatans, and criminals!

In this chapter, I'm going to teach you some of the most popular negotiating tactics used by charlatans, frauds, criminals, and unethical individuals and groups. Now you may be saying, "Peter I'm not unethical, so why are you teaching me unethical negotiating tactics?" Let me explain.

At some point during your negotiations, someone will try to use these strategies against you! Believe me when I say *beware*! These tactics are used on unsuspecting, vulnerable people every day. In fact, hundreds of salespeople and strategic negotiators are using them on unsuspecting buyers as you read this.

You have to know each of these strategies inside and out, so you can spot them and protect yourself from these con artists!

Let me start by defining the term *unethical negotiating tactic*. **An unethical negotiating tactic is a tactic designed to give the initiator an advantage by deceiving you or leaving out valuable information regarding your actual purchase. It's simply tricking you into thinking you've obtained a better deal than you really did. Or it can be outright stealing!**

I'm not only going to teach you unethical negotiating tactics and how they'll be used against you; I'll also teach you how to counteract them.

The following are five of the most widely used unethical negotiating tactics:

1. Misleading Receipts and Quotes

This is when an unethical negotiator changes numbers on a quote or receipt so the price appears to be in your favor, or they leave out valuable information that can sway your purchase decision in their favor. The real cost is hidden. This tactic is used over and over by many salespeople. How does it work?

Example: A furniture salesperson writes out an order per your request. They seem to add up all of the furniture's costs and give you what you think is a really good price. The salesperson gives you the receipt. As an astute, aware buyer, you read the receipt and notice the salesperson didn't charge you for a footrest. You think that you're going to put one over on him by not saying anything and taking it home for free. You feel that you've won! Well, you may have paid a decent price, but the salesperson was the person who got the better deal. How?

The deceptive salesperson purposely left out the price of the footrest. You're probably saying, "Peter, why would he do that, won't he get fired for ripping off the company he works for?" Keep in mind that the salesperson knows the amount of profit margin he has to bargain with. The price of the footrest was probably miniscule. He figured that by letting you think you got a free footrest, you would be eager to agree to purchase everything else at a higher margin today.

Let's break this down even further. When you walked in the store, you asked the salesperson to give you the price on a certain set of furniture. The price was $850. At this time he already knows he's built in a certain profit margin above the price of the furniture (including the footrest). The footrest may have actually cost the company $50. But the salesperson more than likely had more room to negotiate on all the rest of the furniture. The salesperson may have added an additional $400 margin on the price of the furniture when he gave you the quote. He gained in two ways. First, he got you to make a buying decision on the spot (remember, when the buyer leaves the store, chances are that they'll never come back).

And second, he kept you from negotiating a better deal for yourself by deceiving you. Is a $50 footrest worth giving an additional $400?

How to counteract someone who gives you a *misleading quote or receipt*

If you notice that the other side has made a questionable error, bring it to their attention and ask them why they did it. If it seemed deliberate, either make a deal elsewhere, or ask them to adjust it accordingly.

2. Contract Additions or Omissions

This refers to clauses, amendments, and various other types of verbiage that seem to mysteriously show up in contracts, warranties, and guarantees without warning.

Throughout my career, I've had various vendors try to pull the wool over my eyes by padding contracts with false terms, clauses, and amendments. Many of these items were already negotiated and agreed to at far different terms.

Some of your vendors will do this assuming you'll be too lazy to want to go back, renegotiate, and rewrite the contract. On many occasions they'll just change the contract and hope you won't notice. In most instances, vendors will try to get away with small changes. Most realize that if the changes are too flagrant, they'll get noticed. However, there will be many instances where you'll find major changes in an agreement. (I wish I had a dollar for every contract that was returned to me with erroneous information. In fact, I'd be well off if I just had a quarter for every incorrect contract that I received.)

For several weeks, I was negotiating with a manufacturer's representative who represented one of America's top corporations. Finally, we came to an agreement. Two weeks after we settled the negotiation, their attorneys sent me the final contract. Ninety percent of the agreed-on points were either missing or changed. Many of these were major points.

I called their attorney and questioned the errors. They told me the executives I negotiated with didn't give me realistic terms. So rather than renegotiate—they tried to slip the new terms in without telling us. Needless to say, we never finalized the deal. I hate to say it, but this is all too common.

Some of the more flagrant problems found in contracts include changes or additions to:

▶ **Price of the product.** Always check to make sure the price you agreed to pay is the same as the price you're being charged. Always *check your purchase orders and contracts very closely.*

▶ **Exclusive agreements.** Sometimes distributors will try to get you to agree to let them exclusively sell your product or service. This means they're the only vendor that can sell the product or service on your behalf. I even had one agreement come back that was written in such a way that my company couldn't distribute its own product.

▶ **Discount rates.** Make sure the contract clearly spells out the discount rate that you previously negotiated. Many times you'll negotiate discounts based on the quantity purchased. For instance, you may buy 100 units at $50 each and if you purchase 150 units, the price drops to $45. Sometimes they'll be expressed in terms of percentages such as 50 or 75 percent off.

There are two types of discounts to negotiate:

1. **Cumulative discounts. To have a cumulative discount means the quantity for each order is added together for a specified time period. The discount will be based on the running total.** The typical duration for this type of discount is one year. This means if you place three orders over a year, one for 50 units, another for 75 units, and the last for 200 units, your final discount is adjusted by adding the total quantity already purchased to the new order quantity. Your discount would be based on a total of 325 units.

2. **Per order discounts. This means you only get a discount based on the quantity you purchase at one time.** (All previous purchases are irrelevant.)

Examples of Discounts

Let's say that you have a discount rate schedule as follows:

1–50 units will cost $200.

51–100 units will cost $175.

101 plus units will cost $150.

Buyer A—Cumulative Discount Example

1. First order: 48 units at $200 per unit (you have now purchased 48).

2. Second order: 12 units (you now have purchased 60). (Two units of the 12 will be purchased for $200 each and the next 10 units will cost $175 per unit.)

3. Third order: 300 units (you now have purchased 360). (Forty units will be $175 each and the next 260 units will cost $150 each.)

Buyer B—Per Order Discount Example

1. First order: 48 units at $200 per unit.

2. Second order: 75 units at $175 per unit.

3. Third order: 50 units at $200 per unit.

Notice how these two examples differ? Had Buyer B negotiated for a cumulative discount, he would have been receiving a 25 percent discount starting with his second order. By using the per order method of payment to attain the best price, he needs to buy 101 units every time he purchases. He needs to renegotiate!

▸ **Shipping terms.** Always make sure you negotiate delivery times. I always negotiate one-week delivery times in contracts. I can't tell you how many times a vendor has received a purchase order, and then just let my order sit. Usually it's because they're not stocking a fair amount of product. They purposely wait for another large order to come in so they can run the production line at one time. Therefore, they have better economies of scale. Make sure you put your shipping parameters in writing!

▸ **Inventory parameters.** This goes right along with shipping terms. Here, I'm referring to the amount of inventory you and your vendors have on hand to send out to buyers. Always try to get your vendors to keep a set amount of units in stock so you can quickly replenish your inventory without disrupting service to your buyers.

▸ **Carrier agreements.** Remember that some freight carriers don't go to every destination. Make sure that you negotiate with a worldwide carrier for all of your freight needs. Also, if you plan on receiving merchandise through a post office box, you must use the *United States Postal Service.* **Other carriers do not deliver to P.O. boxes.**

▶ **Payment terms.** Make sure your agreement contains payment guidelines. Payment terms refer to how many days your vendors have to pay you for products and services. On the other hand, it also refers to the amount of time you have to pay your suppliers for their products and services.

Make sure the other side doesn't try sneaking terms such as 90 or 120 days into the agreement. Many businesses go bankrupt daily due to insufficient cash flow. At the same time, I encourage you to request 60 or 90 day payment terms for yourself. Why? In many cases, you can sell the merchandise before you put out any of your own money. You'd be surprised how many companies have issued me 60 and 90 day terms just because I asked.

▶ **Indemnity clauses.** These clauses guarantee that if one of the parties is in breach, or does something illegal, *they're responsible for all damages.* Always get the other side to agree to an indemnity clause.

▶ **Guarantees.** Guarantees (written or implied) are formal promises or assurances that a product or service will meet the promised or implied expectation. A guarantee will usually state the refund, return, and/or maintenance procedures.

There are two types of guarantees you must know and understand:

A. **Written guarantee:** This is a formal written document that comes from the manufacturer or distributor. Written guarantees usually state some sort of promise (100 percent satisfaction guaranteed), and return procedure (if you're not satisfied, we'll issue you a prompt, courteous refund).

B. **Implied guarantee:** Implied guarantees are either verbal or tacit. If a salesperson states that you can return merchandise you're not satisfied with, it's considered an implied verbal guarantee. If you go to a local McDonald's and purchase a hamburger and you're not satisfied, even though you didn't get a written guarantee, you expect that they'll give back your money because of their reputation for service.

Because we live in such a litigious society, I have to suggest that you *obtain all guarantees in writing*. Implied guarantees are not as stable in court as a written one. If a company doesn't want to issue you a written guarantee, then you have to question their reasoning. Usually, it's because they know they're selling you a product or service that's inferior or won't meet your expectations.

Now that you understand the difference between *written* and *implied* guarantees, I want to alert you to a subset of them. They are *conditional* and *unconditional* guarantees.

As a negotiator, you have to know and understand each of these guarantees:

A. **Unconditional guarantee:** An unconditional guarantee is a written or implied guarantee stating that you can return merchandise and receive a refund for any reason whatsoever. Unconditional guarantees vary with the purchase. For the most part, you can receive a refund for any reason.

B. **Conditional guarantee:** A conditional guarantee is a written or implied guarantee that requires you to meet some sort of obligation before returning merchandise or obtaining a refund. Some of the conditions include obtaining return authorization numbers (stores will be hoping that you're too lazy), trying the product, or paying stocking and rehandling fees.

▶ **Royalty rates.** Royalty rates are commissions paid to authors or companies after you sell their works. These types of arrangements are typical of publishing and recording companies. Most royalties are expressed either in dollars or percentages. Always check your contracts and agreements to make sure the amounts are both clear and accurate. Many times lawyers and agents will change the royalties due, hoping you won't notice.

▶ **Purchase orders.** Make sure that every part of a purchase order is filled out correctly and *draw a line through any blank areas*. Never let the other side have an opportunity to write in information on your behalf.

▶ **Ownership clauses.** Check to make sure the other side has legal right to sell you their goods and services. You'd be surprised at how many companies distribute products illegally to unsuspecting companies in the United States and abroad. Always make sure they include a clause in the agreement or contract stating that they have full right to distribute and sell merchandise to you for resale.

▸ **Down payments.** Check to make sure the amount of the down payment that is written on the contract or agreement matches the agreed upon amount.

▸ **Contract duration and expiration date.** Always make sure you and the other side agree on the duration of the contract. Keep in mind, many contracts will work out and many won't. By setting the duration, you can adjust your business strategy if you run into any problems. Most contracts run between one and two years. Usually high priced goods and services require longer contract durations.

Look for the expiration date in your agreement. It's not enough to know the duration. You need to know the exact expiration date so you have plenty of time to renegotiate terms in the future. *(This is especially important in union and labor contracts.)*

▸ **Handling damages or faulty merchandise.** Make sure both sides agree on terms for handling merchandise that's delivered broken or contains imperfections. You'll find that a great deal of merchandise will arrive smashed, cracked, and broken. Who's responsible? *Make sure you get it in writing.*

As far as faulty merchandise—you need to make sure the manufacturer backs their product's quality in writing. Also demand in writing proof that they carry product liability insurance. Don't sign a contract without it. (If you're the manufacturer, make sure you have proper product liability insurance.) It's a small investment that can save your business from disaster.

Everyone seems to be suing everyone. Let me say this with emotion and admonition. **Cover your butt!** *Absolutely, positively, under no circumstances, accept a contract for merchandise without proof of liability insurance.*

▸ **International and overseas rights.** Look for the clause stating international and overseas distribution rights. Make sure that if you plan to sell merchandise and services abroad, you get the right to do so—in writing! I can't tell you how many times I've seen distributors conduct long contract negotiations and forget to negotiate for overseas rights. If you get caught without overseas rights, you can get sued for all monies collected and even damages.

▶ **Distribution parameters.** Check for any distribution limitations.

Back when I was in sales, I used to sell customers a world-famous speed-reading program. (Our company had the distribution rights to sell anywhere in the United States.) After reading the contract further, we discovered that a deal was struck years earlier between the manufacturer and a franchisee in Wisconsin. The deal clearly stated the franchisee has lifetime rights for all sales in the state of Wisconsin. Any sales collected in Wisconsin had to be remitted to this franchisee. It was a legal nightmare!

Always write down detailed notes during every negotiation regarding any and all agreed upon terms. Before you finish the negotiation, make sure to read the terms back to the other side and ask them if they have any questions. If they have any challenges with the terms, you can settle them on the spot. Then, when the contract arrives or is drawn up, take the time to *make sure all of the agreed upon terms are in the document and check for any unauthorized additions or omissions.*

If you find that someone has added fallacious information or omitted terms or conditions, bring the mistake to their attention and ask them to clarify their reasoning. As they're answering, check their physiology, tone of voice, and body language for signs of nervousness. If they seem nervous or uncomfortable, it was probably deliberate instead of an honest mistake. At this point, call their bluff and renegotiate a better deal or walk away smiling!

Under normal circumstances, I usually never renegotiate after I make a deal. In the event that I catch someone lying or trying to pull a fast one, I will go back over the offer and go for his or her throat in the renegotiating process. In many instances, I will back out of the deal. It's nothing personal—just smart business.

3. Lying

It's pretty obvious that *lying* **plays a part in the negotiation process. The only difference is that we tend to call it** *bluffing* **or** *stretching the truth.* Call it what you want, the truth of the matter is that if you lie, you must face the consequences. And if the other side lies, they too must face what's coming to them.

Each negotiation brings the potential to bluff the other side into thinking a certain way. Some lying or bluffing is going to be expected by both parties. Keep in mind that while some seasoned negotiators may expect it, some inexperienced negotiators may not. Getting caught lying may put your deal in jeopardy. *Use your best discretion* in this area.

Example: Many years ago, I was in the market to buy a new car. I picked one out and approached a salesman. He was very friendly as we talked about the car for several minutes. He discussed price, warranty, and other issues pertinent to purchasing the car. Next there was big trouble!

He asked me if I was going to trade in my current car. I told him I was (never make this mistake). A moment later, he had the used car manager take my car out for a test drive and appraisal. He came back and told me that my car was virtually worthless because it had a connecting rod that was knocking (this means that there was serious engine damage and potential danger if I drove it). I asked what it meant to have a rod knock. The salesman suspiciously pulled out a connecting rod from his desk and explained what was wrong. I grew scared and intimidated.

At that point, the salesman tried to get me to buy the new car and take it home that day. Luckily, I declined and took my car to a local mechanic who had done a great deal of work for me. I explained to the mechanic that the salesman told me I had a rod knock, and I asked him to look at my car. My mechanic told me that my car was in fine shape and the salesman was simply trying to scare me into making a purchase. To make a long story short, I didn't buy the new car.

And there was a happy ending! Not too long ago this auto dealership went bankrupt and the parent company is facing massive financial difficulties. I guess there is some justice in this world!

Tell the truth—what goes around comes around.

How to counteract *lying*

It's very difficult for me to give you advice on counterattacking a liar without having a lot of details about your specific situation. My best advice is to see if you can work around the lie. If you don't believe you can, cancel the deal if possible.

In general, *if someone lies to you one time, the chances are they'll do it again!*

4. Inflating

Inflating is trying to demand more money after an agreement has been made.

Example: Let's say you're negotiating the purchase of a brand new convertible. You finalize the agreement with the salesman and it looks like a win/win situation for both of you. Great! All of a sudden the salesman comes back and says his manager (using final decision-maker or good guy/bad guy strategies) has rejected the deal and wants a higher down payment. This is unethical. Why?

The salesman probably feels you're easy prey for extorting a few extra dollars. The salesman will then try to resell you the car by reminding you of every great feature and benefit the car has to offer. All of it is a bunch of hot air—he's just trying to rip you off.

How to counteract the *inflating* strategy

Here are some tips on counteracting inflators:

♦ **If a salesperson tries to inflate a deal or extort money from you, ask them to stick with the original deal or reject the deal and walk away smiling.** Call their bluff and tell them "a deal is a deal." Either they give you what they promised or you'll make a deal elsewhere.

♦ **From the beginning, try to establish a friendly, professional relationship with the other side.** Isn't it harder to try to rip off a friend than a stranger? In some cases this answer scares me!

♦ **Tie up all loose ends before the deal is finalized.** Never leave any details to be "worked out later." Loose ends invite inflation and extortion.

- **Another great strategy is to call their bluff.** How? Tell them you want to renegotiate. Be more ruthless than ever. Make such high demands that they'll be begging you to accept the original deal.

If someone tries to pull an unethical deal, you're better off going somewhere else. The chances are better than not that they will try to pull other stunts such as adding or omitting information in their contract.

5. Strategically Placing False Information

This is taking false or exaggerated information and strategically placing it somewhere to mislead the other side.

Let's say, for example, that you're an executive who is meeting with a prospective consultant. Your goal is to try to bring the consultant's hourly rate down by 30 percent. If you were going to use this unethical tactic, you would leave false quotes from other consultants lying on your desk, where he is sure to see them. Some unethical negotiators will go as far as to actually present the quote to the consultant and tell him that he has to beat it!

As much as I want to win every negotiation, I'm smart enough to understand that you should value someone's skills. Pay people fairly—*just don't get ripped off!*

Throughout my career, I've had many people try to pull this strategy on me. The way to counterattack is to use the walk away smiling method. Tell the other side, "Wow, what a deal they're offering you, I can't beat it. In fact, you'd be crazy not to accept it." If they're bluffing, they'll immediately reconsider using the false bid. Don't let yourself be manipulated by false or misleading information. Follow your intuition. If you feel like the other side is trying to rip you off or take advantage of you—walk away smiling!

Quick Review

Do you feel you can spot frauds, charlatans, and criminals? Do you feel comfortable counterattacking them?

The following is a summary of the five unethical negotiating tactics:

1. *Misleading receipts and quotes*: This is simply changing numbers on a quote or receipt so the price appears to be in the other side's favor.

2. *Contract additions and omissions*: This refers to clauses, amendments, and various other types of verbiage that seem to be mysteriously added or omitted in contracts, warranties, and guarantees. Always check for them!

Some of the more common additions and omissions include:

+ **Price of the product or service.**

+ **Exclusive agreements.**

+ **Cumulative and per order discount rates.**

+ **Shipping terms.**

+ **Inventory parameters.**

+ **Carrier agreements.**

+ **Payment terms.**

+ **Indemnity clauses.**

+ **Written, implied, conditional, and unconditional guarantees.**

+ **Royalty rates.**

+ **Purchase orders.**

+ **Ownership clauses.**

+ **Down payments.**

+ **Contract duration and expiration date.**

+ **Damaged or faulty merchandise procedures.**

+ **International and overseas rights.**

+ **Distribution parameters.**

3. **Lying:** It's pretty obvious that lying plays a role in the negotiation process. The only difference is that negotiators tend to call it *bluffing* or *stretching the truth*.

4. **Inflating:** Inflating is trying to demand more money after an agreement has been reached.

5. **Strategically Placing False Information:** This is taking information and strategically placing it somewhere to mislead the other side.

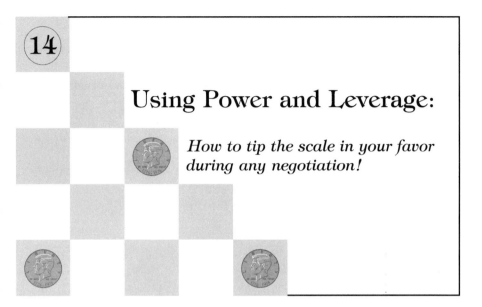

Using Power and Leverage:

How to tip the scale in your favor during any negotiation!

Power seems to have both positive and negative connotations. Some people use their power for doing well in the world and some use it to strong arm and coerce others into doing horrible things—many times against the other person's will!

Power can be your best friend or your worst enemy: It depends on how you use it. This means that you have to understand how much power you bring to the negotiation in order to use it effectively. You also must understand how much power the other side has, and predict how they'll use it. The game is tricky, and when it comes to power, everyone puts on a good poker face. And some players are better than others.

The truth of the matter is that both sides in a negotiation bring different types of power to the table. To negotiate effectively, you need to understand how to leverage all of your power and diminish the other side's.

9 Types of Power

The following is a list of the nine different types of power that you'll need to understand when negotiating. I've also included several questions you must ask yourself when considering how much power both you and the other side really have.

1. Power of options

Options include all of the various choices available to both you and the other side.

The more options you have, the stronger your position in the negotiation.

Ask yourself the following questions in regard to options:

- Can I purchase this product or service elsewhere? Is it readily available through a number of distributors?

- What is my timeline for finishing the deal? Do I need to make a decision quickly? Can I slow the process down?

- Is this the best price available? Is it less expensive somewhere else?

- Does this vendor give me the best quality merchandise or service? Can I buy a superior product at the same price from another company? Is it worth the savings to buy a lower quality item? Can I buy it for less?

- Is there any long-term business potential with this supplier? Is this deal a one-shot sale?

- Do I trust this person? Do I have trust in other vendors with the same product or service?

- Can this product be purchased internationally? Can I buy the product in Japan, China, Russia, or anywhere else for a much cheaper price?

- Does this vendor have any other buyers other than me? Am I the only organization who supplies this product or service?

The bottom line is that you must keep several options open. The more options the better. And remember to *remind the other side of all your other options*. (Never tell them what they are—be vague!) And always, always, always, make sure to seek out new opportunities and keep your eyes open for better deals.

2. Power of risk

Whenever possible, try to minimize your risk. **Whoever carries the most risk has the least power in the negotiation. And whoever who has little at stake, holds the cards!**

Ask yourself the following questions:

♦ Can I afford to take this risk? Is this risk too costly?

♦ Do I have the potential of losing more than I'm risking? Are there long-term ramifications to taking this risk?

♦ Can taking this risk devastate my organization? If I take this risk and fail, will I set my organization back too much?

♦ How much risk is the other side taking? Compared to myself, are they taking a substantial risk?

♦ Can I recover from the worst-case scenario? If I fail, will I lose everything?

♦ Have I taken this sort of risk before? What was the outcome?

♦ What is my gut feeling about taking this risk? Remember to follow your intuition. For most people, this is the greatest guide.

Before taking any sort of risk during a negotiation, make sure the other side bears the majority of the risk.

3. Power of knowledge

The person who knows more and executes has the advantage in the negotiation. There are no exceptions to this rule!

Ask yourself the following questions:

♦ Do I know enough about the other side to trust them? Have I received information from other vendors about past dealings with them?

♦ With the information I have, should I make the deal or walk away?

♦ Have I investigated this product or service in depth? Do I know what the fair price is for this product or service? Have I truly done my homework?

♦ Does this distributor have the highest quality product or service? Do I have knowledge about their competitors and the quality of their goods or services?

♦ Does the other side know me very well? Have they demonstrated that they know anything about me or my organization?

♦ What's their financial situation? Are they wealthy or poor? Is their business large or small? Do they need me more than I need them?

♦ Are they known to be good negotiators?

As I said in the *information gathering* chapter, you cannot have enough information about the "other side." Obtaining mass amounts of information is one of the keys to success in negotiations.

4. Power of time

The individual or organization who has the luxury of time has the upper hand in any negotiation.

Depending on your situation, time can work for or against you. It's very important to take time to negotiate major issues before time starts to work against you. **By giving yourself more time, you have more options at your disposal. As time ticks away, your options start lessening at record speed.**

Example: Let's use a teachers' strike as an example. Usually, the school board knows well in advance that teachers' contracts are up for renewal. They know the exact date they expire. It's usually the union that's ready to sit down and start negotiations way ahead of time. The school board always seems to feel they have plenty of time for a quick renegotiation. And what ends up happening? They start negotiating less than three months prior to the opening of the new school year. They run out of time and schools end up opening late. And in many cases, they end up having to give in to the teacher's union out of desperation. Time always seems to work against the school board and every year thousands of students suffer due to these deadlocks.

Example: Not too long ago, the National Basketball Association (NBA) was in the middle of a strike. It seemed as if the players had tried to resolve their issues for quite some time. The owners took more time than they should have. Had these issues been resolved the year prior, when they knew a strike was possible, the NBA players would have started work on time and millions of fans worldwide would have been buying tickets and merchandise. The route that the owners and players took proved to be a long-term losing situation.

As it turned out, many fans became disgruntled and passed on buying NBA tickets and merchandise. The strike season proved to be a disaster for the sport. It'll probably take three to five years for the sport to make a comeback.

Ask yourself the following questions in regard to time:

♦ Have I given myself proper time to analyze the whole situation? Do I have a deadline to make this deal? If so, what is my deadline? If not, how much time do I have?

♦ Do I feel pressured to make this deal right away? Do I feel comfortable with the time that I've allowed myself to negotiate for this product or service?

♦ Is the other side on a tight timeline? Do they seem in a hurry to make this deal? If so, why do they seem in a hurry? Can I benefit as a result?

♦ Can I stall the negotiation? Do I need more time to make an educated decision?

♦ Are diminishing financial resources going to make negotiations difficult?

Time is crucial to successful negotiations. With the proper amount of time, you'll have more time to strategize and analyze all of your options. Without it, you're doomed to failure, and will play into the hands of the negotiator who has plenty of time to make the deal. **Whoever has the most time to make the deal usually has the most power in the negotiation.**

5. Power of expertise

This is similar to knowledge power, except here we are strictly referring to the knowledge of an *outside expert*. This is a very useful strategy when dealing with issues you don't fully understand. The challenge is to find an expert having both the credentials and the ability to read the situation and its variables properly.

Ask yourself the following questions in regard to expertise:

- Do they really have full knowledge of the subject? Have they handled this type of situation before?

- What are their educational and professional credentials? Do they have a successful track record?

- How long have they been involved with this product, service, or industry?

- What other organizations have they consulted with? Are any of these organizations similar to yours?

- Can they show you samples of their work?

- Do you trust them?

- Do you have to oversee their day-to-day work, or can they be trusted to work independently?

6. Power of perception or reality

In many instances, the other side will try to pull the wool over your eyes and attempt to mislead you into thinking their organization has more power than they really do. Trust me when I say that a little research will go a long way.

Ask yourself the following questions in regard to perception or reality:

- Is this individual the final decision-maker?

- Does this organization have adequate financial resources? Can they support the needs of our organization?

- Does this person have more power in the deal than I do? Can he or she prove it?

- What is his or her formal title? Is he or she the president? Vice-president? Director? Manager?

- Does their position in the company make these types of decisions? Have they referred to any bosses or higher authorities?

- Have they handled these types of decisions before? If so, what was the outcome?

Many times inexperienced negotiators will try to reach high-level executives. Often, these executives will utilize lower level managers to handle all of their negotiations. Therefore, always make sure you're pursuing the true *final decision-maker*. I can't think of a bigger waste of time than trying to negotiate, sell, or bargain with someone who doesn't have the power to negotiate, buy, or bargain with you.

7. Power of personality

This is an individual's ability to influence you based on charm, enthusiasm, or a host of other deceptive psychological methods.

Always make sure to analyze the other side in two ways:

1. **Analyze all of the elements of the deal—what is the other side offering and what is their overall attitude?** Always keep in mind that the deal has to be good for your organization. You have to analyze both long- and short-term profit potential. If you don't feel comfortable with the elements of the deal, you simply must go with your gut feeling or do more research on the company.

2. **Make sure that you're objective about the individuals you're negotiating with.** Many times, people will lower their terms on the fast-talking promises of some charismatic salesman. This is sometimes referred to as the "halo effect." We tend to think that just because we like someone, they'll be good to do business with in the future. Think about how many times you have heard horror stories from individuals who purchased a car from some smooth-talking salesman, only to find that once they signed the contract and drove off the lot, the salesman would never help them ever again. (Some people have discovered that their salesperson will not even return their phone calls!)

Consider the following questions in regard to the other side's personality:

♦ Is this salesman even remotely believable? Is he or she fast talking?

♦ Do they seem as if they're putting up a front?

- Have I checked with other people they've done business with in the past? If so, did they have any reservations after their dealing?

- Does this person seem overly friendly? Does he or she always agree with you?

- What does he or she have to lose by not completing the deal? Does his or her livelihood or income depend on this sale?

- Have you dealt with this individual before?

8. Power of reward

Whenever you feel that someone has the ability to reward you with cash, promotions, raises, or significant contracts, they automatically have psychological power over you.

Keep in mind that power is all in your head. True, many people can reward you with all sorts of things. But the only time this power is really legitimate is when you let the rewards cloud your better judgment.

Consider the following questions in regard to reward:

- Is this reward deserved?

- Does this reward fit the situation?

- Am I being swayed by this reward?

- Do I feel right accepting a reward?

- Will my organization approve of this reward?

- Can I be fired if I accept this reward?

- Should I accept this reward?

9. Power of the iron fist

This is the perception or reality that the other side has the ability to intimidate, punish, harass, or embarrass you into making a deal.

You may be asking yourself, "Does this really happen?" Not only does this happen, but it's more common than you think. If you ever have someone trying to twist your arm to make a deal, run the other way. If you don't, you're setting yourself up for long-term problems and challenges. The second the other side thinks they have you intimidated, they'll demand more and more from you.

This happens quite a bit with savvy merchandise buyers. Many times, buyers will coerce people into giving them special perks such as cash, company merchandise, sports tickets, and other gifts in exchange for orders. Believe me when I say, there are plenty of honest buyers. Turn away from the dishonest ones and go elsewhere. These types of negotiations are a waste of time and can land you in a great deal of trouble.

Consider the following questions if you're feeling intimidated or coerced:

 ♦ Do I feel as if my arm is being twisted?

 ♦ Is this person looking out for him- or herself or their company?

 ♦ Does he or she have something to gain personally?

 ♦ What are they asking for that's making me uncomfortable?

 ♦ Are they making implications? Do they seem dishonest?

 ♦ Can I deal with another individual at this organization?

 ♦ Do I have another company ready to take on this task?

 ♦ Do their demands seem unreasonable?

 ♦ Are they asking for anything completely unrelated to this purchase?

 ♦ Can I buy this product from another vendor?

 ♦ If I don't purchase this product or service from this individual, are there any short- or long-term repercussions that can come back to haunt me in the future?

 ♦ What will happen if I walk away from this deal? Is that ok?

Quick Review

The following is a summary of the nine different forms of power in negotiations. Take the time to memorize each one before you go on to the next section.

1. *Power of options*: The more choices you have, the more power you have.

2. *Power of risk*: Whenever possible, try to *minimize your risk.* Whoever carries the most risk has the least power in the negotiation. And whoever has little at stake holds all the cards!

3. *Power of knowledge*: The person who has more knowledge and executes has the advantage in the negotiation.

4. *Power of time*: The individual or organization with the luxury of time has the upper hand in any negotiation.

5. *Power of expertise*: This is similar to knowledge power except that here we are strictly referring to the knowledge of an outside expert. Use experts to help you make your case during negotiations.

6. *Power of perception or reality*: In many instances, the other side will try to pull the wool over your eyes and try to mislead you into thinking that they and their organization have more power than they do.

7. *Power of personality*: This is an individual's ability to influence you based on charm, fervor, or a host of other deceptive psychological methods.

8. *Power of reward*: Whenever you feel someone has the ability to reward you with cash, promotions, raises, or significant contracts, they automatically have power over you.

9. *Power of the iron fist*: This is the perception or reality that the other side has the ability to intimidate, punish, harass, or embarrass you into making a deal.

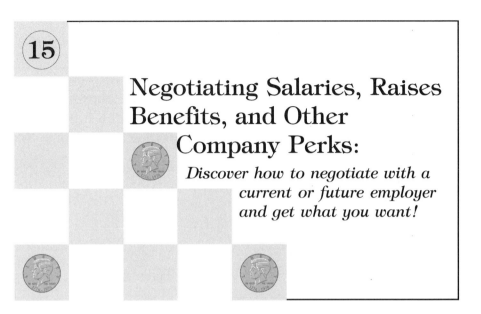

15

Negotiating Salaries, Raises Benefits, and Other Company Perks:

Discover how to negotiate with a current or future employer and get what you want!

If you're not satisfied with your present salary, benefits, perks, or for whatever reason, you just want more from your career, this chapter is an absolute must. This information is vitally important to anyone working for someone else.

Read and reread this section until you memorize all of these negotiation principles. Make these skills a part of you. This section alone can be worth hundreds of times the investment you've made in this book. Use it to your advantage!

Let me start by emphasizing that everyone gets butterflies in their stomach when negotiating for a new position, promotion, or a raise. It's normal to feel scared when facing the boss and negotiating for a higher salary or bonus. The good news is that it's doable; the bad news is that there are risks involved in asking for a raise.

The truth of the matter is that excellent, qualified employees are a valuable asset, and should be rewarded in relation to their contribution. Many executives may disagree with me, but the bottom line is that *the best employees need to be well compensated.*

I recently read a human resources textbook that stated that money is not considered a motivator for good on-the-job performance. I say that's a lot of bull. We live in a Western culture, where money is not only important, it has to be considered one of our top priorities.

If you're going to spend at least one-third of your life at work, it makes all the sense in the world that you *leverage your time financially*. Would you rather make $8 per hour or $80? The truth is that you can earn far more money per hour or per year by following my strategies. By learning how to negotiate with your boss, you can also secure a great deal of company benefits for yourself.

These benefits include:
- Higher salaries and raises.
- Additional vacation or personal days off.
- Tickets for workshops and seminars applicable to your position.
- Subscriptions to business newspapers and magazines.
- Larger bonuses.
- Signing bonuses.
- Health club memberships.
- Country club memberships.
- Interest-free loans to cover home and auto expenses.
- Financial planning assistance.
- Profit sharing or performance bonuses.
- "Golden parachutes" to protect you from any layoffs.

You can also negotiate non-monetary company benefits:
- Time off for extra training.
- Overtime hours at one and a half times your pay rate.
- Reimbursement for suits and other work clothes.
- Stock purchase plans and pensions.
- New homes and boats.
- Additional days off for personal or vacation use.
- Additional medical and dental benefits.
- Payment for sabbaticals.
- Expansive expense accounts.
- Company cars and jet usage.

To most people, some of the company perks and benefits that I've listed may seem a little outrageous. However, people are receiving them every day! Why not you?

Negotiating With Your Employer

I previously mentioned that there are some risks associated with asking for a raise. Let me share some caveats and advice with you.

You must follow the next three steps when you negotiate with your employer:

1. Time your strategy

Before anything else, you need to understand how timing plays a role in negotiations. There are good times and bad times to ask for a raise. Let's go over them individually.

Good times to negotiate a raise:

- After you've successfully completed a major project.
- While the boss is in a great mood.
- When the company announces excellent earnings.
- When you've learned a new skill the company will benefit from.
- After you've made a high-ticket sale.
- When you feel that your employer has the utmost confidence in you and sees you as indispensable.
- After you've brought in a significant amount of money.

Bad times to negotiate a raise:

- When layoffs are announced or shortly thereafter.
- After you're reprimanded.
- When your boss is feeling angry.
- When the company announces poor earnings.
- After you've failed to come through on a major project.
- After a major argument with your boss or another coworker.
- After being involved in any company scandal.

2. Figure out your real worth to the company

Once you feel you have the timing right, you have to figure out what you're worth to the company.

Too many people make the mistake of asking for a raise or promotion with no justification. To get a raise or promotion, you must not only know what salary, benefits, and perks you're looking for, but you must also be able to prove you're worth them.

Ask yourself the following questions:

How much am I making right now? You need to know where you currently stand in relation to where you want to go. Figure out your hourly, daily, weekly, monthly, and yearly salary. Write out each amount and study them very carefully.

What are all my yearly commissions, medical and dental benefits, bonuses and incentives worth? Some jobs and positions include sales commissions, medical and dental benefits, end-of-the-year bonuses, dollar incentives, and special perks such as free products. Total it all up. If you've been in a position for two or more years, average these out for the duration of the job.

If these numbers change every year, simply add them together and divide them by the number of years you worked for the company. If you've been in a position for less than two years, simply add the figures for every month of service and divide them by the number of months that you've been with the company.

How much do other people earn who are doing the same job? This is a very important area for you to understand, so I'm going to spend extra time here.

As I've stated over and over, information is the most valuable asset to a negotiator. To ask for better salaries, raises, benefits, and other company perks, you need to have knowledge of not only your worth within the company, but also what you would be worth to other organizations.

The following are several ways to get salary information:

- ♦ **Ask other people within your field.**
- ♦ **Interview personnel recruiters.**
- ♦ **Interview executives in major companies.**
- ♦ **Read business magazines.**

You may also use publications at your library including:

◆ **Trade journals and other magazines relevant to your industry.**

◆ *The American Almanac of Jobs and Salaries.*

◆ *The Encyclopedia of Associations.*

◆ *The Occupational Outlook Handbook.*

◆ *National Survey of Professional, Administrative, Technical, and Clerical Pay.*

Am I truly successful at what I do? Many times, salaries are based on performance. Think really hard and determine if you're actually doing your job well. Generally, successful, high performers who are successful in their positions are paid much better salaries than a person who simply shows up to work and does the minimum amount of work it takes to get by. Be honest with yourself.

Can I quantify my performance? If you've determined that you're excellent at your present job, you now need to prove it to your employer. You need to list all of your accomplishments on paper. If you've brought the company extra money, you may be entitled to a higher salary based on these figures. List them on a sheet of paper (preferably a spreadsheet). If you can't quantify your contributions, list every day-to-day responsibility you have done throughout the year, and everything you've done that goes beyond the normal call of duty. Were you on special committees? Did you help out on different projects? Did you exceed expectations in sales? Did you bring a profitable, new idea to the company? If you did them, write them down.

How much is my performance really worth in terms of dollars and cents? Based on your answers to the previous question, calculate an estimate of what you think you're worth to your employer and write it down.

How much do I realistically think my employer can afford to pay me? Keep in mind that not every company can afford to pay huge salaries, give extravagant benefits, and provide big incentive plans. Most businesses in the United States are small. For instance, not every company can afford to have a Michael Eisner or Jack Welch on their payroll. Be realistic when you figure how much your employer can afford. Write the figure down.

What salary am I going to request? Now that you've figured out what you're worth to the company, as well as what you feel the company can reasonably pay you, figure out the dollar amount you're going to ask for.

Then *you must decide what you're willing to accept if they don't meet your requested salary.*

What will I do if my salary request is denied? It's very important that you lay out a long-term battle plan based on the following three scenarios.

1. **Play out the best-case scenario—you get what you asked for.** At this point you must decide if you'll accept the offer or shop other companies and have them bid against your employer.

2. **What will you do if your employer says, "No, we can't afford to give you any sort of extra compensation at this time"?** Will you quit? Or will you continue to work for them at your present salary?

3. **What if your employer's counteroffer falls slightly short of the salary you desire.** Will you quit? Or will you renegotiate and see if your employer will meet you at least halfway? At this point, *I recommend that you renegotiate and win!*

As you can see, there are a vast amount of considerations when it comes negotiating with your employer. Now that you've formed your long- and short-term strategies, you're now ready to begin the negotiating process. The next step gives you some key points that you must remember when sitting down with your boss. The negotiation process will go much smoother if you follow them carefully.

3. If you have a legitimate request

If you feel that you have a legitimate request, make sure that you:

A. **Maintain a positive mental attitude.** No matter what, be positive and cheerful. Never ask for a raise with a negative or nasty attitude. Never make demands such as, "Give me a raise or else" or say things such as, "You've been ripping me off all these years." Doing this gets you nowhere. For starters, they may not be in a position to give you a raise—sometimes the company simply doesn't have the money.

By maintaining a friendly, positive attitude, your boss will be 100 percent more receptive to listening to you.

Some quick tips to keep in mind during the negotiation process:

♦ Smile; never frown.

♦ Never seem nervous and try not to feel uneasy.

♦ Keep straight posture and maintain eye contact.

♦ Avoid confrontation or making your boss defensive.

♦ Ask a lot of questions about you and the company's future.

♦ Keep calm and speak in a soft, friendly tone.

♦ Think hard before you agree to anything or answer any questions.

♦ Keep the discussion lively.

B. **Prove to your boss that you deserve a raise.** Present your case using the steps you previously took to determine your worth to the company.

C. **Remember who the boss is…and who needs a raise.** Due to the fact that you live in a Democratic society, you may technically be your own boss and could leave the company at any time. However, when you ask for a raise, remember that it is your boss who controls the cash.

D. **Ask questions.** Ask your boss how you can earn an extra $10,000 a year. Years ago, I tried this strategy and my boss gave me a dollar figure to hit and said if I made it, the money was mine.

E. **Find ways to become more valuable to your boss.** Tell your boss that in return for your raise, you'll put in extra hours and go beyond the call of duty.

F. **Don't take the outcome personally.** Getting a raise usually depends on more factors than just your boss's positive relationship with you. He or she probably has people they have to answer to. If your boss denies your request, it may be for reasons other than how the two of you get along.

Always remember to walk away from every negotiation with a positive mental attitude. Even if you didn't get what you asked for, maintain a good working relationship with your boss.

Keep in mind that there's always a chance that the boss may not have been in a position to give you what you asked for. Treat them fairly. Some people get denied simply because of the way they handled the negotiation.

The following list contains some of the typical mistakes people make. Avoid them at all cost!

- **Giving free concessions.** As you've already learned, when you give a concession, always ask for one in return.

- **Reaching an agreement too quickly.** This is a great place to use the *let me sleep on it* strategy. Never make a decision without thinking it through!

- **Making unreasonable demands.** Always ask for what you really think you're worth and what the company can really afford.

- **Hastily negotiating the deal.** Keep negotiations moving at a comfortable pace.

- **Giving in to surprises.** If you feel dissatisfied or insulted, take a breather and come back to the negotiating table later.

- **Not getting the offer in writing.** I wish I had a quarter for every time a boss reneged on a promise. Make your boss write down all of the details and sign their name to it. Unfortunately, most won't!

- **Negotiating when you're tired.** Never negotiate an offer unless you're 100 percent alert. You must be fully awake to truly understand all of the terms of the deal. *Be sharp at all times.*

- **Giving in too quickly.** Make sure you plead your case. Asking for a justifiable raise makes you look ambitious and serious about your career path.

Some of you are probably asking, "That's great, but what do I do when I negotiate for a new position at a company where I have no track record to speak of?" Great question! When you approach a new employer you have to play every card possible. Let's use an example!

Let's say you're applying for a copywriting position in the advertising industry. You scan the newspaper and notice a position is available at the ABC Advertising Agency. You send in your resume and they call you to schedule an interview. Good job! But what do you do next?

Here are the three steps I recommend:

1. **Take what's called a "Specialty Skills Assessment" based on the needs of ABC Advertising. This will enable you to figure out what skills ABC Advertising needs.**

Write down every possible skill that would interest ABC Advertising. Consider the following skills as an example:

♦ **Writing skills** (Technical writing, copywriting, and business correspondence).

♦ **Relationship skills** (Networking, team building, outside consulting).

♦ **Graphic design skills** (Formatting, color matching, painting, charcoal imaging, drafting, balancing, use of high end software).

♦ **Psychological skills** (Persuasion, leadership, negotiating, positioning, subliminal).

♦ **Intern projects** (Any advertising projects worked on during or shortly after college).

2. **Take what's called a "Skills Inventory."**

   Write down any additional skills you can offer ABC Advertising, such as the following:

♦ **New negotiating skills** (negotiations handled as a result of reading this book).

♦ **Educational credentials** (high school, junior college, undergraduate, graduate, doctorate, special certifications, etc.)

♦ **Software skills** (Microsoft Word, Adobe Illustrator, Flash Media, Director, QuarkXpress, AdobePhotoShop, Microsoft Power Point, etc.)

♦ **Special projects completed** (any projects showing a major commitment).

3. **Tell your prospective employer several personal things. These are traits that typically don't come across on resumes.**

   These can include, but aren't limited to:

♦ **Eagerness to start early and stay late.**

♦ **Strong personal references.**

♦ **Willingness to travel anytime to anywhere.**

♦ **Professional clubs you've joined.**

♦ **Business books you've read.**

- ✦ Seminars on business skills you've attended.

- ✦ Attendance record.

- ✦ Sports you participate in that show dedication and teamwork.

- ✦ Continuing education programs you're currently enrolled in or starting in the near future.

You're probably wondering why offering this type of personal information is important. Let's go through a quick example to illustrate my point. If you were the human resources manager for ABC Advertising and you had to hire a copywriter from the following two candidates, which would you choose? Let's call them Candidate A and Candidate B.

To help you make a choice, consider the following two scenarios:

Scenario 1: Candidate A walks into your office looking average. His clothes are of mediocre quality and his grooming is average. When you ask him why he wants this position he exclaims, "The money seems decent, and I heard back in college this company gives great benefits." He mentions that he's a graduate of a state university and has little background in advertising. While in school he wrote a couple of short stories for the school newspaper. He knows how to use some word processing software packages and has worked on quite a few long projects for his past employer—an office copier dealer. You might say, "Good, he seems like a committed employee who may be helpful on the computer." He seems responsible and with a little training he may work out. Out of a possible 10 points, what would you score him? Maybe a 6?

Believe it or not, this person is the average employee today. *Let's move on to Candidate B.*

Scenario 2: Candidate B steps into your office. To start with, he's dressed very well. His clothes are of excellent quality, pressed, and he exudes self-confidence. He seems a little nervous, but not out of the ordinary. He sits down and you start the interview. Here's what he tells you. First he tells you that he's a graduate of a state university where he had some advertising and marketing classes. In his tenure there, he's completed several marketing plans. After school, he started working for a small newspaper cleaning up the office and occasionally writing some classified ads. The pay was low, the hours were high, but he did what it took to get the experience he would need to get to the next level.

At the same time, he worked for the school newspaper, read the latest business books, studied new marketing techniques, and worked on his copywriting skills at night.

He also recently joined the American Marketing Association for two reasons:

1. **To learn new marketing techniques.**

2. **To network with marketing professionals, hoping to break into the advertising industry.**

Candidate B also mentioned his willingness to travel and how well he gets along with other people. Last but not least, he tells you that in fairness to the newspaper, he would need to give them a full two weeks notice before he would leave.

How would you rate Candidate B out of a possible 10 points? I would personally give him a high 8. Why? Although he seems to have limited experience, his desire to learn will definitely catch up with him. If he keeps practicing his copywriting skills, networking with other professionals, and reads the latest business books to further educate himself, he'll no doubt become more and more valuable. He's expressed his willingness to go the extra mile and has a good image.

Candidate B will be in a much better position to negotiate a higher salary. I'm a true believer in telling a prospective employer everything. If you don't, who will? Resumes can only get you so far! When negotiating with a prospective employer, you must pull out all the stops, pull no punches, and take no prisoners. Remember: This is at least one-third of your life that you're negotiating.

Remember what we talked about earlier. Negotiating is based on leverage. The more leverage you have in a negotiation, the easier it'll be to get what you want and accumulate riches in every area of your life.

Quick Review

Some of the benefits you can receive include:

- Higher salaries and raises.
- Additional vacation or personal days.
- Tickets for workshops and seminars applicable to your position.
- Subscriptions to business newspapers and magazines.
- Large bonuses.
- Signing bonuses.
- Health club memberships.
- Country club memberships.
- Interest-free loans to cover home and auto expenses.
- Financial planning assistance.
- "Golden parachutes" to protect you from any layoffs or downsizing.

Other non-monetary benefits include:

- Time off for extra training.
- Overtime hours at one and a half times your pay rate.
- Reimbursement for suits and other work clothes.
- Stock purchase plans and pensions.
- New homes and boats.
- Additional medical and dental benefits.
- Payment for any sick days or leaves of absence.
- Expansive expense accounts.
- Profit sharing or performance bonuses.
- Company cars and jet usage.

To negotiate for salaries, raises, benefits, or additional perks, you must:

1. **Time your strategy.**

   Good times to negotiate a raise include:

   ♦ **After you've successfully completed a major project.**

   ♦ **While the boss is in a great mood.**

   ♦ **When the company announces excellent earnings.**

   ♦ **When you've learned a new skill the company could benefit from.**

   ♦ **After you've made a high-ticket sale.**

   ♦ **When you feel your employer has the utmost confidence in you and sees you as indispensable.**

   ♦ **After you've brought in a significant amount of money.**

   Bad times to negotiate a raise include:

   ♦ **When layoffs are announced or shortly thereafter.**

   ♦ **After you're reprimanded.**

   ♦ **When your boss is feeling angry.**

   ♦ **When the company announces poor earnings.**

   ♦ **After you've failed to come through on a major project.**

   ♦ **After a major argument with your boss or another coworker.**

   ♦ **Once you've been involved in any company scandal.**

2. **Figure out your true worth to the company.** Once you feel the time is right, you have to figure out just what you're worth to the company.

   Ask yourself the following questions:

   A. **How much am I making right now?**

   B. **What are all my yearly commissions, medical and dental benefits, bonuses, and incentives worth?**

   C. **How much do other people who are doing the same job earn? The following are several ways to get salary information:**

      ▷ Ask other people within your field.

      ▷ Interview personnel recruiters.

- ▷ Interview executives in major companies.
- ▷ Read business magazines.

You may also use publications at your library including:

- ▷ Trade journals and other magazines relevant to your industry.
- ▷ *American Almanac of Jobs and Salaries.*
- ▷ *The Encyclopedia of Associations.*
- ▷ *The Occupational Outlook Handbook.*
- ▷ *National Survey of Professional, Administrative, Technical, and Clerical Pay.*

D. Am I truly successful at what I do?

E. Can I quantify my performance?

F. How much is my performance really worth in terms of dollars and cents?

G. How much do I realistically think my employer can afford to pay me?

H. What salary am I going to request?

I. What will I do if my salary request is denied?

Use the following three scenarios to guide you:

- ▷ What will you do if your employer agrees to all of your terms?
- ▷ What will you do if your employer says, "We can't afford to give you any sort of extra compensation at this time"?
- ▷ What will you do if your employer's counteroffer falls slightly short of the salary you desire?

3. If you feel that you have a legitimate request, make sure you:

A. Maintain a positive attitude.

Some quick tips to keep in mind during the negotiation process:

- ▷ Smile; never frown.
- ▷ Never seem nervous and try not to feel uneasy.

- Keep straight posture and maintain good eye contact.
- Avoid confrontation or putting your boss on the defensive.
- Ask a lot of questions about you and the company's future.
- Keep calm and speak in a soft, friendly tone.
- Think before you agree to anything or answer any questions.
- Keep the discussion lively.

B. Prove to your boss that you deserve a raise.

C. Remember who the boss is and who needs a raise.

D. Ask questions.

E. Find ways to become more valuable to your boss.

F. Don't take the outcome personally.

Avoid making these eight mistakes with your boss:

- Giving free concessions.
- Reaching an agreement too quickly.
- Making unreasonable demands.
- Hastily negotiating the deal.
- Giving in to surprises.
- Not getting the offer in writing.
- Negotiating when tired.
- Giving in too quickly.

When you approach a new employer, you have to play every card possible. Let's use an example!

Here are the three steps I recommend:

1. Take a "Specialty Skills Assessment."

- Write down every possible skill that would interest your potential employer.

2. Take what's called a "Specialty Skills Inventory."

- Write down any additional skills you can offer them.

3. **Tell your prospective employer several personal things about yourself. These are traits that typically don't come across on resumes. These can include, but aren't limited to:**

   ♦ Eagerness to start early and stay late.

   ♦ Strong personal references.

   ♦ Willingness to travel anytime to anywhere.

   ♦ Professional clubs you've joined.

   ♦ Business books you've read.

   ♦ Seminars you've attended to learn new business skills.

   ♦ Attendance record.

   ♦ Sports you participate in that show dedication and teamwork.

   ♦ Continuing education programs you're currently enrolled in or starting shortly.

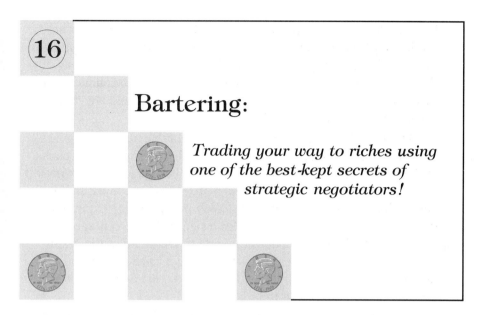

Bartering:

Trading your way to riches using one of the best-kept secrets of strategic negotiators!

In this chapter, I'm going to teach you one of my favorite forms of negotiation. It's the oldest and one of the most profitable secrets! It's called *bartering*.

The Oxford Desk Dictionary and Thesaurus defines *bartering* as exchanging goods and services without money. Now you may be saying to yourself, "How can I get anything without paying any money for it?" Good question! In fact, that's a great question! Not only can you do it—you've probably been doing it all your life without even being aware of it. Before we go into the skills and strategies of *bartering*, let's look at a few quick examples.

When you were a child, did you ever exchange dolls, baseball cards, or your school lunch for something else? Did you *barter* for a more valuable card or a better tasting lunch? These are all forms of *bartering*!

Basically, when you *barter*, you exchange something of value for something of even more value to you. The beauty is that what you have is perceived by the other side to be of more value to them. This leads to a win/win situation for both of you. Here is an example of how I put this skill to work.

Example: I decided to launch a new business on the Internet and wanted to build a state-of-the-art Website. The site was going to have the latest bells and whistles, as well as some of the most aesthetically pleasing graphics, pictures, and symbols. I conceptualized the site from top to bottom and realized it would cost tens of thousands of dollars to build it. Tens of thousands of dollars that I wasn't willing to spend! There wasn't any need to spend any money when I can *barter* the deal. How?

The first thing I did was come up with a "needs" list. The list consisted of three major needs. **First**, I needed strong copy for each of the Web pages. Here I had no problem, I could just write it myself. **Second**, I needed state-of-the-art programming. It just so happened that a business partner with Web programming experience decided to go in on the company for a significant percentage (also a *barter* deal). **Third**, I needed someone to create all of the graphics, pictures, and symbols. This was my major challenge because I didn't want to spend any money. I decided to *barter* for this service 100 percent. It turned out to be really easy!

I decided to look for a promising young designer in need of some credibility. My search was easier than I planned. There was an experienced designer working for one of my clients. I asked her if she'd be interested in doing the design work. She immediately said yes. I found out that she had no experience designing graphics on the Web; however, she was a great designer off the Web. Here's where I was able to barter. If she would agree to design all of the Web pages, logos, and additional graphics, my partner would teach her how to convert her graphics into Web applications. She agreed and we completed the Website with **no money out of pocket**!

You, too, can *barter* these types of deals quickly and easily. The power of *bartering* can be yours once you learn how to apply it. I've seen *bartering* create huge fortunes, save companies from financial ruin, add profit centers, improve people's lifestyles, open up tremendous new capital opportunities, and stretch people's minds to incredible levels of possibility, fulfillment, and achievement.

You may be asking yourself, "What if I don't have anything to *barter*?" I'll guarantee that if you stop and think about it, you probably have more to *barter* than you give yourself credit for. Let me prove it to you.

First and foremost, you have to keep in mind that everyone in every business has specific needs, just as you do. We all have to eat, drink, have transportation, etc. The point is that you have negotiable skills you're more than likely overlooking because you're used to having them and taking them for granted. We all do! These skills can be *bartered* over and over again. I call these skills "Your Personal Riches."

Now, you will learn how to discover "Your Personal Riches." I'm going to walk you through what's called a *personal riches analysis*. In this analysis you'll write down some of the things you'd like to *barter* for. You'll then analyze all of your skills and talents to determine what you'll use for bartering.

Personal Riches Analysis

Write down your answers to each of the following questions:

▶ **List five skills you can use for *bartering*.** For instance: Are you handy? Do you play a sport particularly well? Can you cook something better than anyone else? Do you format resumes better than anyone else? Write them down.

1. _____

2. _____

3. _____

4. _____

5. _____

▶ **Out of the five skills you just listed, which skills do you enjoy using the most?** List them in order from 1 (your favorite) to 5 (your least favorite).

1. _____

2. _____

3. _____

4. _____

5. _____

▸ **Write out the top three skills that you listed on page 217 on the lines below.**

1. _____

2. _____

3. _____

▸ **For each of the three skills listed above, write down five different ways you can *barter* it.** (For instance, one of your skills may be marketing. Let's say that you need chiropractic care. Can you offer to help the chiropractor market his business in exchange for free chiropractic care? Do this for each of the skills you listed.)

Skill One _____

Five ways to barter this skill:

1. _____

2. _____

3. _____

4. _____

5. _____

Skill Two _____

Five ways to barter this skill:

1. _____

2. _____

3. _____

4. _____

5. _____

Skill Three _____

Five ways to barter this skill:

1. _____

2. _____

3. _____

4. _____

5. _____

If you found that you have trouble filling out the three lists, that's okay, it's to be expected. Remember, you're new at this! All you have to do is take some more time to think them through. If you're still having trouble, ask someone who knows you very well for help. Many times when I want to know something about myself, I ask other people for their opinion. Doing this has two major advantages. **First**, you get an objective point of view from an outsider. **Second**, it gives you a fresh perspective.

Now I want you to take a moment and look back at your three lists. Did you find that you have some very valuable talents? Do you see talents that can be *bartered*? Do you now see your true value? I'll bet you did!

The first time I filled out these lists, "writing" was at the top. I love to write direct response sales copy, poetry, and song lyrics. I can't tell you how many times *I've been able to exchange this skill for goods and services.* Every company needs a strong copywriter and they don't come cheap! I'm sure *you have skills that are worth even more.*

Next, you need to make a list of goods and services that you need for personal or business use.

Write down your answers to the following:

▶ **List five goods and/or services that you need right away or use regularly.** (For instance, do you need printing supplies? A new or used automobile? Graphic design work? A haircut?)

1. _____

2. _____

3. _____

4. _____

5. _____

▶ **Of those five goods and/or services you listed, which do you need the most?** List them in order from 1 (most needed) to 5 (least needed).

1. _____

2. _____

3. _____

4. _____

5. _____

▶ **List the top three goods and/or services from the previous list.**

1. _____

2. _____

3. _____

▶ **For each of the goods and/or services listed at the bottom of page 220, write down five gatekeepers (people that can provide them for you and your organization).**

Good or Service One Gatekeepers

1. _____

2. _____

3. _____

4. _____

5. _____

Good or Service Two Gatekeepers

1. _____

2. _____

3. _____

4. _____

5. _____

Good or Service Three Gatekeepers

1. _____

2. _____

3. _____

4. _____

5. _____

Did you list five gatekeepers for each of the three goods and/or services? If so, go on to the next step. If not, go back and list them. Why? To be an effective barterer you need to know who you're going to be dealing with. The more choices you have, the better! With only one choice, you lose your leverage in the negotiation process. Here's a terrific example.

Let's say you're buying a new car. You have a much better chance of getting a good deal on a car if you can walk into Dealer A's showroom and say, "Dealer B says I can have it for $2,000 less and Dealer C said I can have this same car for $4,500 less." What's Dealer A going to say? Dealer A will not only match the best offer, they'll beat it 90 percent of the time.

However, without options (remember the *power of options*), you'd be stuck paying a premium price from Dealer A!

As you can see, *you're worth far more than you've ever dreamed possible*. And keep in mind that I only gave you enough room to list a few of your skills to *barter*. You probably have several others.

In the next chapter, you're going to learn one of the most overlooked opportunities of all. But first I want to give you a quick review of bartering skills!

Quick Review

Let's take a moment and review the fundamentals of *bartering* and how you can apply them to become as rich as you choose!

The Oxford Desk Dictionary and Thesaurus defines *bartering* as exchanging goods and services without money. Follow these four steps to effective *bartering*:

1. Fill out a *Personal Riches Analysis*. In this analysis you'll write down all of the goods and services you want to *barter* for.

2. Analyze all of your skills and talents to determine what you'll use to barter.

3. List all of the gatekeepers you can barter with to obtain the good or service.

4. Contact the gatekeepers and barter!

People Skills:

How to get others to gladly give you what you want!

There are three constants in life: death, taxes, and the fact that *if you're going to be a successful negotiator, you must become excellent at dealing with people*.

The focus of this section is to teach you how to get along with other people. By the end, you'll have learned all of the key techniques you need to get along with others, and *convince them to give you what you want*.

In the workplace, there are a variety of people and personalities you'll have to learn to deal with. And to make matters even more difficult, you also need the ability to convince them to see things from your point of view as well as be cooperative. These people can include, but are not limited to, executives, managers, directors, secretaries, receptionists, supervisors, vendors, customers, suppliers, employees, and peers. This is a mighty tall order, but very doable!

Every time you come in contact with someone else, both you and the other person walk away with an opinion of the encounter. Your success as a negotiator depends on your ability to have positive encounters with everyone you negotiate with. Everything hinges on the strength of your people skills. To negotiate effectively and build long-term relationships *you must have better than average people skills*.

There are no ifs, ands, buts, ors, or any shortcuts here—make sure you read this chapter over and over again, and practice these skills until you master them.

Stellar People Skills

One of your goals as an effective negotiator is to have people want to work with you instead of against you. This means that by getting along with the other side, you'll easily come to agreements quickly and effectively. Therefore, you'll establish a long-term, friendly business relationship. To do this, you must know how to get people to see you as a partner! And to do this, you must display *stellar* people skills!

What are people skills? *People skills are the skills you use during all interpersonal contact.*

People skills are the skills you use to:

♦ Encourage people to happily sign on the dotted line.

♦ Get other people to like you.

♦ Persuade people to cooperate with you.

♦ Show people you're giving them a great deal.

♦ Get along with others.

♦ Mend preexisting poor relationships.

♦ Show goodwill toward others.

♦ Express genuine sympathy and empathy.

Seeing as this is a negotiation book, I'll touch on the most important people skills and how they apply to negotiations. (We'll leave the other issues to the psychologists.)

The following are the fundamental people skills you'll need to develop and use consistently for success as a negotiator:

▶ **Positive mental attitude.** Most people want to spend time with people who possess a positive mental attitude. Positive people are friendly, gregarious, helpful, considerate, fun, loving, optimistic, and believe in the power of community. If you're positive, people will generally drop their defenses and side with you. Being positive will help people lower their guard when they deal with you. And *getting people to lower their guard is one of the keys to successful negotiations.*

You also have to consider the relationship from the other side's perspective. They're going to be considering forming a long-term relationship with you. You need to put your best foot forward and give them reason to believe that working with you will be smooth, friendly, efficient, and profitable.

Remember the famous quote "**your attitude determines your altitude**." To soar to great heights and get others to cooperate with you, you must develop and maintain a positive mental attitude.

▸ **Strong communication skills.** Strong communicators get their point across clearly, articulately, effectively, efficiently, and concisely. During negotiations, you need to have strong verbal skills. You have to be aware of your tone of voice, vocal inflection, rate of speech, and facial expressions. Whoever you're negotiating with is sure to look for congruency and consistency in everything you say and do.

I also recommend developing a strong vocabulary. Use the same level of vocabulary the other side uses and you'll build stronger rapport. Never pontificate or condescend anyone! Strong communicators elicit respect and trust in business.

▸ **Trustworthy.** All good relationships are built on trust. People who possess this characteristic are trusting, reliable, and honest. If a person who's trustworthy says they'll be there at 3 a.m., you can set your watch by it! By having a reputation of being trustworthy, you'll stand out amongst your competitors.

People won't do business with you if they don't trust you. They'll either reject all of your negotiation efforts or slow your efforts with lawyers who'll check to see that every *t* is crossed, and *i* is dotted. They'll also scrutinize your every move, figuring you'll try to pull the rug out from under them somewhere in the deal. By remaining trustworthy, you'll develop a reputation that can't be bought at any price.

Trustworthy people do what they say, when they say they'll do it!

▸ **Good listener.** Being a good listener will give you a major advantage. Why? When you listen to what the other side is saying, you show respect. It shows them you care about their well-being. It shows you care about what they have to say.

Good listeners are quiet when the other side is talking, possess good eye contact, nod their head to show attentiveness, use obvious facial expressions, and genuinely care about the "other side." They also ask many questions and repeat things back to show they're listening. *Good listeners are great candidates for long-term business relationships as well as good friends.*

▶ **Stellar hygiene.** Jim Rohn, the world famous motivational speaker made a profound statement, referring to how people are viewed. He said, "God looks on the inside, the rest of us will take a look on the outside first." What a statement! How about this famous statement, "You only get one chance to make a first impression." What am I getting at?

People will automatically judge you on the following: hair, clothes, jewelry, and cleanliness. When negotiating, you need to not only think sharp *you must also look sharp.* When you look sharp, people will usually assume that you are sharp-minded. They'll take you more seriously and look forward to doing business with you.

The following are seven quick tips on displaying stellar hygiene:

♦ Shower at least once a day.

♦ Wear antiperspirant/deodorant.

♦ Keep your hair clean and neatly combed.

♦ Wear appropriate clothing (nothing ripped, dirty, wrinkled, improperly fitted, or too sexy).

♦ Keep jewelry to a minimum (the other side may think they're going to pay for more of it).

♦ Brush your teeth at least three times a day and use breath fresheners.

♦ Keep facial hair neatly trimmed and clean.

I know all of these sound so basic, yet so many people make these errors every day! The little things always seem to make a big difference.

▶ **Tenacity.** Intelligent tenacity is a highly admired and respected quality. Tenacity means being firm in your convictions. It means you stay with your game plan if you believe in it! Very few people stand up for what they believe in. If you're convincing and you believe your product or service can help someone, the other side will catch on to your enthusiasm. And in turn, you'll close the deal.

▶ **Self-confidence.** Self-confident people, no matter what the situation, are sure of themselves and their ideas. When the heat is on they never crack under pressure and always stick to the task at hand until it's complete. Whenever you're negotiating, you have to be self-confident or you'll never be convincing. Keep in mind that negotiation is all about persuasion. If you aren't confident in your convictions, the other side won't be confident in your solutions to their problems and challenges. Some of the characteristics of self-confident people include being firm, educated, inspired, optimistic, and possessing a positive mental attitude.

▸ **Flexibility.** Being flexible means being able to change your strategy at any moment. It means that you're not foolish enough to stand rigid when you're wrong. Flexibility is one of the most important characteristics of successful negotiators.

▸ **Friendliness.** People tend to gravitate toward others who are friendly and easy to get along with. They also tend to work with them instead of against them. When someone is friendly, people naturally want to help them achieve their goals. They also want to be partners instead of adversaries. Being friendly will give you a distinct advantage in business. Even if the deal starts going sour and all seems lost, remaining friendly will make the situation much easier to remedy. Friendly people smile, shake hands, acknowledge others, show respect, and demonstrate good will in every negotiation.

▸ **Sympathy.** Sympathetic people show understanding when people are down or have major problems and challenges.

If you're negotiating with an individual that's down on their luck, do not take advantage of them. Always keep in mind that those situations can happen to anyone—even you. You can be assured in most scenarios that *the same person who is down on their luck will come out of it at some point and they'll remember how you treated them*! Sympathetic people are supportive, caring, concerned, consoling, comforting, and kind-hearted toward others. They want to genuinely help other people!

▸ **Empathy.** Empathetic people identify and understand other people's challenges. By being empathetic, you temporarily stand in the shoes of the other side and feel their emotions. Based on what you feel, you have to consider their perspective during the deal-making process.

Unfortunate situations happen to all of us and on occasion they happen during negotiations. For example, I was negotiating with a contractor for some construction services I needed in a timely manner. (He was the best at a particular craft.) Part way through the negotiation, he broke three much-needed fingers. He apologized and told me his recovery would take two to three months, but still wanted the job. I instantly remembered a time when I was injured on the job and how valuable my job was at the time. I decided to await his return and let him do the job. What happened and why do I share this example?

Even though I wasn't the only customer awaiting his return, I was the first customer he called back. As a matter of fact, he went to work on my job right away and finished it within a couple weeks. Not only that, but because I was so patient, he gave me an extra one-third off the originally quoted price. It pays to be empathetic!

Negative People Skills to Avoid

Just as there are positive people skills that you want to develop, there are also negative people skills that you want to avoid. The following are negative people skills that can deadlock or kill negotiations:

▶ **Negative mental attitude.** I can't think of anyone who wants to spend time with or do business with a negative person. All they do is drag everyone down. Generally, if you're stuck negotiating with a negative person, they'll try to stymie your efforts and make the whole process more difficult, taking at least twice as long as expected. On the other hand, positive people believe deals are doable and should be done in the most efficient, profitable, and timely manner.

Negative people are pessimistic, nasty, and have a sour countenance. Avoid them at all costs. They're not usually worth building a long-term relationship with.

If you find yourself in a situation where you have to negotiate with a negative person, you can do the following:

♦ **Try to end negotiations as quickly as possible.** As I said before, negative people try to hold up or kill negotiations.

♦ **Remain positive and hope they become more enthusiastic.**

♦ **Choose to walk away and deal with another company.**

♦ **Remind the other side of the benefits of purchasing your products or services.**

♦ **Keep alluding to the importance of dealing with a company like yours.**

♦ **Keep a cool head and never crack under pressure.**

♦ **Tell the other side to remain positive and you'll arrive at a resolution much quicker.**

▸ **Bossy.** *Bossy people tend to make high demands and give low returns.* They also tend to have poor reputations and make horrible team players. They're generally one-sided and care little about anyone but themselves and their organization.

Some of the characteristics of bossy people include negative attitude, frowning visage, argumentative demeanor, poor posture, and never satisfied with what they're offered. Nothing is ever good enough for them. I've seen it time and time again—bossy negotiators tend to blow almost every deal they get involved in.

▸ **Elitist.** Negotiators who fall into this category think they're better or smarter than everyone else. They act as if doing business with them is a privilege. They have a "we are the big and powerful company and you're the little insignificant company" approach.

What the smaller company usually fails to understand is that the big elitist company must need something from them or they wouldn't be negotiating with them in the first place. This is a great tool for leverage.

Elitist negotiators have a tendency to ask for anything and everything. They not only ask for the kitchen sink, they demand the bathroom faucets, the lightbulbs, and all the dimmer switches. And they do it in a way that makes you feel inferior to them. The challenge is that they tend to give little, if anything, in return.

When negotiating with elitists, you can do any of the following:

♦ **Stroke their ego and give them what they want in return for what you need.**

♦ **Play hardball and never give in to unreasonable demands on you and/or your company.**

♦ **If you have a one-of-a-kind product or service, be prepared to walk away smiling and see if they come back with a counteroffer.**

♦ **Tell them you don't have the authority to give any more concessions and refer to the final decision-maker.**

♦ **Explain that you cannot afford the terms they're offering. Stroke their ego and tell them you're nothing but a little guy who simply doesn't have the resources to give them what they want.**

♦ **Remind them of the benefits of your product or service and how it will affect their bottom line in both the short and long term.**

It's very important that you realize the true worth of your product or service. Just because another company is bigger and more powerful than yours doesn't mean they can easily get what you're offering. You're more than likely in a better bargaining position than you think.

▶ **Judgmental.** A negotiator who is too judgmental quickly jumps to conclusions. They also tend to have preconceived notions about everything. This is a major challenge. Preconceived notions tend to cloud our judgment, make us overreact, allow us to misjudge people's intentions, and make people defensive.

Before you become too judgmental, do your homework, and investigate the person or company first. Refer back to Chapter 3 on information gathering!

Judgmental negotiators have preconceived notions about the following three things:

A. **The Situation:** Whenever you go into a negotiation, make sure you have a firm grip on the details of the deal. If you don't have all the details, wait and negotiate when you have your facts straight. Too many people negotiate based on little, if any, factual information. By being too judgmental, you can make poor or detrimental decisions. **Always do your homework!**

B. **Attitude of the Players:** Never assume that people will automatically have a positive or negative attitude. I've walked into negotiations expecting the worst and found the best—and vice versa!

Earl Nightingale, the famous philosopher, used to tell a story about people entering a certain town. Some people would enter the town expecting to find positive, happy, cheerful residents. And that's what they'd find. Others would enter the same town expecting to find negative, frustrated residents. And that's what *they'd* find.

The point is to never have preconceived notions about anyone. The person who originally gave you information about a person or a company may have an ax to grind or had tried to deal with them for a different reason than your own. Maybe their chemistry didn't work, but yours will!

C. Agendas: It's okay and recommended to be a little paranoid during negotiations. Concurrently, you need some basis of information before you judge a person's hidden agenda. If you feel someone is out to wrong you, don't enter the negotiation to start with. If you must negotiate with this type of person, make sure you keep an eye on them and carefully check your agreements. Make sure you dot the *i*s and cross the *t*s.

The most successful negotiators I've worked with or studied have excellent people skills. There have never been any exceptions to this rule.

Take it from someone who's been on both sides of the people-skills fence. Early in my management career, I had questionable people skills. I used to fly off the handle, boss people around, and always act like I knew it all.

As a result, I never obtained cooperation from my peers, causing me to miss deadlines. People acted indifferent and nasty toward me. I was skipped over for many new jobs and promotions. To sum it up, I always felt like the enemy. The saddest part was that I was always excellent at the technical parts of all my positions. People skills were my major flaw!

Finally, I was fortunate enough to go work for someone who sat me down and told me my people skills were horrible. He went on to explain that no matter how competent I was at my job, he couldn't keep me if I didn't change my approach to working with others. He worked with me for a few months and I changed!

All of a sudden, people were working with me instead of against me. I built a network of business contacts and closed more deals than ever. Take it from me: **People skills make the difference between success and failure in any endeavor...especially negotiations!**

Quick Review

Let's take a moment and review all of the people skills needed to be a successful negotiator.

What are people skills? *People skills are the skills you use during all interpersonal contact.*

People skills are the skills you use to:

♦ Encourage people to happily sign on the dotted line.

♦ Get other people to like you.

- Convince people to cooperate with you.
- Show people you're giving them a great deal.
- Get along with others.
- Mend preexisting poor relationships.
- Show goodwill toward others.
- Express genuine sympathy and empathy.

The following are the fundamental people skills you'll need to develop and use consistently for success as a negotiator:

▶ **Positive mental attitude.** Positive people are friendly, gregarious, helpful, considerate, fun, loving, optimistic, and believe in the power of community.

▶ **Strong communication skills.** Strong communicators get their point across clearly, articulately, effectively, efficiently, and concisely.

▶ **Trustworthiness.** People who possess this characteristic are trusting, reliable, and honest.

▶ **Good listener.** When you listen to what the other side is saying, you show respect. Good listeners never talk when the other side is talking, possess good eye contact, nod their head to show attentiveness, use strong facial expressions, and genuinely care about the other side. They also ask many questions and repeat things back to show they're listening.

▶ **Stellar hygiene.** People will automatically judge you on the following: hair, clothes, jewelry, and cleanliness. When negotiating, you need to not only think sharp, *you must look sharp.*

The following are seven quick tips on stellar hygiene:

- Shower at least once a day.
- Wear antiperspirant/deodorant.
- Keep your hair clean and neatly combed.
- Wear appropriate clothing (nothing ripped, dirty, wrinkled, improperly fitted, or too sexy).
- Keep jewelry to a minimum (the other side may think they're going to pay for it).
- Brush teeth at least three times a day and use breath fresheners.
- Keep facial hair neatly trimmed and clean.

▶ **Tenacity.** Always be firm in your convictions. It means you stay with your game plan if you believe in it!

▶ **Self-confidence.** Self-confident people, no matter what the situation, are sure of themselves and their ideas. Some of the characteristics of self-confident people include being firm, educated, inspired, optimistic, and possess a positive mental attitude.

▶ **Flexibility.** Being flexible means being able to change your strategy at any moment. It means that you're not foolish enough to stand rigid when you're wrong.

▶ **Friendliness.** People tend to gravitate toward others who are easy to get along with. Friendly people smile, shake hands, acknowledge others, show respect, and demonstrate goodwill in every negotiation.

▶ **Sympathy.** Sympathetic people show understanding when people are down or have major problems and challenges. They're supportive, caring, concerned, consoling, comforting, and kind-hearted toward others.

▶ **Empathy.** Empathetic people identify and understand other people's challenges. By being empathetic, you temporarily stand in the shoes of the other side and feel their emotions.

Just as there are positive people skills you want to adopt, there are negative people skills that you'll to avoid!

The following are negative people skills that can deadlock or kill negotiations:

▶ **Negative mental attitude.** Negative people are pessimistic, nasty, and have a sour countenance. Avoid them at all costs; they're not usually worth building a long-term relationship with.

If you find yourself in a situation where you have to negotiate with a negative person, you can do any of the following:

♦ **Try to end negotiations as quickly as possible.**

♦ **Remain positive and hope they become more enthusiastic.**

♦ **Choose to walk away and deal with another company.**

♦ **Remind the other side of the benefits of purchasing your products or services.**

♦ **Keep alluding to the importance of dealing with a company such as yours.**

◆ **Keep a cool head and never crack under pressure.**

◆ **Tell the other side to remain positive and you'll arrive at a resolution much quicker.**

▶ **Bossiness.** Some of the characteristics of bossy negotiators include negative attitude, frowning visage, argumentative demeanor, and poor posture. They're never satisfied with what they're offered.

▶ **Elitist.** Negotiators who fall into this category think they're better or smarter than the person they're negotiating with.

When negotiating with elitists, you can do any of the following:

◆ **Stroke their ego and give them what they want in return for what you need.**

◆ **Play hardball and never give in to unreasonable demands on you and/or your company.**

◆ **If you have a one-of-a-kind product or service, be prepared to walk away smiling and see if they come back with a counteroffer.**

◆ **Tell them you don't have the authority to give any more concessions and refer to the final decision-maker.**

◆ **Explain that you cannot afford the terms they're offering.**

◆ **Remind them of the benefits of your product or service and how it will affect their bottom line both short and long term.**

▶ **Judgmental.** A negotiator who is too judgmental quickly jumps to conclusions. They also tend to have preconceived notions about several aspects of the negotiation.

Judgmental negotiators have preconceived notions about the following three things:

1. **The situation.**

2. **Attitude of the players.**

3. **Agendas.**

Again—**people skills make the difference between success and failure in any endeavor—especially negotiations!**

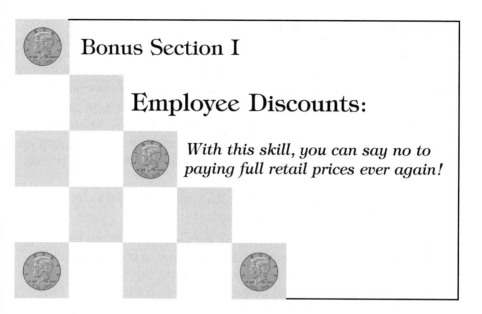

Bonus Section I

Employee Discounts:

With this skill, you can say no to paying full retail prices ever again!

Did you ever walk into a retail store and see an item that you want, but either couldn't afford it or felt guilty thinking of spending money on it? Of course! We all have. Do you know that there's a way to get a 10, 25, 50, or 70 percent discount on any of the merchandise? I've even obtained new products below wholesale! How is this possible? Simple! Take advantage of employee discounts!

Retail employees are always using each other's discounts at stores everywhere! It's *one of the best-known secrets among store employees for obtaining significant discounts.*

CAUTION: Some companies do not approve of their workers using their employee discount for anything except purchases for the employee's own personal use. Some employees may be even be terminated or sued if they're caught. Make sure you ask the employee if their company allows them to make unconditional employee purchases. If so, take advantage of the discount. If not, you may want to reconsider putting them in jeopardy.

What Are Employee Discounts?

An employee discount is a price reduction that an employee gets off of merchandise from the store or company they work for. (With few exceptions, employees will automatically get them just for working there.)

It is pretty common for an employee that works for a retail store to get 10 to 15 percent off, or more, for any personal purchases. Many times an employee can even save extra money on sale items. In many cases, retailers give good employee discounts to compensate for the low hourly rates they pay.

How do you make the employee discount work to your advantage? Consider the following personal example.

Example: Many years ago, I was a manager for a major retailer specializing in lithographs. The store was located in a very affluent shopping mall. Everyday at lunchtime, one of the mall employees used to visit my store and admire the lithographs. One day, she asked me about prices. I could tell by her reactions that the prices were too expensive for her. (She either had little money or she was great at using the surprised look strategy that I taught you earlier.) Finally, one day we struck up a conversation. I found out that her name was Emily and she was an employee of a major bookstore in the mall.

At about the time we met, I was buying a lot of books. So I decided to strike a deal with her. She could have whatever she wanted for cost plus 10 percent if she would allow me to purchase books from her store, using her employee discount. Emily showed up the next day and I told her how lucky she was to have access to so many books for free. She said she couldn't get books for free, but she could buy them for 35 percent off the retail price. I said to myself, "Bingo. I hit the jackpot."

She came back the next day and I broached my idea. I told her that I'd be more than happy to let her purchase the $89.95 picture she wanted for only $10.75. And in return, I told her that I'd like to purchase whatever books I wanted with her 35 percent employee discount. Emily happily agreed, and the next day we gave each other our wish list and made our purchases. It was a win/win situation. She was able to buy the picture and several other items she wanted and I was able to buy books at a 35 percent discount for the rest of the year. Since then, I've done these deals over and over again!

You can use employee discounts to exchange:

♦ Products for products.

♦ Services for services.

♦ A product for a service.

♦ A service for a product.

Always *remember to exercise stellar people skills when initiating these types of bartering agreements and negotiations.* How can you make this work for you today? Let's form an action plan for using employee discounts!

▶ **Make a list of 10 products and/or services you would like to purchase.**

1. _____

2. _____

3. _____

4. _____

5. _____

6. _____

7. _____

8. _____

9. _____

10. _____

▶ From the list, write down three products and/or services you need right away in order of importance (1 being most important and 3 being least important):

1. _____

2. _____

3. _____

▶ Next, list the names and phone numbers of three stores that sell each:

Product 1 Stores and Phone Numbers

1. _____

2. _____

3. _____

Product 2 Stores and Phone Numbers

1. _____

2. _____

3. _____

Product 3 Stores and Phone Numbers

1. _____

2. _____

3. _____

▶ Next, you have to design a plan.

Now that you know what you want, simply call any of the stores you listed and ask to speak to a salesperson or the manager. After they answer, inquire about the product or service you wish to purchase. Ask the salesperson detailed questions about the product or service's features and benefits. Then ask for the retail price. Once you feel comfortable that you have all the necessary product or service information, ask for the employee's name, telephone extension, and normal work hours. (Use the following sample log to take notes.)

Why is this important? Simple—you'll have more options at your disposal! Now that you know what you want, get in the stores, meet these people, and get chummy. Perhaps you have friends or family members that can help you.

Product and Service Log Worksheet

Name of Product or Service

Item Number

Features

Benefits

Store Name

Store Address

City _____ **State** ____ **Zip Code** ____

Telephone Number

Salesperson

Extension

Salesperson's Hours: Sunday _____

Monday _____

Tuesday _____

Wednesday _____

Thursday _____

Friday _____

Saturday _____

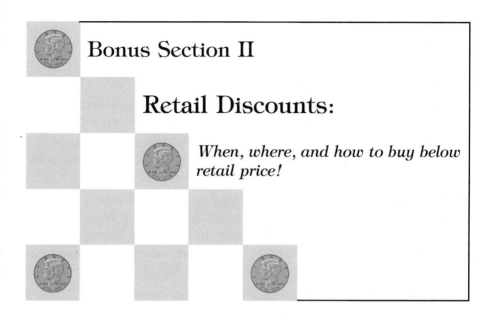

Bonus Section II

Retail Discounts:

When, where, and how to buy below retail price!

Are you aware that there are some people who never pay full retail price for anything? They get exactly what they want at bargain prices all the time. These astute shoppers have figured out how to work the system, doing something that 99 percent of people don't. They take advantage of all types of retail discounts and sales.

Here are a few examples:

▶ **Clearance sales.** Many stores run clearance sales to clear out last season's merchandise so they can make room for new products. Discounts of 50 to 60 percent are very common.

▶ **Seasonal sales.** Astute shoppers buy one year in advance of each season. For instance, I purchased all my winter clothes for next year at the end of winter this year. Doing this enabled me to buy all my clothes at clearance prices. If I were to buy all my winter clothes at the beginning of winter, I'd have to pay premium prices. Taking advantage of seasonal sales will enable you to save 30 to 90 percent.

▶ **Fire sales.** There are many businesses that experience fires and have to shut down. Many liquidate merchandise that survived the fire. Here you can save 75 to 90 percent.

▶ **Damaged merchandise sales.** Often, you can purchase things such as slightly dented furniture, stained clothing, and other items that aren't quite perfect at prices 10 to 50 percent off the retail price. Many times, the imperfection isn't even noticeable.

▶ **Overstock.** Often, retailers will buy a vast amount of a certain product, anticipating huge sales. This happens quite a bit with faddish or trendy items. In many cases, the trend or fad falls by the wayside and they're left with too much merchandise. This triggers a huge sale! Here you can save 40 to 80 percent easily!

▶ **Loss leaders.** Many retailers will advertise things like laundry detergent, toothpaste or other typical household items at too-good-to-be-true prices to get you into their store, in hopes you'll purchase other high profit items at the same time. By just purchasing the original items in quantity, you can easily save 10 to 40 percent.

▶ **Volume discounts.** Many times, you can talk to a manager or other decision-maker and convince them to give you a volume discount if you purchase two or more items. This works very well with higher priced merchandise. Typically you can save 10 to 25 percent.

▶ **Grand opening sales.** Many times when a new store opens, retailers hold grand opening sales to encourage people to stop in the store for the first time. These sales run from one to 30 days. Scan the newspapers for grand opening announcements and buy in quantity. Savings of 5 to 40 percent are very common.

▶ **Holiday sales.** Most retailers hold special sales during major holidays. Some great holidays include Christmas, New Year's, Valentine's Day, St. Patrick's Day, Easter, Graduation, Mother's Day, Father's Day, President's Day, Memorial Day weekend, Independence Day weekend, Labor Day weekend, Columbus Day, and of course the day after Thanksgiving. Savings of 20 to 75 percent are common.

▶ **Store celebrations.** Many stores celebrate their founders' birthdays or the company's birthday or any number of other special store holidays. Watch for them and you could typically save 25 to 80 percent

▶ **Special store sales.** These include one-day-only, 13-hour or 24-hour sales at certain stores. Sometimes stores have midnight sales where the store opens at midnight and discounts on a first-come-first-served basis. These are variations of clearance sales where you can typically save 40 to 90 percent off merchandise.

▶ **Frequent buyer programs.** This is where you get points or rewards for every time you purchase. Typical examples are coffee cards from Starbucks, sandwich cards from Subway, or frequent flyer cards from airlines. Savings vary from 20 percent off to free merchandise.

▶ **Private or closed-door sales.** Many major department stores and designer boutiques will invite their best customers to special private sales. Here you'll be able to take advantage of special sales only available to people invited to the event. You'll be the first to see new and limited merchandise as well as meet designers and other celebrities who may be in attendance. Discounts of 10 to 20 percent are typical.

▶ **Garage sales and flea markets.** These are great places to buy all kinds of new and used merchandise at 40 to 95 percent discounts.

▶ **Going-out-of-business sales.** Every year, hundreds of businesses close their doors for a number of reasons. They typically liquidate all leftover merchandise at huge discounts. At these sales, you can typically purchase the store's merchandise and store fixtures for 60 to 95 percent off the retail price.

▶ **Bankruptcy sales.** Many businesses close down because they've gone bankrupt. And many times, they have to liquidate their entire inventory for pennies on the dollar to help pay off their creditors. Discounts of 50 of 95 percent are common.

▶ **Sidewalk sales.** Every year, thousands of businesses get together and have outdoor sidewalk sales. Typically a group of retailers on the same block or in the same area have an outdoor sale to clear out slow-moving merchandise. Many times you'll see a whole city block or two with loads of merchandise for sale outside on tables. Discounts of 25 to 60 percent are pretty common.

▶ **Catalog and Internet sales.** Watch catalogs and Internet sites very closely for any number of the same discounts offered in the stores. Many times you can purchase through catalogs and Internet sites for 10 to 15 percent less than shopping in stores.

As you can see, there are vast opportunities to buy anything below retail price if you know where to buy, how to buy, and when to buy. And the real beauty here is that you can even negotiate better deals on any of the sales above.

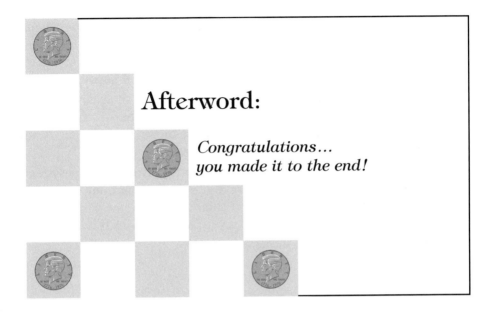

Afterword:

*Congratulations...
you made it to the end!*

$\mathbf{B}$e proud of yourself! You've gone the distance!

How does it feel to know you have learned strategies and tactics that can help you convince just about anyone to give you anything you want on your terms? Just think about it. You've been introduced to the same skills and strategies used by the world's smartest strategic negotiators. The big question is: How are you going to use these new skills? I have a few ideas to help you.

First and foremost, I suggest you *work very hard at developing and fine-tuning your negotiator's mindset.* Look for opportunities to negotiate everywhere you go. Try to find an opportunity to use each of the 36 strategies I gave you. (In fact, try to develop your own!) Then, turn shopping into a game where the score is reflected in your wallet. Whenever you make a purchase, *refuse to pay full retail or asking price.* Remember my favorite saying:

The more you rant and rave, the more money you'll save.

Keep in mind that occasionally you may fall short of your goals and not be able to complete a negotiation as successfully as you'd have liked. That's okay, it happens to all of us at one time or another. You just have to pick yourself up, brush off, and get ready for your next challenge. Mark my words—if you've carefully studied and practiced the negotiation methods I've taught you, your chances of failure are slim to none! You're now on your way to becoming a more successful negotiator.

Don't be afraid to refer to this book often. Reread the chapters until these strategies are as routine as breathing, brushing your teeth, or tying your shoes. Eventually, you'll automatically use these strategies each and every time you purchase a product and/or service.

In closing I'd like to say thank you for making my negotiation system a part of your life. It's been a pleasure and honor to share my strategies and experiences with you. Put them to good use! Write me with all your success stories. Best of success to you as you *Negotiate Your Way to Riches*!

Wishing you the best of success,

Peter Wink

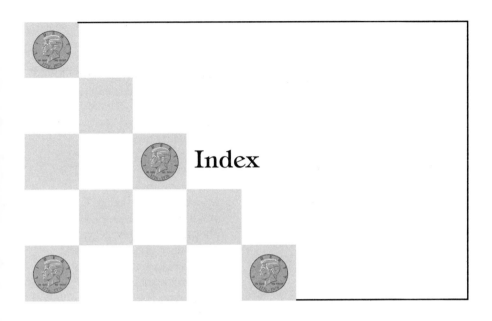

Index

About the Author

Peter Wink is the president of his own management and marketing consulting company, Promoter Extraordinaire. His past and present clients include Sweet Traditions L.L.C./Krispy Kreme Doughnuts, BluBlocker Corporation, HairDiamond International, Information USA, Brian Tracy International, LifeSuccess Productions, Aesop.com, and PSI Seminars.

Wink served in management or marketing for United Parcel Service, Gold Standard Enterprises, Successories of Illinois, Rockwell, Jamba Juice, and the world-famous Nightingale-Conant Corporation.

Wink has successfully negotiated hundreds of deals throughout his career, covering a wide variety of products and services. His office is located in Chicago, Illinois. For information on Peter Wink's private consultations or seminars send an e-mail to questions@peterwink.com.

Peter Wink, Chairman and CEO
Wink Publishing Group, Inc.
1926 Prairie Square, Suite 334
Schaumburg, IL 60173
Phone: (847)303-9421
E-mail: questions@peterwink.com